Permanent Connections

—•—❧—•—

Sue Ellen Bridgers

1 8 ┃f 1 7
——————————— HARPER & ROW, PUBLISHERS ———————————
Cambridge, Philadelphia, San Francisco, Washington, London, Mexico City, São Paolo, Singapore, Sydney
NEW YORK

Permanent Connections
Copyright © 1987 by Sue Ellen Bridgers
Designed by Joyce Hopkins
1 2 3 4 5 6 7 8 9 10
First Edition

Library of Congress Cataloging-in-Publication Data
Bridgers, Sue Ellen.
    Permanent connections.
    Summary: Forced to spend a semester in his father's
small hometown up in the mountains, seventeen-year-old
Rob finds his feelings of alienation and self-hatred
diminishing as he forges relationships with relatives
and new friends.
    [1. Interpersonal relations—Fiction.   2. Self-
acceptance—Fiction.   3. Mountain life—Fiction]
I. Title.
PZ7.B7615Pe 1987   [Fic]   86-45491
ISBN 0-06-020711-6
ISBN 0-06-020712-4 (lib. bdg.)

for
Judith Hummell Budd

1

Rob awoke slowly, pulling himself out of a foggy dream of being trapped somewhere, a steeply rising place tangled with rhododendron and blackberry briars. Above him, beyond this thick wet mist, there was a summit familiar from some other dream, and so he wasn't frightened, just disgusted with his stumbling, backsliding climb. He could feel his limbs fighting against him as his body tried to sink back into sleep, but his mind darted upward, tugging him out of the nightmare, away from the rumbling sound of a storm he heard moving toward him in the distance.

He opened his eyes to the rosy glow of the streetlight

on his window shade. Without even looking he could sense the evenness of every surface, the smooth desk and dresser, the straight shelves, all the angles clean and perfect. There was no danger here, no slippery surface to send him tumbling in an avalanche of slimy rocks and thorny brambles. He would not be broken at the bottom.

He lay watching the ceiling and waiting for a sound, because he suspected the storm in his dream was real. There was a hissing along the wall, his mother's anxious voice kept low, spitting in frustrated rushes so she would not alarm his sister, Allison, who slept across the hall. The rumble was his father, heavy thunder before the squall, in control as he always was but pushing, always pushing like the wind behind a bank of dark clouds, bringing the storm relentlessly on. They were arguing about him.

Rob got out of bed and slid the shade up. The suburban street was quiet, wrapped in a predawn glow of fluorescence meant to make them feel safe. He glanced back at his alarm clock. Two fifteen, the safest part of the night. He had read somewhere that crimes against property—burglaries, breaking and enterings—took place at four, felonies perpetrated by strangers, their faces hidden behind ski masks, gloved fingers jimmying doors and window latches. But what about crimes of domesticity, of passion, of love turned explosive? Those eruptions occurred anytime—at breakfast or dinner, after the eleven-o'clock news, at two fifteen A.M.

He knew what they were saying.

Dad, the grumbling thunder: He's not going to amount to anything. Seventeen years old and the only job he

could find was cutting three lawns! And somebody has to remind him to do that.

Mom, defensive but fretful, too, panicked by the possible accuracy of his dad's opinion: He looked for a job. What do you want him to do, work nights at one of those convenience stores or a hamburger joint where he could get killed?

Dad: He'll probably kill himself in that car of his the way he drives.

Mom: You bought it! You said give him responsibility and he'd be responsible.

Dad: Obviously I was mistaken. I certainly expected him to pay his own gas bill. No telling what else we're paying for. That crowd he hangs around with, they're lowlife, Carrie. They're not even pretending to be interested in high school, much less getting into college. He should have participated in sports. He was a good little athlete. He could have made the J.V. basketball team—he was quick enough. He just didn't try.

Mom, sharply, a thin brilliant edge of lightning: You wanted him to play because you didn't get to. He's not you, Davis.

Dad: He sure as hell isn't. I didn't get everything handed to me on a silver platter. I didn't coast through high school. I wasn't out half the night, doing God knows what. Papa would have beat hell out of me if I'd come in at three in the morning with liquor on my breath.

Mom: I don't want him drinking either. I'm as scared as you are.

And they would fall into each other's arms, defeated by their fears. His mother's face would be blotchy and flat with exhaustion, her eyes wet, but she wouldn't cry. There was still enough anger to keep her from grieving, enough hope to make her shudder out one gasping sob and be still. They would finally fall asleep barely touching each other, maybe just his dad's foot against her ankle. She had broken her leg years ago, and Rob knew that where the nerves were damaged, even the lightest touch could bring her pain.

He waited for the silence. Old wearying discussions sparked these outbursts, and exhaustion always dissipated them. There was no resolution. He was not a solvable problem. He wished he had some dope, at least a cigarette. Warm smoke in his lungs—just a couple of drags—would make him feel better. But he'd never kept paraphernalia in his room like his friends did, stowed over window valances, rolled in socks, taped inside bed rails. He was too lazy to be that careful; besides, his mother knew where to look.

He heard the john flush next door, a heavy tread—his dad lumbering to bed. His mother's voice was pliant now, inviting forgiveness as if she, rather than her son, were to blame. Rob strained, his eyes closed, to concentrate on every sound. He heard the slight rustling movement of the bed, the clink of the chain against the metal lamp as the light went out, then the quiet.

Holding his breath, he waited for the light-headed rush oxygen deprivation could bring. The pink glow on the lawn outside brightened, then paled, brightened again, turned rusty brown like old blood. He exhaled, took a deep breath and turned back toward bed. Downstairs the liquor cabinet was empty, no beer in the fridge, temptation removed. They had done all they could to make him safe and it wasn't enough.

He fell forward across the bed and pulled the pillow over the back of his head, hands latched over it to keep the silence out. All he could hear was the muffled wind of his shallow breath, the pounding of his heart reverberating through the mattress.

You are going to sleep, he said to himself. You are not going to think about anything.

The clock hummed, doing its digital magic; minutes replaced each other on the plastic screen. Two years ago he would have had something to read, but no book had held his interest in a long time. Allison had taken his earphones to her room, so he couldn't listen to his stereo. If he went downstairs to watch television, they would hear him, want him back in bed. They needed him to be asleep. He needed a drink, a smoke, something to do with his hands, his mind. He could think when he was high; he saw things clearer, could make connections.

Once he had written a paper stoned. It was a brilliant paper; he could feel it while he wrote, how strong the language was, how precisely he'd developed his theme. He'd loved writing it. The pen had felt powerful in his hand, like a gigantic metal hook that could pull everything he wanted to express into shape. His ideas flew as if magnetized to the hook. The paper became beautiful before his eyes. He had done something great.

His grade was a D with an admonishing note attached. His penmanship was atrocious, his points underdeveloped and flighty. He had done much better work, which was the only reason he didn't get an F. The teacher was illiterate, he told himself. She'd never liked him. He'd show her. He didn't hand in the next assignment at all.

Right now he should get up and write something. He would write about how it feels when you wake up in the night because your folks are arguing about you, about how lousy it is to never be left alone, about what a pain in the butt your twelve-year-old perfect sister is, about how you're already messed up. Already, at seventeen, boxed in with no way out. Not enough guts to scramble, never enough bucks to float. Sinking, always sinking. Holding tight and falling away at the same time.

He flung the pillow against the headboard and looked at the clock. Three forty-five. He would keep watch, that was what he'd do. He would stay alert through the hour of breaking and entering, his guard up to prevent crime. He would keep his parents and his sister safe. They would never know how diligent he had been. It would be his secret, a silent defense against their barrage of criticism. He stared at the clock, watching the minutes form flickering red lines. His eyes closed, blinked open, closed again. He slept.

2

They broke through the clouds, and there were the mountains beneath them. August green undulating, here and there open flinty shelves of yellow rock, narrow twisting ribbons of road and river splitting the valleys. Rob studied the terrain searching for landmarks, some sign that would distinguish it from other ranges in the southern Appalachians. There was a sudden sheet of mist against the window, a damp translucent drift of cloud, and then the sky again, pale blue and hazy. The sun had been shining in Newark.

After a few minutes he could see the interstate, two strips of shimmering concrete poured down rocky gaps, rolling and wavering past ragged fields, isolated houses, then a small community with a few brick buildings clustered at one end surrounded by a crowded parking lot; a double row of flat-topped two-story structures; houses scattered behind the business section on either side and up the hillsides, pushing the forest back with hedges and flower beds. A church steeple. Then they were over the country again, flying above a dam and a lake of dark water trapped by dense woods. No smooth boat landings, no beaches.

He wanted to ask if that had been Tyler Mills, but his dad's eyes were closed. It's just as well, Rob thought. He didn't want to show interest or make any gesture that Davis could interpret as a concession. He'd been forced to come, had had to give up a week of his summer. He was silent, savoring his anger.

The jet droned, its engines close and fierce as they dropped altitude, seeming to pick up speed. Rob felt pressure on his chest and he stared down at the hills coming up, trees now separate, clumps of pines on the ridges, thick stands of conifers, wild laurel thickets, black-trunked oaks, then a fringe of dogwood leafing toward the light, weedy patches of wild daisies and black-eyed Susans. They bumped onto the runway, lurching forward slightly, the engines roaring as the plane settled to the ground.

"Terra firma," his dad said, opening his eyes. Davis Dickson was smiling as he leaned toward Rob to peer out the window. There was nothing to see but the border of trees and weeds. His smile drew in, becoming abruptly tight and nervous, and he squeezed Rob's thigh quickly as if he needed contact with a fellow traveler, even if it was his hostile child.

Rob didn't respond but looked out the window, watching as the dinky brick airport came into view. The plane nosed toward it while the stewardess reminded them to remain seated. Her mouth pressed to the microphone, she watched them like a prison guard addressing the incorrigibles in her charge. Behind the fence people waited with their fingers hooked in the chain links, grinning with anticipation.

No one had come to welcome the Dicksons. There would be a rental car to take them farther into the country, up a narrow snaking highway, until they finally turned onto a road that would wind down into the valley where four generations of Dicksons had lived. The house would be standing alone because most of the outbuildings were shacks now, the fences in tatters, the orchard and garden stymied with weeds. Davis' sister Rosalie had told him how it was. She had been telling him since Christmas how the place was falling apart.

"Papa's half senile," she'd huffed on the phone, being dramatic. "Brother does all he can but he's by himself in it. And Cora, well, I don't really know what ails her. You ought to see for yourself, Davis. You ought to come."

He'd promised he would, but then he didn't. He had trips to make. His job as a management consultant kept him in the air too much as it was. He had his own family: a troubled teenager, his wife teaching a full load, a daughter they were watching like hawks. He couldn't just pick up and go because Rosalie overreacted to every situation that came along.

All through the winter and spring Davis had put her off, promising a summer visit when Rob and Allison, perhaps even Carrie, would be free. But Carrie had ended up teaching summer school at the college; Allison was at a local camp for the gifted, and Rob was—well, here he was scowling as he lifted his duffel bag out of the overhead storage bin. He wouldn't bring anything but T-shirts and jeans, his running shoes and some shorts. Carrie had put a pair of chinos in Davis' bag, just in case, but Davis doubted he'd be able to get Rob to wear them. There was no need to dress up to visit Fairlee in the hospital, anyway.

"We'll go to the house first," Davis said at Rob's shoulder as he followed him through the airport lobby. They were moving quickly, although there was no need to. "We'll get the car and go on out there, see what's what before we visit Fairlee." He seemed to think that making their plans clear would ease the tension between them, but Rob moved on ahead, out of range of his dad's conspiratorial tone.

Confined in the plane he'd had no choice but to cooperate. He'd accepted the noon snack, thumbed through

9

the magazine the stewardess handed him, but now with this momentary space between them he was going to avoid contact with his father. Soon enough they'd be in the car together, probably sleeping in the same room, touching whether he wanted to or not, breathing the same damp musty air in that old falling-down excuse for a house. For the time being he was going to stay out of reach.

In the parking lot Davis handed him the keys to a new Oldsmobile, then waited on the passenger side while Rob opened the door and tossed their bags into the backseat. The interior smelled strong, the ashtray was clean, the dashboard clock worked. While the engine idled, Rob switched on the radio, but the only clear station twanged with country music and he clicked it off with a groan.

"Left," Davis said, "then west on the highway." There was a lightness in his voice now, as if he were expecting to make an adventure out of the trip.

Rob caught his profile, just a quick glance away from the road no one could criticize, and saw that his dad's face betrayed him. The flesh seemed to be sagging away from his cheekbone; the corners of both eye and mouth drooped slightly. There was a pouch of flesh under his jaw, a scattering of gray hair at his temple. Rob looked back at the road while Davis loosened his tie and slid deeper into the seat. Although he didn't seem interested in Rob's driving, Rob stayed defensive, ready to balk against any advice Davis might give him.

After he'd turned onto the highway, Rob glanced in his father's direction again, expecting an interrogation.

Neither of his parents could get him alone in the car ten minutes without wanting to know all about him. "What do you think?" they would ask, waiting anxiously for his reply. He had learned to be careful. The comradery of the journey, the steady engine music, used to lull him sometimes, and he would inadvertently show them a vulnerable spot they could pounce on, investigate, pick clean with their sharp little know-it-all teeth. He had learned to keep his mouth shut.

"How far is it?" he was forced to ask after a long silence.

"Thirty miles or so. The farm is six miles past Tyler Mills. Of course, we could go by now to see your Uncle Fairlee. Do you want to do that? It would keep us from having to come back to Tyler Mills tonight. Maybe that would be better."

"Whatever." He wasn't accustomed to being asked to make such specific decisions. "What do you want?" was what they asked him. "What's the matter?" Questions too big to respond to. There could be so many wrong answers.

"Let's stop at the hospital and see Fairlee then. It's still midafternoon. We can see him, find out just how he's doing and then we'll have something to report to Papa and Coralee when we get to the house. Maybe we'll stop and get a few groceries, too. Things you like. No telling what they've been eating without Fairlee to go to the store."

"Aunt Rosalie brings things out," Rob reminded him.

"And complains about it, too. I don't want her to have to do anything while we're here," Davis said, sitting up

11

straighter. "We'll stop and see Fairlee first," he said. "And get some groceries." This plan encouraged him. "According to Rosalie your Uncle Fairlee is going to be helpless for quite a while. A broken hip at his age doesn't mend quickly. Now, you'd be on your feet in no time. Of course, I've never heard of a young person with a broken hip—collarbones, legs, necks, that's what kids break. And hearts, of course. Not you, though, no girl breaking your heart. Not yet."

He seemed to want Rob to respond, but what was there to say? Rob didn't trust this talkative person with a sudden interest in his love life. It was his mother who was after him to date—not go steady, of course, but take a girl to a movie on Saturday night, get a pizza, go to the dances after the football games. She could imagine those settings, make a pretty picture in her head that included elegant manners on his part, the care he'd take driving, maybe even a gentle, innocent kiss under the porch light. No groping. No French kissing, no joints passed between them while they parked in the littered clearing behind the municipal park. He had managed to keep Marsha a secret for the past six months. Maybe he thought she wasn't worth the hassle, maybe she never would be. He knew she wasn't the kind of date he'd voluntarily bring home to dinner. She wasn't the girl his mother would want to take to her heart.

The thought of what his mother wanted sent a swift ache across Rob's chest. He shuddered with it.

"You cold?" his dad asked, reaching over to adjust the air-conditioner vent.

"Yeah," Rob said. It was easier than telling the truth.

3

The hospital was a one-story concrete-block building with a brick face. Rob turned the car into a visitors' space facing the glass entryway. He could see into the lobby: chrome and vinyl sofas, scraggly overgrown plants tilting out of plastic pots, a television attached to the wall projecting a rolling colored picture.

"This is the hospital," he said sarcastically, but his dad didn't bite. The drive seemed to have exhausted him. He didn't have any fight left, or else he'd tuned Rob out.

"When I was a boy, it was two rooms attached to the doctor's house," Davis said. "Nobody wanted to go to the hospital anyway. People thought you were bound to die there and they'd rather take their chances at home."

They got out slowly, stretching and frowning in the heat. The air was still. No cool mountain breeze or smell of dark mossy soil like Rob remembered.

"I hope the place is air-conditioned," he said.

"Don't count on it," Davis answered, but in the lobby they were met with a blast of cool air. "There are only twenty beds, so we ought to be able to find him."

They turned down the right hall and went past the X-ray and lab rooms before they came to the little cubbyhole that served as the nurses' station. "Fairlee Dickson," Davis said to the nurse. "I'm his brother."

"I think he's asleep, Mr. Dickson," the nurse answered, "but you go on in. He doesn't have anything to do but sleep, so I know he'll be glad to see you. It's the second room on the left."

The door was slightly ajar, and through the opening Rob could see the bed with the sheet pulled back so his Uncle Fairlee's legs were exposed below a loose hospital gown. He was bandaged down one thigh and his white legs looked awkward and useless. Rob couldn't remember seeing his uncle undressed, not even in pajamas. Fairlee was always up before everybody else, wearing khaki work pants or jeans that bagged in the seat and slipped down in front below a hefty protrusion of gut.

"Fairlee," Davis said, going past his son in the doorway. "Fairlee, it's Davis."

They waited for the eyes to blink open. A grin appeared at the same moment. "Well, if this don't beat all! I thought I was dreaming there for a second. That's the truth. I saw you through the slit of my eye. That nurse always thinks I'm sleeping—she don't know how I can lie like the dead an hour or two. I learned how to be quiet hunting, boy. Out in the woods, the critters know. You got to still your breathing and not make a sound when you're squirrel or rabbit hunting. Come on in here! Lord-a-mercy, it's little Robbie come all the way down here to see us!"

He twisted toward them in the bed and put out his arms for Rob to come into his embrace. There was nothing to do but oblige. Rob leaned down onto the thick chest, felt the warm shoulder against his face, smelled after-shave and tobacco smoke. He had not hugged a man in so long he'd forgotten the feel of it, the rightness of equal contact. There was no reason to be gentle, no fear of crushing. Fairlee pounded him on the back, solid thuds that didn't hurt but sprang off his shoulder blade easily, like he was being pumped up. They let go of each other.

"And you, little brother," Fairlee boomed.

Davis took Rob's place but didn't linger. He pulled himself up but kept his hand on his brother's shoulder for an awkward moment.

"You look fine, Fairlee," he said. "To hear Rosalie tell it, you're in quite a lot of pain."

"Naw." Fairlee motioned for them to sit down. He folded one arm behind his head, ruffling his thick graying hair as he did. "They had me in traction for a part of a day and one night to keep me still until they could do the operation, and that was mighty uncomfortable. But since the surgery—that was two days ago—I've been doing all right. Got a pin in here, boy," he said, "a pin and a metal plate. Going to have 'em in there for the rest of my days, so they tell me. Going to have to take it easy for a spell, too. Can't pull my full weight on this bum hip." A fleeting sadness crossed his broad face but then he grinned again.

"Fell out of the hayloft, Rob. Did you hear that? Up there sweeping a little, planning to store some odds and ends out of the damp, and lo and behold, the floor gives way right under me and next thing I know I'm sprawled out on the dirt. Couldn't get up, either. Couldn't stand is what I'm saying. Crawled to the house, dragging this leg along like it was a soaked log. I knew there was something wrong in there. I could feel it all crackling and loose inside, stinging and carrying on. I pulled myself right up on the back porch and banged on the door for Cora. Finally she came. Scared to open it 'cause she looks

15

through the curtain and don't see a thing. I'm lying on the floor banging and her looking out at nothing. 'Coralee, open this damn door,' I yell, and the door flies open. I can tell you she was white as a sheet and trembling like a leaf. Both of us was. She pulled me in and called the emergency number on the telephone. They came, too. Brought me right here with the siren going and the light flashing. Those boys love that equipment and they make the most of it. Well"—he sighed, grinning at them—"that's the gist of it."

4

The car stirred a cloud of dust off the side of the road. They rode along in the gray bubble, the air conditioner chilling their bare arms and necks. Davis was driving now, maneuvering around potholes and ruts, holding the car in second gear as they went winding down the dirt road toward the farm. Queen Anne's lace was growing among the other weeds on the ditch banks, hiding the falling fences and rocky fields. Dust, dry and sparkling, flew up around them so that Davis leaned forward into the wheel to peer through the windshield.

Someone was walking ahead of them, a tall, lean figure slightly stooped, wearing a flat-brimmed hat that shielded him from the sun on all sides. Hearing the car, the figure moved to the edge of the road but didn't step completely out of the way.

"Owns the road," Rob said as they passed the figure, spinning dust onto his ancient clothes—a collarless shirt, tattered pants pulled high with buttoned suspenders.

Davis put on the brakes, sliding a little on the loose gravel, and flung open the door. "Want a lift?" he asked into the thick gray air behind him. The car engine idled loudly, making a troubling sound in the silent valley.

"Can't say as I object." The old man came forward slowly. He was no hitchhiker racing for a ride that could at the last minute pull away from him. Finally he climbed into the backseat, his hat low on his forehead, sparkling powder lifting from every surface as he dusted himself off.

"Much obliged," he said, no gratitude apparent in his gravelly voice. "Need rain," he went on, mumbling in the quiet interior of the car. "Been needing it. Every car comes by here stirs up a storm of dust somebody's got to clean off. The garden didn't make worth nothing. Puny old thing. Corn ain't half tasseled."

Davis cleared his throat as if he had swallowed a mouthful of road dust. "Rob," he said, "son, speak to your grandpa." He concentrated on the road, never glancing into the rearview mirror. "Papa," he said more loudly, "it's me, Davis. I've come down here to see how you're doing."

There was no movement from the backseat. Then the head came up, the exposed face looking tight and hard. "I knowed it was you, boy," he said, angry at them both. But they knew he had not.

The house was two story with a porch running the width of it. Two long windows stared blankly from either

17

side of the front door, and there were three gabled windows above the tin porch roof. The side of the house they approached from the lane had a porch, too, which Rob remembered connected the house to the kitchen.

When his family had come for a visit six years ago, his dad had told him all about the house, how when his great-grandfather built it to replace the original cabin, the kitchen was a separate building because they were afraid of fire, although they eventually linked it to the house with a porch. Later they got an iron wood stove so big the floor had to be reinforced to support it. It had been Grandpa who had put in electricity, gotten a hot water heater, a modern stove and refrigerator, had put screens on the windows and a bathroom where the hall closet used to be. "Protesting every minute," Davis had said.

Rob remembered because, even at eleven, he had struggled with the idea of being attached to such a person. How could it be that ever in the world there were people opposed to progress, who would rather stumble in the dark to the outhouse than flip a light switch in a warm, clean bathroom?

5

They pulled up facing the side porch, where snowball bushes drooped heavy with fat blossoms turning rusty with age. Under the porch roof the splintery white wall was mildewed, but where the boards were exposed to the weather they were clean, bare and gray.

"You ought to get the house painted, Pa," Davis said, irritated by the sight of the place. What could he have expected, Rob wondered, after all Rosalie had complained about? Had he imagined everything magically perked up to welcome him home? Had he expected a welcome at all?

The house was quiet, but Rob thought he saw a movement at the kitchen door window where the curtain fluttered lightly as if someone had breathed on it. Or maybe it had been parted slightly, held back by a thread. Coralee was watching them.

"I'll get the bags," Davis said, and hurried to lift them off the seat so Rob was left to tend to his grandfather.

Rob opened the back door and waited for the old man to pull himself out of the car. His grandfather came through the opening with his tough, gnarled fingers gripping the doorjamb and armrest, his head bent low under his hat. He didn't acknowledge Rob at all but went on toward the house, his steps wandering a little as if he had to get used to walking again after the motion of the car. He grabbed hold of the post to pull himself up the porch steps and banged heavily on the kitchen door.

"She's got everything locked up tight as a tick. Ain't nothing in there nobody wants, but she thinks she'll keep the boogeyman out," he mumbled.

The house responded with silence.

"Cora! Dad-blame it, gal. We got somebody here!" he boomed suddenly. He took off his hat and slapped it on his thigh, then stomped his high-top work shoes on the floor, stirring the dust that settled right back into place. He had a thin neck, crisscrossed with deep ridges and sprouts of wild white hair growing at random below his hairline. There was a narrowness about him and a hard quality, too, like a locust post long set that leans a little and gives in a hard wind, but if need be can bear weight.

"Maybe she went out," Davis suggested. He was on the porch holding his suit bag over his shoulder. Rob waited on the steps.

"Huh!" Grandpa snorted. "Not likely." He tried the doorknob, which turned easily in his hand. The door sprang open and there was the kitchen just as Rob remembered it. A round table covered with yellow floral oilcloth, a lightbulb dangling below a fluted milk-glass shade, open shelves exposing stacks of mismatched dishes, rows of jelly glasses, tomatoes, beans, corn and pickles put up in Mason jars, black skillets resting inside each other, clear glass canisters of beans, rice, tea, coffee, flour, sugar, cornmeal. Under the narrow counter a skirt of blue calico hiding whatever Cora couldn't bear to throw away—a handleless saucepan, an enamel footpan eaten thin with rust, a heavy container of rat poison marked with skull and crossbones.

"She seen us coming and opened the door, that's what she done. Gone upstairs to put on them diamonds of hers." Grandpa hung his hat on a wobbly coat tree in the corner. The room was close with heat and smells of vegetables stewing in bacon drippings.

"Leave the door open, boy," Grandpa ordered Rob. "And put up every window. I knowed it'd be hot as a cracker in here. I tell her, cook of a morning and let it set all day, but Cora does her own way."

"And what are you goin' on about, Papa?" Cora asked from the doorway. She was gray headed, hair cut short and blunt as if she'd done it herself. Her skin was pale and clear, as unwrinkled as a child's although she was sixty years old. She wore an old-fashioned print dress with a scallop-edged collar that formed a V above her breasts and buttoned down the front. It was too long, halfway down her calves, floating above her worn tennis shoes.

"Sweet Jesus, it's Davis come all the way down here!" She sucked in her breath as if to gather with it such extraordinary news. Her lips quivered, eyes glassed over to cry, but then she saw Rob and forgot everything. "Look, Papa! It's Robbie. God love us and now I know He does. Why, he's handsome, Davis. Better-looking than all of us put together. A movie star! Why, he could get on television just like that, if'n he wanted to, but we wouldn't see him, would we?"

"Not in this house!" the old man shouted at her. "No sirree! People coming at you selling things, wanting you to buy. Telling what's going on halfway round the world when it ain't none of your business."

"No TV?" Rob mouthed toward his dad before Cora had him in her embrace. She hugged him against her thin chest so he felt her ribs, the fluttery breath pushing in and out, her hands on his back, kneading the flesh gently as if she must get the feel of him to be convinced he was there. She seemed intent on holding him forever.

Davis looked embarrassed, waiting his turn. "Let him

go, Cora," he said finally. "He's not going anywhere."

"Who says that?" But Cora turned Rob loose, leaving her arms open for her brother. "Who knows what will happen outside of here?" she asked with a stern look that melted immediately into a little smile. The two of them hugged.

"Cora, you going to put supper on the table or not?" the old man fussed, scraping his chair out from the table.

But Coralee held on to her brother. "What's the hurry, Papa? You didn't even wash up yet."

"It's six o'clock, I know that much," Papa barked, "and this here table is bare."

Undeterred, Cora hugged Davis even harder. "You been gone too long. You don't feel right," Coralee said. "He's too skinny, Papa. Look at him. He's skin and bones. You stay around here and we'll put some meat on you." She released him reluctantly.

"Don't see how," Grandpa grumbled. "We're all near 'bout starved and you ain't doing nary a thing about it."

"He's all the time complaining," Coralee said lightly, turning to the shelves above her meager counter space. She lifted down the plates, heavy chipped ones with faded wreaths of flowers on the rims. One of them had a thin black line across its yellowed surface where it had been glued.

Who would mend a plate? Rob wondered. Why bother? His mother would drop it in the trash without a thought.

"Let's help get the food on the table then," Davis said, almost gaily. His eyes searched Rob's face looking for a congenial response, but Rob would not give in.

He forced his face into sullenness, averted his eyes,

pushed a ribbon of disgust across his forehead. There, he thought. Deal with that, Daddy.

"Push up them windows, boy, like I told you," Grandpa ordered from his place at the table. "I'm sweating like a pig."

"I'm going to the john," Rob said, ignoring the old man. It was the only escape he could think of, a contrived exit, but it pleased him to leave his father there.

6

The kitchen air was still thick with greasy smells when Rob came down at dawn. He opened the back door quietly and touched the screen. The mesh had a chill on it. He breathed deeply, trying to exhale the misery of a wakeful night.

He'd been restless in the bed beside his father, cramped by the small space of the room and the proximity of someone in the bed with him. Preparing for sleep they had both felt nervous, out of sorts. Their rituals were unknown to each other now—there was no tucking in anymore, no recitation of prayers, no familiar, easy method of saying good night. Instead, they'd crept into their separate spaces and drawn up the communal sheet protectively although the room was stuffy with locked-in afternoon heat. They sighed separately, then in unison, which surprised them both and caused them to turn simultaneously away from each other. Rob had spent the night trying not to move.

Now he pushed on the screen door, easing it past a squeak, and sat down on the step with his running shoes in his hand. He was glad he'd thrown them into his bag. Now he saw he'd planned his escape in advance without even realizing it. Already he wanted to get away from the encroachment of these relatives, although last night they hadn't seemed especially interested in him beyond how he liked the beans, the fried okra, the cornbread. He'd heard how he looked like his daddy, which anybody could see wasn't true, how surprised Rosalie was going to be when she came out this morning before work and found him and his daddy here. "She'll be mad as a hornet," Cora'd said happily, as if she were eager to see her sister with her dander up. "She'll be wanting to know how come we didn't call her up tonight," Cora said, "when she ought to know I'd want you to myself for half a minute. She'll want to know why you didn't say you was coming, Davis Lee. She'll get you told but good," Cora ended with a quick, barking laugh. Rob didn't want to have to listen to it.

Mist hung between the barn and the orchard, almost as thick as fog. He wondered how long it would take the sun to burn through. Noon, probably. No wonder the house felt damp; inside the walls it was probably spongy with wood rot. His laces double knotted, he stood in the yard trying to decide which way to go. The road they'd traveled the day before was the only one familiar to him, but he'd probably meet Rosalie on it. He remembered there was another dirt road going up the mountain, though, at about the spot they'd picked up Grandpa. Farther up it would probably turn out to be one of the logging trails that laced the mountains. It would be ragged and brambly but at least he would be off the main road. He stretched a little, leaning against the car to release the tightness of his calves, and then started slowly down the road. He wanted to be gone a long time.

7

Rob met Rosalie at the back door.

"So you're back," she said, standing firm in his way on the steps. "I was just telling Davis what kind of luck I've been having trying to find somebody to come up here and stay. Nobody wants to leave home and hearth if they can help it—they have to be *destitute*—and Papa says he's not having a woman in this house. He and Cora think they can manage fine, but you see how it's going. With Fairlee off his feet for at least two months, we've got to do something. He won't be able to get himself into the bathtub, can't drive, can't do anything without a walker or a cane. And no lifting. He don't know the meaning of helpless, and he's going to try to do just like usual if we don't get some help. I told Davis I've got to work. We can't get by without Avery and me both working. Leanna's got a job, too, at Ennis' char-broil place in town. I told her she'd better keep it during school this year. She'll have to work her schedule around cheer-leading and chorus and all she wants to do."

Rosalie took a breath and grabbed Rob's shoulders. "I haven't got a hug yet, now have I? Down here we hug our kin. Big hugs. None of that cheek-pecking I see on TV like foreigners do."

He was damp from cooling down and smelled sour. Serves her right, he thought, giving her a big hug. She was polyester neat. Not a crease anywhere and her hair teased high with morning light glinting through it.

"I've been running," he said, breaking loose.

"I can see that," Rosalie answered. She was solid on the creaking step. "I reckon you'll be going to see Fairlee today. Well, go by and speak to Leanna, why don't you? Won't she be surprised! You'll have to introduce yourself, it's been so long. She's about forgot she's got Yankee cousins, and you might not know her either. She's all grown up just like you are. A senior in high school! My baby's just about out of the nest and having a fit to go to college. Wants to study those computers. She's going, too—beg, borrow or steal. I told Davis it'll mean something to her because she'll know the sacrifice. Some children think everything's supposed to come to them tied up in a pretty package, but Leanna knows different. She was raised different."

Finished at last, Rosalie pushed past Rob as if he were an obstacle in her path and got into her car. "I told Davis I'd see him later—we've got a lot of decisions to make—so I'll see you, too," she called through the open window. "I want to get some things settled before your daddy takes off. Three days here has always been his limit, and that's not time to decide doodly-squat."

She was gone, her drooping exhaust pipe bubbling a trail of oily smoke behind her.

"She's a nervous wreck," Davis said, stepping out on the porch.

"She's a bitch." Rob dropped to the step to take off his shoes. He spanked them against the edge of the step. Davis didn't respond. He watched the first glint of sun on the barn roof.

"I guess we're going to see Fairlee today," Rob said. "Your sister expects it."

"That's what I was planning to do all along. We never did get the groceries, so I've got Coralee making a list."

"Big plans."

"I think you can suffer through," Davis replied.

Rob heard the screen door close behind him. He was suddenly tired. His body sagged inward so his lungs were scrunched together and his breath was shallow. His empty stomach burned. All this discomfort reminded him of how lax he'd been all summer. Sometimes he'd walked more than he'd run, and he'd skipped days altogether. Once an entire week.

He stripped off his socks and stuffed them in his shoes, then planted his feet in the patchy grass below the step. There was no walk, just a hollowed footpath wandering from the gravel lane toward the house, another ragged trail in the direction of the clothesline. No straight lines anywhere; instead, the sagging barn, overgrown shrubbery, a jagged line of runty hemlocks that separated the yard from the field. Once there had been flowers there, Rob remembered, seeing another summer morning in his mind. Tiny button marigolds of brassy orange and gold that Coralee couldn't bring into the house because

27

Pa hated their smell. Behind them, red plants that grew straight up, a single fluffy spire—scarlet something, he thought it was, that reminded him of soldiers on parade, each one standing at attention. He remembered there'd been hollyhocks behind the house because that day his dad had shown him how to make dolls out of the pink blossoms. It had embarrassed him, seeing his father holding the dainty petal skirt in his hand or slitting the tiny stem of a clover blossom to make a chain, and he'd rushed off to his sister with them to watch her crush the flowers in her baby fist, bruising the petals to a bright red like blood spots in her hand.

"See what she did!" he cried to his dad, forcing the attention on Allison so no one would see how his father's childhood embarrassed him. *I was six or seven then*, Rob recalled, *and I knew what a dump this was.*

They'd visited one other time he could remember, at Thanksgiving when he was eleven. He was cold the entire three days. Rosalie and Avery came on Thursday morning, bringing Leanna along with their three older children, two brawny teenage boys and a married daughter with two babies. They filled up the house, grunting and grinning at each other. He thought they didn't speak the same language he knew. The men clustered in the living room in front of the stove listening to Fairlee tell stories that always ended in quick, explosive bursts of laughter unless Grandpa interrupted the tale midway, impatient to be the center of attention himself.

Meanwhile, the women bumped into each other as they talked and cooked in the crowded kitchen. Even his mother had joined in, rocking Rosalie's grandson to

28

sleep, learning about cracklin's because Grandpa wanted cracklin' bread, no matter what kind of meal they were having. It turned out to be thick greasy cornbread with hard bits of bitter skin in it.

Now as he sat in the narrow patch of sunlight that had eked through the mist, Rob could feel his old humiliation return, for he remembered how, when he spat the rancid, unchewable kernels into his hand, his daddy had sent him away from the table. Leanna had enjoyed his exile, he remembered that. He knew from the smile hidden in her eyes.

She must have been twelve, a stringy-haired, pale little girl wearing a frilly dress meant for a spring party, not a family gathering in November. She'd followed him out onto the back porch as soon as she could and stood there in the cold, not shivering a bit, just looking at him while he watched the bank of clouds rolling across the mountain, blocking the winter sun with their gray foam. He was the one shivering under his creased corduroys, his button-down shirt, his Izod crew-neck sweater.

He'd felt miserable, cold inside his skin but sweaty, too, and panicked by his dad's hard expectations for him. All day he'd been getting messages off Davis' creased brow, from his clenched jaw, the way he worked his hands, kneading his fingers as if recovering from the contact of a hard punch: Behave yourself; don't shame me with your privileged life; don't give Rosalie or Papa reason to criticize.

The men hadn't talked about their jobs or vacations or politics or movies or the national news. There was nothing they could agree on, no safe subject that didn't point relentlessly toward the differences between themselves and Davis. So they focused on hunting and fishing stories and, those topics finally exhausted, they turned mercilessly to Rosalie's grandchildren and Allison, who giggled in Uncle Fairlee's arms, unaware of her responsibilities to be entertaining; then eventually on Rob, the only Dickson heir, the unacknowledged title holder at odds with his skinny body, his brace-packed smile, his smarting, intractable anger at his father who, without warning, suddenly expected so much.

On the porch Leanna said as if addressing an assembly: "When it's time for dessert, don't touch the mincemeat. Sissy made it and she's the worst cook in the world. Besides, it's got suet in it." So she had come to warn him, to form an alliance.

He had turned toward her gratefully, thinking he'd acknowledge this friendly gesture, but his first skittering glance reminded him how she looked like her mother. A miniature of Rosalie's sharp face stared back at him full of cocky insulated pride, intent, he saw, on explaining everything because he was so pathetic, an ignorant city boy disconnected from real life.

"Then we'll all have wine. Daddy makes scuppernong, and every year we all have a glass at Thanksgiving and Christmas. Even the children." Leanna pushed her hands deep into her ruffly pockets, tightening her dress across her thin chest. Rob, who had just begun to notice the changing shapes of girls in his class, didn't see any sign that Leanna was going on thirteen, older than he.

"I drink wine every Sunday," he said solemnly. "At church."

Leanna's mouth dropped before she could get control of her face. "You do not!"

"I do too."

"It's grape juice. Welch's grape juice. I know it is."

"It's real wine," Rob said slowly. "Fermented. We're Episcopalians."

Leanna stared at him, made speechless by this horrible admission, and then she flew away, fluttering in her summer dress back to Rosalie's nest.

Later that afternoon, his head buzzing, he raised his glass to her and downed the last drop of her daddy's scuppernong wine, swallowing hard on its fruity sweetness. Across the room Leanna took another dainty sip, frowning into her juice glass while Rob watched her movements rippling in and out. Slowly she blurred into an adumbral figure, insignificant and unnecessary to him.

Leanna, he now recalled with a smile, had been the cause of his first drunk.

8

There was a girl on Fairlee's bed. Perched on the edge, one bare leg crossed under her, the other dangling so her sandal hung from her toes, she leaned toward Rob's uncle to whisper something, then tilted backward to make room for the laughter between them. Fairlee was sitting up, his slick damp hair struggling back into curls, the creases in his pajamas still evident from where Rosalie had taken them from the package. He was all spruced up and looking delighted with himself.

The girl had brown hair, cut very short except along the neckline, where it was long enough to give in to natural curl. Her shoulders seemed broad and solid, an athletic girl with tanned arms and legs. This couldn't be Leanna, Rob thought. He had a permanent image of his cousin—pale, her Rosalie bird face giving him quick, piercing looks that Thanksgiving afternoon.

"Rob!" Fairlee called. "Looky here, girl, my nephew's come!"

The girl turned toward Rob, half a fading smile visible, an interrupted face, words stopped on a mouth that twisted suddenly away from him. She chewed at her lip and murmured "Hi" too softly for him to hear what her voice sounded like. She slid off the bed and plopped into a vinyl chair. The place she left on the bed was rumpled.

"Sorry to butt in," Rob said. He didn't like his own voice. He stood at the end of the bed and hooked his thumbs awkwardly into his jeans pockets. The girl slumped deeper into the chair, steepling her hands under her chin. She hadn't looked at him for more than a fleeting glance, but he saw her eyes were dark and hooded in a sulk familiar to him. He felt as if he had glimpsed himself.

"You're not bothering a thing!" Fairlee boomed. "This is Ellery, a friend of mine from up the ridge. And honey, this here is my nephew Rob, come to see us from New Jersey. Sit yourself down right here, boy." He patted the place Ellery had just vacated.

32

"Dad stopped by the business office. He'll be here in a minute." Rob tried to settle on the bed but the edge felt too narrow for him.

"I was going to send Ellery down to see you today," Fairlee said. "I thought you'd be about the same age. Both turned seventeen this summer, if I got it right. Going to the eleventh grade. I thought to myself there's no reason these two don't get to know each other, even if it's just a week. To hear Ellery tell it, there's nothing to do around here, Rob, and I reckon she knows. Course, there's the natural things—hiking, fishing, just lying back in the woods enjoying the day, but you young folks don't get much outa that. Got to be going somewhere in the car to call it doing."

"This is his old-fogy act," Ellery said. Her smile had reappeared but she was looking at Fairlee. "In a minute he's going to tell us how *grateful* we should be."

"That's because it's the truth. 'Fore you know it, you're both going to be tied down in the classroom, stuck in those tight little desks with no leg room. You ought to be out running the ridge right this minute. Doing something besides sitting around in a hospital with an old geezer like me."

"I tried to run this morning," Ellery said irritably. "I told you somebody else was up there." She was frowning again. She stretched her legs out, caught her sandals on the undergirting of Fairlee's bed, and left them there. The bed moved slightly against the pressure of her feet while Rob tried to hold it steady with his own foot.

"Ellery's mama just built a house up beyond us, and

33

now Ellery thinks she owns the mountain," Fairlee said as if he saw the need of an interpreter. The two faces looking at him were so dependent, so ill at ease without him. "That's how foreigners are. They come in here and put down money for a piece of land, they cut through a road, dig a well, put up a house. They think they own it. They put up a no-trespassing sign. They get a shot-gun."

" 'Good fences make good neighbors,' " Ellery said, the beginning of a smile creeping onto her flushed face.

" 'Something there is that doesn't love a wall, That wants it down,' " Rob shot back.

"Robert Frost." Ellery aimed the words with her eyes, then offered her smile to Fairlee instead of Rob. "Do you know him? He wrote a really neat poem about mending fences. I'll bring it to you sometime."

"I knew you two would get on!" Fairlee squeezed Rob's knee. "You ought to get outa here right now. Do something. Ellery's got her mama's Jeep, and I'll tell Davis you're gone. Make a day of it."

"I'd better wait for Dad." Rob hesitated. "We've got to buy groceries."

"And I've got to do some shopping, too," Ellery said. "I need some stuff for school."

"Well, go along together!" Fairlee roared. "Go by Ennis' and get a burger. It'll give me something good to think about while I'm lying up here twiddling my thumbs. Well, go on."

9

She had two hundred dollars in her pocket, guilt money from her father, who had not come from Charlotte for her birthday. Four new fifty-dollar bills that had come in a silly card, just the kind he would pick because it expressed in cartoon fashion sentiments he couldn't seem to say straight out. For the past month she'd kept the card and folded money in a brass jewelry box he'd given her for Christmas. The box had contained diamond stud earrings, small enough to be tasteful for a teenager but large enough to look expensive. She had worn them once, when the chorus sang their spring concert. The earrings were the first thing Leanna noticed.

"Good gracious, look at those!" she'd squawked, getting the attention of the entire alto section.

"They're just zirconia," Ellery had said. "Fake."

But she was the fake. Here in Tyler Mills she imitated life—smiled, studied, walked, sang medleys from Broadway shows among forty untrained, exuberant voices, drove a Jeep up a winding, ragged road to an unfinished house her mother had built, chunks of beam exposed, fieldstone piled in the red clay yard.

She patted her hip pocket where her driver's license and money were stowed in an envelope. She never carried a pocketbook unless it was a big one stuffed with half her belongings. "It's all or nothing with you," her mother Ginny would say, "about everything."

Well, then, she'd spend every cent of the money. She'd clothe herself in revenge.

Rob trailed along behind her, not really wanting to go. He hoped he'd meet his dad in the hall, but Davis didn't appear and they were out in the hot sunlight before he could think of a reason not to go with her. The Jeep was a station wagon, high and bulky. He felt like he was crawling into a tank.

"There are three places to buy clothes in this town," Ellery said, fishing under the seat for the keys. She raked them out along with a paper cup, some soiled napkins and a coat hanger. When she'd turned the key and the Jeep had coughed itself into an even roar, she looked at Rob. "So your misery won't last long."

"Good," he sighed under his breath, but he thought she heard.

A few minutes later he was standing around while she ran her hand through the racks, pulling out an outfit now and then.

"Look," she'd say, "what do you think?" holding a bulky jacket in front of herself, swinging a shirt in his face. Everything she picked looked dull to him—gray, tan, green, camouflage colors, black pants, a motley sweater that came to her knees.

"Why don't you just go to the thrift shop?" he asked finally, half joking, but she had him by the arm and they were two doors down in a crowded storefront smelling of must and mothballs and other people's lives. She bought a man's jacket two sizes too big and several oversized shirts with soft worn stripes and ragged collars, the kind of shirts his grandfather had been wearing for years. All this amounted to eight dollars, and they were back in the department store buying what she'd left flung on the counter.

"Shoes," she said.

"No way." They were headed for the Jeep with Rob carrying the thrift-shop purchases in a wrinkled grocery-store bag.

"Just a pair of sneakers. It won't take fifteen minutes." She stuffed the bags in the backseat.

"I'll wait in the car."

"I think I'll get black high tops. What do you think?"

"I think you're going to look like an idiot." Rob got into the front seat.

"You don't even know me."

"Does anybody else here dress like this?"

"Not yet."

"So you want to be different?"

"I already am. In case you haven't noticed, I'm not from around here."

"I noticed." Rob beat out a rhythm on the dashboard. "Don't take too long. It's hot out here and I'm starving."

She slammed his door and he watched her going up the street, all legs, white shorts sparkling. He could see why Fairlee liked her. She was bright and fine to look at, opinionated and clever. Glib. The colors of her— dark hair and tanned skin contrasting with the pink T-shirt and white shorts—were meant to attract attention, to hold interest.

So why was she spending a small fortune on drabness, clothes to get lost in? Did she intend to hibernate through the winter? Actually, that seemed like a good idea to him. Hiding could be his junior-year project, too. He would speak only when spoken to, act only when the consequences would be worse than those of inertia. He would eat, sleep, wash, smoke, fill his days with droning classroom lectures while his empty notebooks and useless texts stayed piled in his locker. He could pass without studying; last year he'd proven his ability to slide. He'd be like an earthworm hidden in the dirt. Exposed, he'd just dig deeper; chopped in two, he'd heal himself. No problems in that furry place his mind could create. No confusion, no mental forages into the meaning of things. He would be loose and contained at the same time. It could be done.

"Hey, one pair of black high tops." Ellery plopped the bag between them and climbed in. "Now a burger at Ennis'. Really big-time. You will find, as a visitor from worlds beyond, that the resources of this planet are quite limited, as in nonexistent. There is Ennis', where char-burnt burgers await with canned chili and lettuce and tomatoes when in season. Then there is Bert's Serice Center, where on odd nights—e.g., when there's a full moon or an electrical storm, both occasions when respectable folks are not abroad—you can buy bootleg beer, even a pint of something akin to gin. This is a dry county, you see. No brew locally made anymore either, according to Fairlee, who knows the back roads like the lines in his palm. But plenty of car trunks. Bert's is the place." She started the Jeep. "Although I don't suppose you'll be here long enough to sample the stuff."

"Just through the week."

"Good for you, kiddo! Fly in, fly out. I envy your wings. I, like Icarus, flew too close to the sun once. It was a warning I heeded."

Rob wanted to ask how she'd come to live in Tyler Mills but something in her voice stopped him. He recognized its slow rolling movement, like smoke trapped in a bottle. Someday it was going to spew up, heat churning into anger. Maybe she was there already.

"Ennis'," she said, sailing into a parking place. "Let's go in. At least it's air-conditioned."

"You want to lock the car?"

"We can watch it." She pushed the keys under the seat. "If you close the windows, it'll be an inferno. Besides, nobody wants this stuff."

"Not if they look at it first," Rob agreed, following her into the restaurant.

The place looked like a takeout business with a recent addition to provide seating. Orange vinyl booths lined a new concrete wall. The tile floor was sticky where a spilled cola had been tracked across it.

"I'll buy," Rob said, heading for the counter.

"No, I will. I've got five dollars left and I want to spend every cent." Ellery pushed in front of him. "Two burgers, a large order of fries, two large Cokes," she said to the girl. "That okay?" to Rob.

"You doing all right, Ellery?" the girl asked, her back to them while she stuffed fries into a carton.

"Yeah, just bored out of my skull. Hey, Leanna, don't you know who this is?"

Leanna, bringing the fries to the tray, looked at Rob for the first time. "What are you doing here?" she blurted.

"Dad and I came last night."

"Well, thank the Lord. Mama's been harping on Uncle Davis coming for months. It's about to drive Daddy and me crazy, listening to her all the time. She's having a nervous breakdown, that's what I think."

"She seemed just the same to me." Rob sipped from the cup she handed him.

"You've seen Mama?"

"And Uncle Fairlee twice. That's where Ellery and I got together. She was visiting him too."

"I told Travis last night we ought to go by there, but he has this aversion to hospitals. The last time he went was to see his mama after her gall-bladder surgery. She had a tube coming out of her side, and that black bile was collecting in a bag hanging from the bed. Travis threw up right there! He's got the weakest stomach." Leanna put the wrapped burgers on the tray. "Four fifty-two," she said to Ellery and took the money. "How long you staying?"

"Just a few days. I don't want to waste my whole summer."

"School starts here in two weeks, if you can believe it. I dread it so bad, don't you, Ellery? Travis and I are going to the drive-in tonight to see *Psycho II*. Why don't you-all come along? I don't give a fig about seeing it—I hated the first one when it was on TV—but Travis says we probably won't be watching the show anyway." Leanna giggled. "Of course we will if you two come along."

"I've already seen it," Ellery said. "Two years ago in Charlotte."

"Me too," Rob said.

"We'll do something else then. Meet us down here at seven o'clock and we'll decide."

"I don't know," Ellery said.

"Me either."

"Well, call me later." Leanna had that bossy edge on her voice Rob remembered. "And take this food before it's cold." She leaned toward them. "It's not all that good when it's hot."

10

"I'll take you home," Ellery said.

"I can walk from your road." They were bumping along because Ellery didn't bother to avoid the chuckholes.

"I don't mind. Maybe I'll go in and speak to your aunt. Isn't she the saddest thing you ever saw?"

"I hadn't noticed. Why do you think so?"

Ellery took her eyes off the road long enough to squint at him. "How obtuse can you get?"

"You're dying to tell me, so let's have it, for God's sake."

"I think she's got agoraphobia."

"She's got what?"

"Agoraphobia. She hasn't been out of the house in at least three years. Not even in the yard. Fairlee had to get a clothes dryer because of it, and you can see how the garden's all grown up. That was Coralee's thing, according to Fairlee. She had a green thumb. She planted flowers everywhere and grew enough veggies to keep them fed all winter. Now he and Mr. Dickson try to manage a row of beans and a few tomato plants."

"I don't care about the garden. What about Coralee?"

"I don't know anything except what Fairlee told me, which wasn't very much. He didn't even know there was a name for it. Mom and I figured it out."

"So tell me," Rob said, then waited while Ellery swung the Jeep into the Dicksons' lane. It grumbled and churned in the dust.

"Get Fairlee to tell you," Ellery said. "He was there."

The rental car was parked at the edge of the house beside Fairlee's old Dodge truck. Ellery pulled in beside them, letting the motor idle while the dust flew into the open windows. "About tonight, you can forget it if you want to."

"You've got something better to do?" Rob had his hand on the door handle.

"Are you kidding? I keep telling you there's nothing happening here. It's the twilight zone."

"Then let's go. If nothing else, my spending some time with Leanna may appease Aunt Rosalie. She treats us like we think we're too good to be here."

"Maybe you are. I know I am." The Jeep bucked under her foot.

"I'll come get you," Rob said, grinning at her.

"Watch it on our road," she said when he was out of the Jeep. "Can you drive a stick? If you can, come in Fairlee's truck. When we get to town, we'll ride with Travis anyway." She backed up, arching across the stubby grass, then gunned down the lane and disappeared.

"So that was Fairlee's girlfriend," Davis said from the porch.

"She thinks a lot of him." Rob went past his father into the empty kitchen.

"He's coming home in a couple of days."

"That's terrific." Rob ran water, swished his hand under the flow, then filled a glass. "Then we can get out of here."

"I've spent most of the day talking to social services, the employment agency, talking to everybody Rosalie's already talked to, and I came up with zilch. Some management consultant I'm turning out to be."

"Oh, come off it, Dad. Giving advice to companies is hardly the same as finding a baby-sitter for three grown people." The water had a sweet taste he'd never noticed anywhere else, and he held it on his tongue for a moment.

"Maybe so," Davis replied, "but I can't leave here without some arrangement for their care. Rob, I do have one idea I've been mulling over. It came to me while I was studying the job description. You see, what we're looking for is a physically fit person, someone who can do the lifting, get Fairlee in and out of the tub, do the errands and be here at night. Those are the essentials. Between, say, eight and four, I think the three of them could get by fairly well alone now that they've got a telephone. Of course, it would have to be a person they'd feel comfortable with, especially Cora and Pa. They won't tolerate a stranger in the house."

"I think you'll have to stay, Dad." Rob laughed. The laughter hung there. In a moment of pure silence that followed, he put the glass carefully in the sink.

"I was thinking of you, son," Davis said. "It is a very possible solution."

"A solution? I'm not a solution! I'm going home with you." He slapped the glass over, shattering it in the sink. "I'm not staying here, Dad. They're all half crazy—"

"They'll hear you!" Davis gripped the back of the chair, then pulled it out carefully and sat down at the table. "Listen, Rob," he said calmly. "I'm not saying this is ideal but it is an answer. You have to admit that. You can go to school here until the end of the term."

"That'll be Christmas."

"Maybe just till Thanksgiving then. Three months, and you'll be out of the house most of the day."

"Yeah, in some rinky-dink school that starts mid-August."

"I don't remember the quality of the school mattering to you before now. You've slept through two years of excellent education so far."

"It's punishment, isn't it?" Rob studied the shards of glass. He could glide his hand across the jagged edges and bring it up dripping blood. He didn't move. "You got me down here to punish me. Or to get rid of me." He turned away from the glass. "You can't make me do this."

"I've never made you do anything, son. I think that's part of your trouble. But it's decided. You're going to stay here. I mean it."

"No."

"You're staying, Rob." The voice was cold.

"I'm calling Mom. She won't let you do this."

"I've just spoken to her, but of course you can call her anytime you want to. She sees the sense of it, Rob. She sees it could be a good thing for you. Maybe you need a little time away from home, away from the city. I know what the pressures are, son."

"You don't know anything! All you know is you need this done and so I can do it. Well, you can forget it because I won't stay. What are you thinking? Make the kid walk five miles to school and that'll make a *man* out of him? It's a crock, Dad, and you know it. You left here as soon as you could, and I haven't seen you rushing back. Three times in seventeen years that I know of. Some fine son! Some great role model!"

Davis was out of the chair. "Hold it, Rob. That's enough. You straighten up and listen, damn it, before we both say things we'll regret. I know this is a surprise, even a shock, but you know damned well it wasn't planned. I thought I'd come down here and find somebody to hire."

"You can't make me stay. I can be out of here in five minutes flat."

"You can, but you'd better not come home."

Rob was too angry to move. Muscles, held so tightly that his body throbbed, gave way suddenly and he crumbled inside, demolished by his dad's power over him. "They don't even have a television set."

"We'll send one. We'll send anything you want. We can rent a box on a moving van and move the entire contents of your room down here in about three days."

"What about my car?"

"There's Fairlee's truck. He won't be driving it anyway."

"What about my school credits? They probably don't have the same classes I've preregistered for."

"Grabbing at straws, Rob. The schedule can be arranged."

"You never had to go to a new school. I don't know anybody, Dad."

"You know this girl Fairlee likes so much. And your cousin."

"There's nothing to do here. Ellery hates it! She's miserable."

"Then she'll be glad to have you. I hear misery loves company."

"This isn't a joke, Dad. It's my life we're talking about."

"It's three months, Rob. Till Thanksgiving—Christmas at the latest. Listen, son, I don't expect you to be happy about this. I'm not happy about it either. But hard times demand hard decisions. You've been making a mess of things at home, we both know that. I know you've been unhappy for a long time. You've been bogged down. Well, you can bungle it here, too, if that's what you want. But you can also do a good thing. You and Fairlee can get to know each other. Coralee, too. I know Pa's cantankerous, but he's an old man and this may be your only chance to know him even a little bit."

"Yeah, this is a great opportunity."

Davis sighed and slumped a little against the table. "I'm going to tell Rosalie you'll do it," he said. "When she gets her chin up off the floor, she'll probably say something encouraging, like you're better than nothing."

"I don't want to deal with Rosalie," Rob said.

"You're not alone in that." Davis smiled. "I think once she sees things are going all right, she'll leave you to it."

"I hate this, Dad."

"I know. Just try it, Rob. Things could work out better than you think."

11

His father left him in the kitchen. The room felt oily to him, full of old smells like souring coffee grounds and rotting fruit. He pushed up a window but there was no breeze. He was locked in. He knew he hadn't fought hard enough. Why was that? Didn't he have the courage even for this, a battle he could possibly win, that didn't center on some previous failure? His arguments with his dad had always been after the fact—after the grades, the speeding ticket, after missing basketball tryouts, after giving up the guitar.

He remembered the struggle his fingers had had on the strings. They had felt like gigantic sores to him. He didn't even wait to get calluses before stashing the instrument under his bed. It haunted him, though. Two hundred dollars of enthusiastic Christmas spending he'd abandoned by February while his dad complained of the waste. "You never try hard enough," Davis had said. "Look at all the kids struggling just to survive—no money, broken homes, living conditions you wouldn't let a dog live in, and they manage. They make something of themselves."

"Just like you did," Rob would egg him on, although he knew this emotional sparring got them nowhere.

It was his mother who always forgave him. She spent her days with college students and so she knew how to forgive. Tolerance with late essays and unexcused absences seeped into her weekends and evenings, making her tolerant when he was an hour late, sympathetic when he needed a loan. Still he knew he drew her attention only in negative ways. She was probably glad to be rid of him.

Then he would oblige her. He would stay. He would hate every minute of it. He would do the minimum. If he failed, no one would be surprised. Nothing he did mattered in the long run. He knew that.

The house was too quiet. Was anybody really there but him? Maybe this was all a dream he was having. His crazy grandfather, these weird aunts and uncles, this dreary old house, even Ellery, maybe they were all some wired fantasy, a long, lingering nightmare he'd eventually pull free of.

"What are you doing, standing in here all by yourself?" Cora asked, coming close to squeeze his arm. She was wearing big gaudy rings, dime-store stones with adjustable bands, that cut into his skin.

"Nothing."

"Thinking, I betcha. You know what's out there, don't you? First time I looked at you yesterday, I could tell you knew."

"Knew what?"

"Ah-ha. About what goes on. You can't be too careful. Fairlee broke his hip from not taking care."

"I'll be careful then," Rob said, waiting for her to loosen her grip.

"See to it," she said. "Ellery brought you back home. She came to see me once. She's ignorant but she's sweet."

"She's a friend of Leanna's," Rob offered.

"Well, that don't go far toward recommending her, does it?"

"I guess Dad's told you he wants me to stay here and help out until Uncle Fairlee's well."

"Pshaw, I can do everything. There's not one thing I can't do."

"What about the groceries? And the garden?"

Coralee stiffened and moved away from him. She looked down at the broken glass in the sink. "Look at this here," she said.

"I know. I did it—accidentally. I'll clean it up."

"I'll do it."

"I broke it. I'll clean it up." Rob swung past her and lunged his hand into the sink. He didn't feel the cut but there it was, a thin line of crimson across his palm. He watched it widen, a red stinging ridge pushing through the skin. "Damn."

"Does it hurt?" Coralee was dabbing at it with the wet end of a dish towel.

"No," Rob said, staring hard at the reappearing rim of blood. "Nothing hurts me," he said.

12

The next morning, there was a soft rain, the kind that lets you know by its steady drumming that it's settled in. Ellery put on her running clothes anyway, raked her fingers through the brush of hair that was beginning to fall toward her forehead, popped a stick of gum into her mouth and went downstairs. The house was quiet and thick with moist air. The all-night rain had drenched the new dry smell of the house with another fragrance, a woodsy smell like wet rotting leaves and moss. The room was hazy with cloudy unfocused light, but she could see the looms, the slick golden wood of the castles, the dull thin steel of heddles laced with yarn.

Her mother was using three looms at once, moving from one to another as the mood struck her—here, pastel cottons for baby blankets; next, cloth as blue-green as fresh water, shot with rust and gold like sunlight. Finally, heavy place mats in a row with lengths of connecting fringe, Christmas green woven with contrasting squares of red, elegantly plain. Only one loom was empty, an old one with heavy oak works, scarred and unstrung. Her mother had found it at an auction, and it had taken Fairlee's truck and three men to get it home. The string heddles would have to be retied, the splintered pegs gouged out and replaced; the cloth beam was missing altogether.

"You've already got three looms," Ellery had protested. "There's no place to sit."

"I can't leave it here," Ginny said, as if that were explanation enough.

It's her stray, just like you are mine, Ellery thought, rubbing her hand lightly along Rufus' back as he slunk against her ankles.

She stepped over the cat and took her shoes and socks out on the porch, where the rain splattered the steps and sent rivulets of red clay down trickling paths between lumps of gravel in the driveway. Shoes on, she stuck her hand beyond the eave and tested the cool drops on her wrists, then went down the steps, turning back to stretch against the porch post. Her calves twitched and pulled. She rolled her shoulders, feeling the light pellets of rain slipping down her shirt. She put her arms behind her head and tugged at them in turn until she felt the stretch down her sides, her shoulder blades giving inwardly, softening.

Then she jumped over the puddles in the yard and walked down the road, welcoming the rain that soaked into her hair and flattened her tank top to her back and breasts. Once in the woods she wouldn't feel the rain except intermittently where the logging road opened to more than a footpath. Most of the trail was canopied with leaves, a massive, lacy umbrella to shelter her.

That was the only kind of protection she needed unless she had to deal with the trespasser again today. Yesterday she'd let him stop her, but today she was prepared. She could outrun him if need be. After all, who knew the woods better than she, after a spring and summer of daily roving? She could follow the ridge absently now, skirting without stumbling the familiar stumps and rotting logs that bordered her path. She knew where the hornets' nest was, invisible in the leafy tent of an oak. She knew which brambles hid holes, which could be traversed. She'd even found a path through a tangle of mountain laurel where she could disappear if she hunched her shoulders and lowered her head against the snare of hard bent limbs. She was glad not to have to think, glad to run and let her mind float. Maybe moving she could keep at bay the lodged memory of last night's fiasco.

The date had been such a disaster, gone awry from beginning to end. She was glad she'd never see Rob Dickson again.

13

The rain's night-long racket on the tin roof kept Rob awake. He heard the leaf-clogged gurgling of water in the drain, then the streaming overflow that eventually spilled onto the ground beneath the window. Beside him his dad slept through it all, snoring lightly so his breath whistled and hissed into the sheet. He was sleeping soundly, like someone who had cleared his mind of all his troubles and was drifting carelessly through his dreams, even though his heavy body was still there, cramping Rob to his narrow half of the bed.

When dawn came, it was in a moment of misty lull that lightened the corners of the dismal room to the color of smoke, and welcoming it, Rob crept out of bed and down the stairs, his running clothes in his hand. He dressed in the cheerless, shadowy kitchen. He had spent the long night with one thought in his head: He couldn't stay here. The rain, the creaky dreary house, the slow gray dawn, all reverberated that single message. Get away. Get away.

All night he'd contemplated where he would go, what he would do. He had never thought beyond complaints until now, had never tried very hard to make his life different. In the ninth grade his dad had taken him to look at a boarding school, and he'd spent a miserable afternoon being led through stone buildings by a smiling woman whose job it was to show the place in its best light. Davis had asked all the right questions, had bragged about Rob as if he weren't there. Later he'd insisted they walk out on the playing field together where they could look beyond the weathered bleachers toward a prospect of dormitories and academic buildings collected on a plateau of thick browning grass and burnished oaks.

"What do you think, son?" Davis had asked.

"I think I'd rather die than come here," Rob said. At home he'd thrown away the colored brochure of pretty faces concentrating in lecture halls and library carrels; girls arm in arm laughing in a row like beauty contestants; athletic bodies swinging tennis rackets and golf clubs.

Maybe he should have applied, but it was too late for that now. He was caught. He had snagged his foot in his own trap. It was a round trap, one that would keep him running in circles, always coming back to the truth of it. He had no choice but to run the trail he knew. He didn't have the courage for anything else.

He stretched out against the wet truck, which felt cold and slick under his hands. There was nothing he could hold on to. The rain was slow and steady now. By the time he reached the woods, he'd be logged with water, but what did it matter how slowly he ran? He knew there was no place to go.

Running, he made his mind push past his misery, although there was very little pleasant to think about. Leanna came at him out of nowhere. He liked her better than he'd thought he would, but she was still intense and full of Rosalie's self-righteous posing. Travis tempered her some. He liked Travis, although he knew he hadn't shown it last night. Last night he'd felt so cornered, his wounds so raw and throbbing, he'd not had the energy to act decent.

And Ellery. What did she think, after the worst date of her life? She'd probably never speak to him again and he couldn't blame her. He knew how his teeth had been set to tense his jaw, how his eyes narrowed against light; he could hear his carelessly slurred enunciation. On the front porch of Ellery's strange house—it seemed ready to fly off the side of the mountain—he'd tried halfheartedly to change his expression, to ready a smile, but it refused to come. He was too angry with his parents, with all the Dicksons, with the mountains themselves, to let go of his resentment, even for this girl who he knew didn't deserve the scowl he presented in the yellow beam of her porch light.

The interior of the house hadn't helped his mood any—one big room cluttered with big wooden looms, baskets of yarn hanging from open beams, strange equipment he assumed had something to do with weaving scattered everywhere. Bright colors in abundance but no plan to it, nothing to make the room comfortable. He had to sit in a kitchen chair at a table strewn with thin S-shaped hooks, wooden boats with metal rods through them, a contraption with ribs like an umbrella attached to the table edge with a vise. He stared at the confusion while Ellery went up the open stairs to fetch her mother, who came down wearing an old madras caftan, barefooted, her red hair tied back with a piece of purple yarn. Her pale face flecked with unconcealed freckles, Ginny Collier looked thirty instead of forty, and she'd thrust out her hand with more enthusiasm than he thought necessary to meet her daughter's date. She asked him questions, too. How was Fairlee? What was happening at the Dicksons'? How long were he and his father staying? Rob had answered halfheartedly, secretively. He didn't want to admit he was being forced to stay. It was Ellery's feigned worry that they were late that rescued him. He promised himself he'd be nice to her, but of course he wasn't.

"Want me to drive?" she'd asked when they'd bumped and scraped to the bottom of her hill in Fairlee's old truck. "I'm used to it. Fairlee taught me."

"I know how to drive," he said through clenched teeth, both hands on the wheel to hold the jumping truck out of the ruts.

"You have to ram the clutch harder," she said, obviously not knowing when to shut up. He didn't speak or look at her again on the ride into town.

They went to an indoor movie instead of the drive-in, then back to Ennis', where Travis and Leanna did all the talking. They didn't seem to mind. All the time they were providing the entertainment, Travis rubbed Leanna's bare arm with his hand. Rob watched the smooth movement, amazed at how gently his heavy fingers seemed to slide against her skin. Leanna seemed unaware of his touch until his hand paused mid stroke; then she leaned into him a little, making contact again. Rob kept his hands on the table. He didn't want to risk touching Ellery by accident.

Somehow he managed to get her home, the old truck shaking and rattling all the way. The interior smelled of greasy tools and old briny sweat. In the dark the pale dials of the dashboard illuminated his hands gripping heavily at the gear shift, jerking into second so the engine chugged, pulling them upward. They finally stalled, shuffling to a halt when he hit the brakes but forgot the clutch, a car length behind the parked Jeep.

"Well," she said, waiting in the dark. "Thanks."

"See you" was all he'd said. No walk to the door, no hand reaching through the greenish light toward hers.

So that was that.

14

Now he followed the logging trail where it cut along the ridge, hidden in foliage. Beneath the trees he could feel only misting rain unless he bumped against a bush or brushed a leafy branch out of his path. Then he was sprinkled with a quick shower off the leaves. Once he shook a tree on purpose, enjoying the soak.

Beyond him the path narrowed and the trees were slick and glossy. Everything was black and green—trunks crusty with wet bark, limbs dripping patches of pale ruffled lichen, the soil mossy and dense, the leaves like glinting jewels. Ahead, he caught a glimpse of color. Maybe a bird winging low between two branches. But then the color pierced the solid bank of green again and hung there, a steady shaft of yellow. Someone was running ahead of him.

Ellery felt movement behind her, but this time she didn't veer off her path as she had yesterday, but clung to the road, her feet pounding solidly in the spongy dirt. She could outrun the trespasser.

"Hey!" she heard him calling. So he had seen her. She sprinted forward, her arms pumping, stride lengthening as she pushed against the solid wall of moist air in front of her.

"Hey, wait up!"

The voice trailed her, punctuated by gasping breaths and a lumbering, uneven tread.

She peered skyward, out of the thick leafing. Above her the clouds were fused to a gray metallic cast. Two hundred yards from here she would turn off, would skirt a tangle of laurel to slip between the firs and go down past the lip of the ridge where poplars and maples grew so closely, they knitted a covering for themselves.

Her legs trembled, pushing her forward. She reached the point and dove past the laurel, skidding over rain-washed outcroppings of rock and the slicks of black glistening leaves in her path. When she reached the stand of firs, she could still hear the runner close behind her.

The needles pricked at her arms, drenched her with their flying water as she scurried between them.

"Hey, stop!"

The voice was at her ear, in her head. It sounded like her own voice. She sank deep into her chest to gather a breath that came sputtering up to lift her forward. At the poplars she would make her own path, bearing to the right down a treacherous shelf of crumbling sandstone toward home.

But yards from the poplars arms latched her waist, tugging her backward. Her legs churned, kicking the air as she came off her feet for an instant, then went tumbling down, flanks skimming the slick leaves as if she were riding a slide. The two bodies, locked at their waists, bumped on a shelf of hard slate and tumbled downward, scrambling against the fall until they landed on a flat protrusion of bedrock.

They lay there heaving, tangled together, arms and legs askew like broken bones. "Are you all right?" Rob gasped. His voice was throaty and shuddering in her ear.

"You are a bastard," she said all in one breath, and pushed him off her.

He let go—one arm released from her waist, the other sliding from beneath her shoulder. "I thought you knew it was me," he groaned, sitting up to examine his shin, which was scraped and puddling blood across the raw surface.

"How was I supposed to know that?" She lay flat on the rock, breathing hard, her shoulders and back sunk into the litter of leaves, twigs, and sharp loose stones. The rain was drizzling on her face. She opened her mouth and caught drops on her dry tongue, ignoring him.

"If you stay like that, you'll drown just like a turkey," Rob said. He was kneading his neck, making circles with his shoulders.

"You're the only turkey around here." Ellery sat up. "It was you yesterday, wasn't it? Why didn't you tell me?"

"How was I supposed to know this was where you ran?"

"Well, if you'd put ten words together last night, maybe it would have come up in conversation. You know about conversation, don't you? It's when two people take turns saying stuff to each other. Sometimes they actually do that on a date." She pushed debris off her legs, then pulled each foot up to her groin, tugging at the tightening muscles as they cooled. "You could have killed me."

"I'm sorry." Rob stood up and offered his hand to pull her up. "About last night, too. I know I acted like a jerk."

"It seems to come natural to you." Ellery grabbed his wrist and came up.

"That's what everybody says." He followed her between the poplars.

"A sad story you've got there, buddy, but I'm not interested. I've got problems of my own." She was walking fast, watching the ground. Rob could see a bruise coming on her shoulder, a scraped line down her arm and across her elbow.

"I think you're hurt," he said, coming close behind her.

"I'll live. I'm used to being run down and knocked over."

"I said I was sorry."

"So you did. The next move, I suppose, is to kiss it and make it better?"

"I hadn't planned on it but that seems like a good

59

idea." He caught her arm and swung around her so he was in the lead. "I think," he said, "this is where you're hurt."

His mouth brushed against her lips before she could stop him. She was on slippery ground. The rotting leaves they were standing in sent up their trembly dank smell.

He moved away, letting her arm go so gently she didn't feel the loss until he was sliding away from her, down the mountain, jumping rocks, his arms flapping to give him balance until he disappeared in the woods below her.

"Rob," she called faintly. Her voice had to travel miles before it was airborne. He was gone.

Her shoulder ached, elbow stung, one knee was tightening. She began walking, following the trail he'd made, but not hurrying. The rain was slackening, the slate sky lifting. She walked on, gathering her breath, feeling the long strength of muscles, the warm expansive sensation in her chest. After a few minutes she began to trot, a slow easy jog. It felt good. She felt better than she had in weeks, in months, since Charlotte. She picked up speed and, without any thought of where she was going, ran all the way home.

15

At home Ellery slumped against the porch post as her breathing slowed, recovering. She couldn't see beyond the pocket of cottony gray mist the house was trapped in. What was it Fairlee Dickson had said about Ginny building so high on the side of the mountain?

"I wouldn't put two sticks together up there myself." That had been his unsolicited opinion that first day, when the bulldozer came in beside his property line to cut the road and clear the site for the post-and-beam house Ginny intended to build. "I sure wouldn't." But he'd said it congenially, tolerant of other people's mistakes. "But, now, you do what you will," he added, as if he might have offended this strange, tangle-haired woman wearing cutoff jeans and high-top brogans with heavy red-rimmed socks poking out the tops. He'd winked at Ellery, who'd stood silently in the background, sulking.

During the spring he'd come up several times a week to look the place over, and Ellery had watched him gradually come to admire the house. It had a rough-hewn look he liked, a sturdiness in the white pine beams he appreciated. "Ordered out of a book," he'd said frequently, shaking his head with disbelief. "Now that's a hoot."

He watched the solar panels being installed in the sloping roof, saw the house become part of the mountain "like it belonged there," he said finally, when it was finished, and they were moving their sparse belongings in. The interior had a raw unfinished look but it was full of light. The bare pine floors were cold and dusty but provided a perfect setting for her mother's looms. On a clear day the view of the valley and the mountain range beyond was spectacular from the front-porch rockers. Fairlee approved.

All along he'd given advice on the well, the septic tank, the price the power company charged for running lines, the setting of a block retaining wall to hold the freshly cut mountain back. He'd helped grade the road because that was what he'd spent most of his life doing, working a grader for the state department of transportation, keeping country roads open and smooth through all kinds of weather. Even with a Jeep their road would be hard going during a freezing spell, but he leveled it where he could and tried to give the slope traction on the north-side curve.

Now he would be housebound for several months, and she was stuck with Ginny for two weeks of silence, of shrugged shoulders and hooded glances before school started and she exchanged one kind of misery for another. Getting the divorce papers hadn't improved her mood; neither had the letter from her dad saying the house in Charlotte had been sold. He was moving into a one-bedroom apartment until he could find just the situation that suited him.

That meant another house, another wife, maybe even other children. Ellery knew he'd marry again. He liked stability just as she did. "I could be living with him," she'd said to Ginny when his letter came.

"In an efficiency apartment?" Ginny replied, implication heavy in her voice. If he'd wanted her, he'd have gotten a place big enough. Even Ellery knew that was true.

"When he gets something permanent, I'm going to stay with him," Ellery said. "I hate it here."

"Just remember how slow he is," Ginny said, seemingly unaffected by Ellery's anger. Over the past year she had toughened up, grown a shell. "Your dad is ponderous." What she meant was boring.

Ellery raked her soles on the step, then crossed the porch and entered the great room that served as kitchen, living room and workroom. Ginny had left all but a few pieces of the good furniture in Charlotte. Most of it had come to them through Ted's family anyway, and she was tired of polishing it. Finished with doing her duty, she'd told Ellery, and with taking care of things she hadn't chosen herself. Years of lemon oil rubbed carefully into gleaming surfaces hadn't made her love the furniture or the Colliers, either. So she had chucked it all, husband, house, furniture, banker's-wife image; watched it sail out the window like dust kitties off a rag.

That was how it looked to Ellery. She's throwing my life away, Ellery had thought, but there was no stopping her. Her mother was an unalterable force once she'd decided—deliberate, diligent, methodic.

"He doesn't deserve this," Ellery had argued, "no matter what he's done."

"He hasn't done anything. There is no other woman, Ellery. No outside interference. He doesn't have the courage."

"He wants us. He loves us," she had pleaded.

"You he loves. Me he tolerates, just like I do him, and it just isn't worth it anymore. I'm not who he thought I was. Look at this house—this is what he thought I wanted!" She was flinging her arms at the decorated rooms, the breakfront crammed with silver goblets and trays, all tarnished, black edged, the dusty silk-flower arrangements, the hand-painted china tea set on the sideboard.

"And you didn't? You didn't want any of this? It didn't just happen, did it? One morning you woke up and all this stuff was here and you hadn't planned it?"

Ellery kept screaming. Those last three weeks in Charlotte she had been hoarse with yelling and Ginny hadn't tried to stop her. Ginny hardly heard, Ellery thought. She had decided, and all the screaming in the world wasn't going to stop her.

But Ellery couldn't stop either. "Well, I want it!" she screeched. "I love this house and this—this," she sputtered, grabbing a silver candelabra off the sideboard.

"Then ask your dad if you can have it," Ginny retorted, dismissing Ellery's feelings as effortlessly as she was discarding everything else.

"I won't go," Ellery screamed. "Daddy will want me to stay with him!"

Ginny sighed. "Then stay," she said finally with a cold calmness that disarmed Ellery completely. "I want you with me. I think we can work it out together, but that's up to you. I know this is hard for you, but we've always been so close. Give it a little time, Ellery. You'll see."

Ultimately, she went. As angry as she was with her mother, there were times when she'd awaken in the night out of some groping dream of displacement, and it would be her mother's face that would comfort her. Memories would flood over her—the two of them at the beach climbing dunes of burning sand, forcing each other to the summit because neither of them would give up; the kitchen table splattered with finger paint or pails of colored water for her to play in; bits of yarn and dogwood branches for branch weaving; her mother at the piano studying the notes with fierce concentration as she accompanied Ellery's flute; a book left on her dresser that turned out to be just what Ellery needed to read, as if Ginny knew her readiness before she did. Ginny teaching her how to stuff a leg of lamb, how to slice potatoes paper thin, how to make a pot of soup out of leftovers and a skinny chicken. Practical things. No instant fudge or peanut-butter cookies. That's not food, Ginny would say, it's junk. You don't want that.

What she wanted was for them to stay, for her mother to love the suburbs, to love her husband, for her to do what Ellery wanted. And Ginny would not. Ted's attempts to keep them seemed feeble to Ellery. Maybe he had felt it coming, knew something Ellery hadn't discerned. Maybe he wanted to be rid of the confusion they brought to his life. After all, he liked the orderliness of the bank, people's lives in computer terminals, not played out in a human frenzy. At home he read studies on the economy and watched television. Three seasons out of four he could play golf; in the winter he went to a fitness center during lunch. He didn't know what to do with a fifteen-year-old who stayed on the verge of giggles or tears. He didn't seem to know anything about women.

This he admitted, sitting on the edge of Ellery's bed the night she decided. Hunched over, only half facing her, he looked forlorn but not broken, not truly in need of her care and comfort. "If it doesn't work out with your mother, you can always come back," he said. He never said: Don't leave, stay with me. If he had to fight to keep her, he'd rather let her go.

She hugged him, leaning across his shoulders, her head pressed to his back. He shivered hard, as if she had touched a sensitive place, and so she let her arms fall away. The heat faded across her chest where moments ago she'd felt warm and hopeful against him.

"Take anything you want," he said. "I know your mother doesn't want anything, but all this belongs to you, too."

So in addition to everything in her room, she had taken an oil painting after the style of Renoir off the foyer wall, the tarnished candelabras, a porcelain box with a sprig of apple blossoms hand painted on the lid that had belonged to her grandmother Collier.

Now the candelabras were on her chest of drawers, towering and out of place with their curling ribs of silver and stubby candles. They'll come in handy when the power goes off, Ginny had said, turning Ellery's symbolic hold on her old life into a practical gesture. But twice already they had been used for emergency light.

Now the house was quiet, with Ginny sleeping upstairs and Rufus dozing on the braided hearthrug, curled up like an emblem of domestic tranquility. He opened his eyes but didn't move, waiting to see if Ellery was about to open the refrigerator or move in the direction of his dish. She didn't but took an orange from a bowl on the counter and went upstairs quietly, her running shoes in her hand.

Her room was full of watery light, and she pushed open the window to let in the thin mist that hovered at her screen. Her end of the house seemed to float off the edge of the ridge, and since the rain had stopped, she could see into the valley toward the Dickson place, had a view of the ragged shelf of rock halfway down but not the open pasture at the bottom or the house and crumbling outbuildings still layered in mist.

The Dicksons were only half a mile away as the crow

flies, their closest neighbors. Rob would be there by now. She could imagine him creeping into the sleeping house, moving carefully through the thin kitchen light, peeling off his soaked shirt. She brushed her fingers lightly across her lips. He would be gone in a few days and that was just as well. She didn't want any complications in her life. She didn't want somebody's anger interfering with her own, didn't need a quickened pulse, a warm damp flush spreading across her chest.

Still she could see him—his bloody knees where they had collided with rock, his tangle of damp hair, longer than hers and speckled with bits of leaf and sparkling shards of mica, his face close to hers, gray eyes she could have seen into had she looked. But she hadn't, knowing instinctively she would have taken whatever sadness she saw there into herself.

"Go away, Rob Dickson," she whispered into the screen. "I've got all the hurt I can handle." But still she saw him.

16

Although the spray stung his scrapes, Rob grimaced and leaned into the hot water. He rolled his sore shoulders under the shower, felt his hair plastered to his scalp, then lifted his face to the water, gasping and blowing to clear his nose and throat. The pain was worth it if he could wash away the clawing rage in his stomach, the topsy-turvy lurching in his chest. He wanted rhythm again, a steady drumming beat he could depend on to march him out of himself, away from this skittish anxious feeling that clung to his skin like wet pine needles.

He would pay fifty dollars for enough grass to roll one joint. Fifty dollars was all he had, money he'd stashed in his shaving kit almost as an afterthought.

He kicked the soap against the wall of the tub and turned off the spray. He should have thought to bring his own money. Why hadn't he seen this whole incredible business coming at him like a steamroller, plowing through his life, its one intention to destroy him? Must have had your eyes shut, you idiot, he said to himself. Or was it one of those times when everything was a blur no matter what he was looking at? He'd have to admit that occasionally something really interesting blew right past him. Sometimes he forgot whose basement rec room he was in or where he was going in the car. Once he had spent two hours in stony silence trying to think of Marsha's name when he could have just asked her. She wouldn't have cared. She probably didn't know who he was either.

Well, let's hear it for the boy, because for two days now he'd been aware of every minute, and it was an exhausting ordeal. On the ridge this morning he'd known he wanted to kiss Ellery. Holding her like that, their bodies thrown together on the wet ground, he'd felt an explosion in himself, a widening of the narrow corridor of his anger as if her skin colliding with his had burned a trail, a smoky opening he wanted to fill with her coolness.

"A smoke. What I need is a smoke," he said aloud to dispel her image. He pulled a worn towel off the shelf and wiped one quick stripe across the steamy mirror to expose his face. It was foreign to him. These were not the features that bloomed, forever growing and changing, out of his childhood photo album. It was not the same face that stared back at him from high-school yearbooks or off the family's stiffly posed Christmas card. This was a different face, more restless than he wanted to admit, more lost, more bewildered. He tried to turn away, but his own eyes held him there. Through the streaky reflection of the mirror he could not avoid the likeness he knew they betrayed. They were his father's eyes.

17

When Ginny was eight years old, she made a list of things she couldn't live without: a silver ankle bracelet like Bonnie Worth had; a Chinese kite shaped like a fish and flecked with gold she'd seen in a magazine; a piano, not new but *one that would stay in tune*; and a doll, life size, that could wear real clothes, from the window display at Dalton's Department Store. At Christmas she got the silver ankle bracelet and the doll, who wore a white sailor suit trimmed in red and navy blue. His outfit made his sex unquestionable, and so she named him Davy and scrounged the neighborhood for outgrown baby clothes, blankets, caps.

He had pajamas and overalls and Health-Tex knitted shirts, a crocheted sweater, a winter jacket, sunsuits, even sandals she forced onto his molded plaster feet. She rode him up and down the street in a rickety stroller she'd once ridden in herself. She made a bed for him out of a cardboard box lined with ragged towels and a soft faded crib sheet. He used her own eyelet-trimmed baby coverlet. His body was cloth, pliant and giving, and she would wrap his molded arms around her neck and carry him on her hip, his legs splayed like a real baby's, bobbing against her side. It felt like he was holding on.

She loved all her dolls. Her imagination lent them personalities that interested her more than real people did. Their demands fitted neatly into her schedule. They never complained when she went to school, when she left them piled on her bed to go skating or biking with her friends. With Davy she was more careful, though, for she put him to bed every night, dressed him every morning.

"That Ginny's going to be a good mother," the cleaning lady said to Mrs. Weston.

"Dolls don't cry all night," Mrs. Weston replied.

Ginny had cried continuously when she was a baby, so she grew up hearing stories of her colicky self, her tiny body stretched out in pain, pulling away from the frightened, exhausted mother who tried to comfort her.

"I did everything anybody knew to do back then. Finally you just grew out of it," her mother said.

Remembering, Ginny sent the shuttle singing through the shed. She was weaving a baby blanket, and the soft colors of blue, pink and yellow on the warp made her think of Davy, her perpetually smiling baby she'd deserted somewhere, probably in her mother's attic among the boxes of hand-lettered grade-school booklets, college term papers, games with missing pieces in broken-cornered boxes. She had given him up for a real baby, her Ellery, who had screamed enough to bring the house down, a nervous, trembly baby who didn't find comfort in her mother's anxious arms. Ellery had blinked in the sunlight outside the hospital and then let out a wail as if to tell the world she wasn't ready for it yet. Ginny hadn't been ready either, not for the tiny fingers clutching wildly at air, the frantic hard-kicking legs, the extended body, taut as wire, her singed, throaty cry.

"What am I doing wrong?" she worried.

"Nothing," her mother answered coldly but perhaps to comfort her. "She'll outgrow it just like you did."

The curved shuttle was warm and smooth in Ginny's hand. Almost mechanically, she sent the harness up, and the shuttle left her hand to shoot between the threads although she wanted to think about every motion. Lately she'd felt the need to concentrate on the moment, to be sure of what she was doing. She wanted to feel the resistant tug of weeds in her flower bed, to know the spongy resilience of bread kneaded under the heel of her hand, the texture of the cotton yarn, so soft and useful you could protect an infant in it.

But her mind took her elsewhere, back into her own childhood, then forward into Ellery's. Sometimes lately she confused the two, couldn't distinguish the child from the mother, as if she were living her young life again in Ellery. How could that be when they were so different? So far apart? They didn't even show any family resemblance, for Ellery had inherited her father's looks. The same mismatch of features that had attracted Ginny to Ted had made their daughter oddly pretty. Those dark round eyes in a heart-shaped face, her mischievous pouty mouth below a slightly bumped nose. Until this summer she'd worn her hair long and shiny, enviable if your own was a tangled mass of curls you'd given up trying to conquer long ago. Ginny had been stunned when Ellery came home with that glossy sleekness shorn two inches from her crown, sides clipped around her ears but left scraggly and grabbing at her neck, but she hadn't expressed a word of disapproval or regret. For once she'd held her tongue, bitten down hard, clenched her jaw— all the clichés in one tight grimace—because only her silence would keep the hair growing through the summer, would prevent bleached tips and colored streaks. Now, with the school year approaching, Ellery was looking human again.

"Oh, child of my heart," she exhaled suddenly as the loom made its rhythmic moans, treadles moving, harnesses bringing the threads up and down, the reed pressing forward to bind the weft. Daughter, where are you going in your life?

The cloth formed before her, a woven length of pastel cotton too small to show the full effect of the pattern. It had been one of her hardest adjustments to weaving— not being able to view the product until it was finished.

Once the piece was done, the warp cut, and the cloth unwound from the beam, there was no changing it, no going back. You had to live with what you'd made.

It is the same with children, Ginny thought, letting the shuttle trail its thread along the warp.

There was enough warp for three blankets. She could change the weft, this one ecru, the next blue, the final one pink. Three choices. Three chances. If she had Davy back, she would wrap him in one of them, the blue one. She'd make a cardboard bed for him somewhere and keep him safe. She would do all the right things. She wanted something to hold again, something sleeping that nestled close against her as if she were the only thing it needed.

The empty shuttle rested in her hand. She pulled out the bobbin and slipped in a full one, then overlapped the frayed ends of yarn. The hand movements were natural to her now—so many hours of winding, threading, tying. After so much practice the weaving had become the easy part, a joyous selfless act. Her body moved to it, welcoming the reaching, the stretching. She played the loom as if it were a musical instrument. Its songs of creaks and moans filled her house, sank into the narrow crevices of her pine floor, tugged at her own senses. It was a patient melody, notated with stops and pauses she had written herself.

Between the gliding notes of the harness and reed, she heard the tearful whispering of Ellery's flute above her head. The tune drifted down, an aching melody, subdued and plaintive. Ginny didn't stop her work. She knew there was no chance of reaching beyond her arms extended at the loom, no contact possible except her hands on the smooth shuttle.

The music hung above her in the still air, her child's secret voice sending the coded message of an adagio, signatured with youthful passion and pain. She yearned to respond. Longing stilled her hands for a moment while the melody poured over her, unanswerable notes she could only take into herself.

Her foot pushed the treadle, the harness went up, the shuttle made its journey, the beater brought the reed forward again. The loom groaned as it moved, gathering the pattern she had set while she and her daughter wove their hurts into a song devoid of harmony but played together just the same.

18

"I think we should go tubing," Leanna said. She had come with her mother to help Uncle Fairlee get settled and to say good-bye to Rob's father.

"He's staying to take care of things, Leanna, not to go gallivanting around with you and Travis." Rosalie was plumping worn flat pillows on the sofa while the rest of them watched. "I think you ought to sit right here, Fairlee," she continued. "It's high enough so you can pull yourself up to the walker. That chair you usually take is too low, so don't go trying it. Of course, I reckon Rob here can get you out of it if he has to, but why not just do the easiest thing?"

"We'll manage, won't we, boy?" Fairlee said, winking at Rob. "You just leave it to us, Rosie. There's going to be three able bodies here fussing over one barely crippled person." But he dropped down heavily on the sofa where she directed him.

"The doctor says you're not out of the woods yet. He's a slow healer, Cora. Mama was like that. Don't you remember when she broke her wrist? Why, it was practically a full year mending and never did get exactly right. She suffered from arthritis in it the rest of her life."

"We could go tubing tomorrow," Leanna said to Rob. "I've got the day off and so does Travis. He's been working on the tree farm with his brothers, and he's got one day off before early football practice. I'll call Ellery, too."

"Don't bother," Rob said. They were circling him. The trap tightened.

"Leanna, you leave that boy alone," Rosalie ordered.

"You can go if you want," Davis said. "I'm catching a seven-A.M. flight."

"No reason to sit around here, Rob," Fairlee said. "Once I'm up and dressed, I can do for myself. You go on while the water's high and fast."

"I think—" Rosalie started, frowning at the whole situation.

"We ought to have a piece of pie," Coralee finished. "It's peach, Fairlee. Davis bought the prettiest peaches at the market this morning."

"Tomorrow at ten. I'll fix a picnic," Leanna said.

"Where's that you're going?" Grandpa fumed at them. "You all ought to be going back where you come from. It's too crowded in here."

"Oh, Papa," Rosalie cried. "It's just the family."

"Well, it's too many." And he banged out onto the front porch, slapping the screen shut behind him.

"He'll calm down," Fairlee said. "I think he's been worried about me, but he'd never say so."

"A family trait," Davis said.

"And what's that supposed to mean?" Rosalie huffed. "I talk."

"At me, Rosalie. You talk at me. We haven't had a conversation since I left for college."

"I can't stand arguing." Coralee's lip was quivering and she rubbed her hands hard in her apron. "I'm going to cut that pie. Fairlee, can you get yourself to the kitchen?"

"Unless you've moved it."

"I'll bring the pie to him," Rosalie said. "Fairlee, you've done enough for one day." She followed Coralee out of the room.

"Well," Fairlee said. "Home sweet home."

"Wear shorts over your swimsuit. And sneakers," Leanna said. "You can't go tubing barefooted."

"I only brought running shoes, expensive ones."

"I'll get you some more, boy," Fairlee said. "You've got to stop putting obstacles in your own path."

"Dad?"

"I'll give you money for shoes," Davis said. "You'll need some clothes for school, anyway."

"And an allowance. I'll have to drive everywhere I go."

"An allowance," Davis agreed.

"My stereo and records. All my tapes. The TV."

"Agreed."

"A phone credit card."

"Okay."

"Why, that's bribery," Leanna whispered, nudging Rob with her elbow. "Mama'd kill me if I tried that."

"I'll try anything once," Rob said, "even tubing."

19

They rolled the inner tubes off the bed of Travis' truck, which he'd parked on the edge of a dirt road. "We'll have to walk up to the head of the creek. There's a trail we can take that runs a mile or so up. That suit you, Lee?" Travis was lifting the cooler off the truck.

"Anywhere," Leanna said. She and Ellery had started toward the creek, bobbling their tubes beside them in the dirt. There were wooden seats tied into the holes of the tubes. "To keep your fanny off the rocks," Leanna had told Rob.

"And the rope gives us something to tie the beer to," Travis had added. "We'll leave the food at the pool— that's about halfway down the creek," he said, "and just hope no bear gets it."

"Bears?" Rob was trying to figure a way to carry the tube without looking like a fool.

"We've got a few. This isn't like the park, though,

where they think they own the place. Those bears in the park will steal you blind, and if they don't like your grub, they'll eat *you.*" Travis was watching Rob wrestling with the tube. "There's no good way to carry that thing, so why don't you drag it? A tractor tube is practically indestructible."

The girls were waiting on the trail. "Leanna's worrying about snakes," Travis said. "She's telling Ellery about a copperhead I killed up here last year. At least I reckon I killed it. Stunned it with a rock, for sure. Didn't have a hoe. Leanna says, 'Travis, why didn't you bring a weapon?' 'A weapon?' I say. 'You want me to carry a *hoe* tubing?' She says, 'Well, you could push off with it when you're not killing snakes.' Sometimes I have to laugh right out loud at her. Now it's the water moccasins you've got to really watch out for. They'll attack you. You don't have to startle them or nothing. Up at Wildcat Lake there's one that'll try to get in the boat with you! Damndest thing I ever seen! My brother Harley's just swimming around enjoying himself, and he sees something skimming the water, say five yards away, just this little ripple, but he knows what it might be and he starts paddling to the boat. That snake comes right on, puts his head up over the side, coming after Harley and him so scared he can't get his breath. I beat it off with a paddle. The next time we went fishing up there, we took a shotgun along, but Harley didn't go swimming."

"He's telling that snake story!" Leanna called. "There's no snakes in this creek, Rob. I wouldn't be coming if there were. Copperheads don't swim, do they, Travis?"

They followed the creek, walking two abreast, with Travis and Leanna in the lead.

"So when are you going home?" Ellery asked Rob when the silence got too much for her.

"Thanksgiving." He tried balancing the tube on his shoulders. "Somebody has to take care of things until Fairlee's able to get around."

"And you volunteered?"

"Got drafted."

"Sorry."

"Me too."

"So you'll be going to school here?"

"Looks like it."

"Try not to get Perkins for U.S. history. I had him for western civ. last year and it was death."

"Hard?"

"Boring."

"Who, then?"

"I signed up for Hardison, the only other choice. Try for him. Maybe we'll get in the same section. For English, go after Ms. Masters. She likes Robert Frost." She was smiling at him.

"You're enjoying this," Rob said. "Dad said misery loves company."

"There's no love in it," Ellery said, "so don't get your hopes up."

Travis stowed their lunch under a ledge of rock that jutted out over a deep green pool. "Let's go on up," he said. "There's a little fall I want you guys to try."

They followed the trail that began now to rise steeply above the creek. They could hear the water and see the

79

pale, sunstruck leaves that rimmed the sky above the flow. At the head the water spilled down over a stone shelf, then swirled between rocks that stood like sentinels in the creek bed. "This is it."

The water was icy cold and faster than Rob had thought. He was floating before he felt settled in the tube. "A natural attitude for you. Head back, feet up!" Ellery called to him.

"How'd you learn so much about tubing?" he asked, catching a hanging branch to hold himself steady while she plopped into her tube and sailed in front of him through the rocky sluice.

"There's nothing to learn. Just watch out in the white water and relax where you can."

"White water?" He spun after her, arching his shoulders forward in time to avoid the wall of rock. Leanna and Travis were coming after them, with Travis holding a six-pack of beer in his lap to keep it from banging on the rocks.

Soon the creek flattened and widened a little, and Rob could watch the bottom as he floated over smooth pebbles, the water flowing in splashing streams over the big outcroppings, then swirling back on itself. He trailed his hands in the slow cold current. The air above him felt warm, and the surface of water beyond was golden with sunlight.

"Don't go to sleep," Ellery said, pushing off a rock and bumping against him. "Before we reach the pool there are these minor rapids."

"You don't scare me." He held on to the rope on her tube, keeping her close. "Where I go, you go."

"I don't think so," she laughed, pulling away from him just as a surge of current caught his tube and sent him plunging between two boulders in a gush of white water. He tucked his arms in just in time. "Some warning!" he called as she came rushing down behind him.

"That deserves a beer!" Travis said when he and Leanna had come hurling through the run. He pulled a can out of the water.

"No thanks," Leanna said. "I wish you wouldn't drink, Travis. Mama would have a fit."

"We'll split one," Rob said. "You first."

Ellery swallowed deeply and handed the can back to Rob. The beer was so cold it made her chest ache. "That's all I want."

"Travis, we'll be having lunch in a few minutes and I brought Kool-Aid."

"She brought Kool-Aid," Travis laughed.

"Well, it's the best thing for thirst, isn't it, Ellery?"

"Leave me out of this. I'm not getting in an argument about Kool-Aid."

"Just about everything else," Rob said. "I bet this woman likes serious arguments, like capital punishment and nuclear disarmament and school prayer. Stuff she can really get hot about."

"At least they are issues. The only thing you're concerned about is yourself."

"Right."

"I wish everybody would try to get along," Leanna said. "This is my day off."

They floated into the pool and climbed onto the flat shelf where Travis had hidden the cooler. "The water's eight to ten feet in the middle," he said, while he and Rob pulled the tubes out and stacked them against a tree on the bank.

Ellery, who had shed her clothes down to a swimsuit and kicked off her shoes, was in the water before Rob knew it.

"I'll spread lunch while you swim," Leanna said.

"She's afraid of the water," Travis said.

"I am not. I just don't want to get my hair wet."

Travis and Rob both jumped in. The water was so cold, Rob came up breathless.

"Takes some getting used to," Travis said, swimming off toward where Ellery was floating in the still water.

That was what his dad had told him this morning. "It'll take some getting used to, son, but you can do it. I'll have your records sent down tomorrow, and you can get an appointment to talk to somebody at the school next week. It'll all work out. Just take it easy, Rob."

Well, he was taking it easy. He was going to do as little as possible. Float through the coming months just like he was floating now. He'd let these people take up his time—it was better than having to be around his grandfather—but he wouldn't give anything back.

Ellery came up beside him, her head rising out of the water at his shoulder. "Going to swim or what?" she asked.

"Or what?"

"Sink!" And she had pulled him under so quickly, he took in a gulp of the icy water.

"Damn it, Ellery!" He came up sputtering.

"That's for tripping me on the trail." She laughed, darting away toward Leanna's rock.

"Okay," he said between ragged coughs and heaves. "We're even."

"It's ready!" Leanna called, and they climbed up beside her, dripping on the faded tablecloth spread with sandwiches and plastic containers of pickles and deviled eggs and potato chips.

"What we need is some music," Ellery said. "Something baroque to go with the contained structure of our environment."

"Whoa!" Travis gulped his beer.

"Bach out under the trees. Sunlight dappling the water. This is a perfect setting for classical music. Much better than a drawing room or a concert hall."

"I'd rather have Pink Floyd," Rob said.

"Ugh."

"Pink Floyd's *The Wall* is a classic."

"Oh, God," Ellery groaned, and rolled over on her back so she could look up between the trees. The light flickering off the leaves hurt her eyes.

"Jerry Garcia singing 'Friend of the Devil' is a classic," Rob went on. "In fact, the whole Grateful Dead repertoire is classic."

"And you're a Deadhead," Ellery said, squinting at the sky. "Literally."

"You got it, sweetheart."

"Naw," Travis said, munching on a handful of chips. "Willie Nelson's 'Whiskey River.' Now *that's* a classic."

"Then what about Paul McCartney singing 'Yesterday,' and John Lennon doing 'Imagine'?" Leanna wanted to know.

"I suppose," Ellery intoned, covering her eyes with

her arm, "your criterion is that if the tune makes it to Muzak, it's a classic."

"Ellery, you're a snob," Rob said.

"I've just got taste." Ellery sat up to get their full attention. "There are twelve notes in a scale. With the same twelve notes, Beethoven wrote nine symphonies, Mozart wrote *Eine Kleine Nachtmusik*, Vivaldi wrote *The Four Seasons*. Surely you'll admit they did more with twelve notes than Michael Jackson ever has."

"I reckon they did," Travis conceded, "but it doesn't make as much sense to me."

"That's because good music takes more effort on the listener's part than junk does. But the rewards are greater. Listening to Puccini's *Tosca* makes me high."

"I'll stick with Pink Floyd and sinsemilla." Rob laughed.

"What's that?" Leanna wanted to know.

"Grass, honey. Perfect grass," Travis said.

"You wouldn't! You don't!" Leanna screeched, upsetting her Kool-Aid. "Good grief."

"What about Elvis?" Rob asked, spearing a pickle on his plastic fork. "He's dead. That ought to make him a classic."

Ellery flopped back down on the rock.

"And Slim Whitman," Travis said. "He's not dead, but he's the most famous recording star in England."

"Dumb, dumb, dumb," Ellery moaned. "You're all hopeless."

"We just don't agree with you," Rob said, leaning over her. She could feel his breath on her cheek but she didn't move.

"You and Slim Whitman will not stand the test of

time," she said, rolling away from him. She jumped off the ledge into the water.

"You didn't wait thirty minutes," Leanna called. "Ellery!"

"I think she likes me," Rob said.

"Whoa!" Travis said. "Is that what you call it?"

20

"In a way it was a gradual thing," Fairlee said to Rob.

They were on the front porch watching the creeping darkness that came from inside out—first the house and porch lost color, then the field lay in shadows and the woods blurred into solid black mounds. Now only the dense mountains themselves were separate from the pale sky, as if the dark were slowly rising out of them.

"She never wanted to get a job or anything, not that there was much she could do. Coralee never was real smart at school, not like your daddy or even Rosalie, for that matter. Oh, she got by, but she was happier following Mama around and helping in the house. She liked the garden, too. That's one of the shames of it, because most ways we get along all right. But Coralee loved nature about as good as anybody, and now that's lost to her, it looks like."

"Even when she was a girl, she wanted to stay inside?"

"Well, not every minute. She went places where Mama

and Papa went, like to church and social gatherings here and about. She went to Tyler Mills on Friday evening or Saturday—nobody got to town more than once or twice a week back then—but looking back on it, I reckon Cora did stay home more than other folks. She didn't seem to have a yearning in her to do anything much. She liked sparkly stuff, though. She's always had a hankering for rings and bracelets and earbobs and the like, but mostly rings. After Mama passed on, I used to get her to town by promising a stop at the five-and-dime. She'd be beside herself when she got a new doodad." Fairlee whistled between his teeth, watching the sky above the barn. "Look at them bats," he said. "If Coralee comes to the door, we'll say they're swifts. She's scared to death of a bat."

"So am I," Rob said. "You could have told me they were swifts."

"Shoot, boy, nothing's going to get you out here. Nothing *wants* you. That's what I tell Coralee, but she don't listen. Her mind's made up. I saw that the day she decided never to come outside again. I was standing at the kitchen window drinking a cup of coffee. Must of been a Saturday. Anyhow, Coralee's at the clothesline. I know it was Saturday 'cause that's when she did up my work clothes and there they were, all them pants flapping on the line, shirts, too. The wind was working them a little. She's got her hand on the line, sticking on a clothespin, best I can tell, and then I see her stop right there, froze it looks like, one half of the shirt pinned up, the other half flapping at her. She's just staring at the sky, so I look too, and there's nothing. Just these clouds, big fluffy clouds with specks of gray in them. Not bad-looking, not a bit threatening. The wind's moving them, though. They're crossing the sky on a high wind and then the wind dips down and catches the clothesline and all those shirts and pants start shaking like folks are dancing in them. It went on like that for just a few seconds. The sun was shining and everything. I'm here to tell you, it was a pretty day. Then I hear Cora yelling. It's one big wailing sound, like she's got a grabbing pain somewhere, and she comes running for the house. 'What's the matter?' I say on the porch, but she goes flying past me and up the stairs to her room. I could see she wasn't hurt anywhere, so I let her be. When night came, I brought in the clothes and fixed me and Papa some food. I thought I ought to take Cora a bite, seeing how she missed dinner and now supper, too. She was in the bed with her clothes still on, all hunkered under the covers and this is the summertime. 'What is it, Cora?' I ask her. You can see I was getting worried. 'I'm not going out there again' is all she said. And she didn't. That was three summers ago, and so far as I know, she ain't been out of this house since. She don't even hardly look out no more."

"What do you think it was?" Rob asked.

"Something in the sky, I think," Fairlee said. "I believe she saw something in them clouds."

"But how could it be that you didn't see it too?"

"Well, I wasn't looking for anything in particular. Maybe Coralee was."

"You think she imagined it?"

"Could be, but that's the worst kind of thing to be afraid of. Something in your head. Who can tell you it ain't there?"

21

"He's staying until Thanksgiving to help Fairlee," Ellery told her mother.

"That's nice." Ginny was stirring custard on the stove. "I'm making a trifle to take down tomorrow. I think I'll take some place mats, too. I've never given Fairlee a thank-you gift for his help with the house."

"He doesn't expect anything." Ellery pinched a bite off the sponge cake on the counter. "And I sure wouldn't give him place mats. Who ever heard of giving a man place mats?"

"He eats at the table, doesn't he?" Ginny asked, watching the steady circular motion of her spoon. "What about a pillow? You pick one for me. You know the house."

"Hardly. I've only been in the kitchen, and it's ancient. The whole place is old."

"Probably a house full of antiques. How about that blue Whig Rose pattern? It's old-fashioned." Ginny set the saucepan off the stove. "This has to cool. So tell me about Rob. He's staying until Thanksgiving?"

"His parents are making him. He's p.o.'d to the max."

"Speak English please."

Ellery pinched off another chunk of cake. The ragged edge she left pleased her. "He hates it here just like I do. Anybody with any sense hates it here."

"Does every conversation I try to have with you have to turn into a diatribe about how miserable your life is?" Ginny pressed waxed paper to the surface of the custard.

"My life *is* miserable, and a day tubing doesn't change that, Mother. Nothing changes that."

"But life changes us, Ellery. You've got to loosen up and let it. I couldn't stay seventeen years old and neither can you. I had to grow up."

"Hoorah for you! Nobody wants to stay seventeen. It's the absolute pits."

"I know it's hard, Ellery."

"Then why don't you try to make it easier?"

"Things aren't so easy when you're forty either. The problems are just different. At least I think they are. I get just as anxious as you. I want to control my life just like you do. Maybe we're actually the same age and I just *look* older."

"Somehow I can't quite manage to feel sorry for you, Mother." Ellery swung open the refrigerator, peered inside and slammed it shut again.

"What are you looking for?"

"I don't know. Something to eat. There's never anything to eat around here."

"I know how you're neglected."

"The least you could do is to take me seriously! I deserve that much."

"Of course you do, sweetheart. You deserve a lot of good things. But most of them you're going to have to get for yourself. Blaming me doesn't get you anywhere." She paused to peruse the kitchen. "Why don't you eat one of those bananas before they go bad?"

"I don't like bananas. I don't like food period." Ellery twirled the fruit bowl around on the counter, making it clatter. "I thought today was going to be fun. Well, it was fun in a way, but I kept thinking I wasn't one of them. Rob's from New Jersey, for God's sake, and he fits in better than I do! At least he's got relatives here. He can act like them when he wants to."

"I doubt he thinks he fits in."

"Travis likes him. He'll be starting school with a friend."

"So will you. Leanna tried all last year to be friends with you and you know it. And now there's Rob."

"They're not my friends."

"Of course they are."

"Mother, you don't know a thing about it! How could you? You don't need anything! You've never needed people like I do. I miss my real friends."

"You could have visited them this summer. You could have spent a week or two in Charlotte. I think your dad was disappointed that you didn't."

"But it wouldn't have been the same, all cramped up in his little apartment. I don't live there now. I don't fit in anywhere anymore."

"You don't know that."

"Of course I know it. I know just what happens when somebody leaves the group. It closes up and that space is never there again. I've seen it happen."

"But you could still visit, Ellery. You can go for Christmas."

"I can't, Mother! Don't you understand anything? I can't go back there and see what I'm missing. I'd go crazy doing that!"

"Then I don't know the answer. You'll have to figure out something for yourself. That's what I'm doing. I'm just sorry I'm no help to you."

"You aren't trying very hard." Ellery stripped a banana.

"Sometimes I can't seem to help more than one person at a time."

"And it's always yourself."

"Not always, Ellery, but you're right, lately I have been trying to take care of myself. That's what women are most afraid of, you know. Being selfish. It's the ultimate sin."

"You want some of this?"

Ginny broke off the tip of the banana Ellery offered and popped it into her mouth although she didn't really want it. It was the gesture that mattered. They were trying to talk to each other.

"Well," Ellery said, dropping the peel into the sink, "I guess I'll go to bed. I can go with you to the Dicksons' tomorrow if you want."

"Thanks, I was hoping you'd offer."

"There's nothing better to do," Ellery said, her old scratchy edge in her voice. She disappeared up the stairs.

The house felt empty to Ginny as she waited for the custard to cool. She wandered among the looms and out onto the porch. The dark enveloped her. She needed to install a couple of lights along the road. The next money she could spare would go for that—to lighten the darkness. She wished she could see down to the Dicksons'. She wondered if lights glowed in their strange, cluttered rooms, if Coralee burned a lamp to ward off whatever fear had crippled her. We are the same, Cora, she thought, although you don't know it yet.

Her need to speak aloud to someone overcame her.

"I am afraid, too," she whispered in the darkness. "Hear me, Coralee Dickson, while you are curled like an animal in a hole away from sky and wind and sun. The demons that devour women are all the same."

22

When Rob heard the car in the lane, he thought it was Rosalie, whom he'd been expecting since the crack of dawn. The old biddy must have overslept, he thought on his way downstairs. She'd called him at eleven thirty the night before to make sure he'd locked the doors properly, pulling him out of that early dreamless sleep that so often evaded him at home. He'd been so tired by the time everybody was in bed that he'd fallen in himself, oblivious of the quiet that used to haunt him. At home he could never stay in a room five minutes without audio—the television, a radio, the stereo, any sound to fill the unnerving stillness.

"It's them two women!" Grandpa yelled from the front porch.

By the time Rob got there, the old man was leaning off the porch with a fierce grip on the post, talking to them. "Fairlee ain't able to do nothing, so you might as well not go a-bothering him."

"I think they're bringing us something," Rob said, urging Grandpa backward toward his chair, but he wouldn't go. He held fast to the post, half blocking the top step.

"Nothing we got use for, be sure of that," Grandpa fussed. "What you holding on to me for, boy? It's Fairlee what's crippled. He's the one what can't do for hisself."

"Hello, Rob!" Ginny called from between the Jeep and the porch. "We just dropped by to visit with Fairlee a minute. Is this a good time?"

"Sure, he's right in here." Rob let go of his grandfather, who fell backward a little, then caught himself and stumbled into his chair.

"I don't want none of it," he complained, not looking at them. His scrawny neck leaned forward out of the frayed collar of his shirt while he stared at the porch floor. He flicked at a dead butt with his shoe and missed. "You tell 'em that, boy."

"They didn't come to see you, Grandpa," Rob said through his teeth. "Just sit there, will you?"

Ellery was carrying a bowl covered with foil as she came after her mother. Without a word she slipped past Rob, who held the screen door open for them. She was wearing jeans and one of the men's shirts she'd bought at the thrift shop.

"It's my best girls!" Fairlee was beaming. "And what's this here?" He took the pillow Ginny offered him. "This is for me? You made it, didn't you? Look here, Coralee, Ginny made this on one of them fancy looms I was telling you about."

Coralee stood in the doorway looking the picture of a pioneer woman who had been isolated from the company of other human beings for years. That was how Ginny saw her, hesitant, shrinking inside as her expression faltered between pleasure and wariness. The design in the pillow Fairlee held out to her had caught her interest immediately, and she wavered there in the doorway like a starving animal who nevertheless mistrusts the appearance of food.

Which emotion would overpower her first, fear or longing? Ginny wondered. Coralee reached out for the pillow, came the five steps required to take it.

"Good," Ginny said under her breath, waiting.

The soft hands moved over the surface of the pillow, reading the intricate pattern of the threads. "I make edges," Coralee said finally, holding the pillow tenderly on her open palm.

"That she does!" Fairlee laughed. "She puts a border on everything. Sews 'em, crochets 'em, tats 'em. Looky there!" He was pointing at the living-room curtains, cheap open-weave ones hanging askew but edged with the most beautiful cotton lace Ginny had ever seen.

"You made that!" she gasped, and went to examine it. "You made it, Coralee?"

"I did." Coralee smiled. "Anybody can tat that's got a mind to."

"No, not anybody. I've never seen anything so beautiful."

"She sews borders, too," Fairlee said. "Every towel in the house she's trimmed out. Everything that's got a straight edge to it Coralee finishes off."

"I close everything up," Coralee said agreeably. "You put a good binding around something and it's sealed. Can't nothing get through it."

"What did I tell you?" Ellery whispered to Rob. She was still holding the chilled trifle bowl, and when he didn't acknowledge her, she moved toward Fairlee. "We brought a trifle—sponge cake soaked in sherry, with layers of strawberry jam, custard and cream. You're going to love it."

"Sounds too good to eat," Fairlee said. "Maybe we ought to just look at it."

"I hope you like it." Ginny felt suddenly shy. "It needs to be refrigerated, Coralee."

"I'll take it," Ellery offered, wanting to get away from Rob, who hadn't shown any sign of life since their arrival.

"No, I will," Ginny said, taking the bowl. "You'll come with me, won't you, Coralee?"

And the two women disappeared down the hall, Cora still holding the pillow.

Ellery plopped on the sofa. "You didn't run today," she said before she could stop herself. She felt herself pulled toward a fray. "Not yesterday either."

"It's your mountain," Rob said.

"I knew you'd say something like that!"

"I reckon that trail's not big enough for the both of you," Fairlee interjected. He was grinning.

"She doesn't think the world is big enough," Rob said.

"Well, it looks like we got ourselves a little territorial dispute right here." Fairlee chuckled, straightening himself up in his chair. "Now, what we could do is make a settlement—the two parties could grant each other right of way."

"I'm not running," Rob said.

"That's what Calvin Coolidge said," Fairlee told him, "but it didn't improve his disposition any."

Rob tried to control a smile but it poked around the corners of his mouth.

"I'll run at six, you at seven," Ellery suggested.

"No way. When school starts, seven will be too late."

"What about afternoons? I'll run mornings, you take afternoons."

"I always run in the mornings."

"You haven't always had a person to help get dressed and do things for," Ellery flashed at him. "Excuse me, Fairlee."

"You're right, girl. Stay at him."

"You could run cross-country at school, you know. I'm sure you could make the team. In these county schools, all the big athlete types like Travis play football."

"Thanks a lot."

"It's the truth."

"And you always speak the truth. The mountain oracle or something."

"I try." Ellery sighed, fed up with his frown and the way he avoided her eyes. "Look, we'll run together until school starts. After that we'll decide. I'll stay in the lead anyway."

"Oh-ho!"

"I think it's settled," Fairlee said.

But nothing felt settled to Rob. She made him so angry. A hot crinkly feeling came into his stomach every time he thought about her. He didn't know what it was—lust maybe, because he was missing Marsha. He missed the feel of a girl. He'd been so lonely last night, he'd called

Marsha, but she was out. He knew better than to ask her mother where. The woman wouldn't know. "Who is this?" she'd asked him. "A friend," he said, suddenly unwilling to admit even to himself that Marsha mattered in his life. "Well, I'm glad to know she's got one," her mother said as she hung up.

What did that mean? He tried to remember Marsha, to get her face exactly right in his mind, but she eluded him. As he had gone back to sleep after Rosalie's phone call, Marsha's features had meshed with Ellery's, and he had focused his closing eyes on a weird creature like a Picasso painting—lopsided eyes, misplaced nose, wildly tinted cheeks. Exotic but sexy. She was the monster he hugged in the night.

Now the apparition was fleshed out, had taken a seat on the sofa while he stood awkwardly in the middle of the room. She was more at home than he was.

"I'm going out for a while," he mumbled, fleeing across the front porch where his grandfather rocked angrily, glaring out at the unfamiliar Jeep and gripping the arm-rest as if to hold himself to ground.

"Come here to me!" the old man barked after him. "You got company!"

"Oh, shut up!" Rob stalked toward the barn. There was no place else to go unless he dug a hole and got in it.

The barn enclosed the damp chilly air of dirt and rotting hay that sickened him, but he slumped into it, leaning against the splintery wall, relishing the dark. He remembered that sudden calm in his gut when, in a game of hide and seek, he knew he'd discovered the perfect place, somewhere he couldn't be found.

But no one will come looking this time, he thought. This isn't a game. Nobody cares. Who had ever cared about him? His mother, maybe, but he couldn't bear to think of her, to imagine her cleaning his empty room, stripping it of his belongings as if he'd died. He wondered if she was mourning, missing him no matter how hateful he'd been to her.

What were her memories like? Did she know about all the uneaten green beans he dropped into his napkin? The times he'd cheated on grade-school spelling tests or taken change from her wallet? Had she recognized scents on him—stale beer spilled on his clothes, semen on his sheets, grass in the hazy distance he kept from her?

How could she love him, knowing all of that? The interior of the barn was like his insides, empty and cold. He slid to the dirt floor and buried his face in his hands. He was still there when he heard the Jeep pull away.

23

What can I say to her? Ginny wondered, following the woman down the dark hall. All the doors were shut, and the narrow wall boards and the stairwell were painted oxblood, the color of the mud in Ginny's yard. The stairway that rose up through the center of the house was steep. No light splashed down on them, because the doors upstairs were also closed. There was no air to breathe except the damp residue of cooking steam and the dust lifting around their feet off the scatter rugs. What can I say that won't threaten her?

Ginny felt a cold spiraling cylinder of regret rising into her chest as she grappled with her predicament. What did I think I was doing, she wondered, coming to befriend a woman years older than me, someone whose life is already structured, already buried in oppression? Can I really be this arrogant, so sure of myself that I think I can help her?

Coralee pushed open the swinging kitchen door, and for an instant Ginny saw her bathed in light, her plain thin dress diaphanous, her white hair glinting as if it were shot with stars. She saw her as a child in a communion dress, as innocent and expectant and fearful as that. "Then we will be afraid together," Ginny thought, and came herself into the light, where her vision bumped against the ordinary kitchen, its painstaking cleanliness, the old worried smells of cooking, disinfectant, laboring.

She went to the refrigerator and put the trifle in without a word while Coralee watched as if she were the visitor and unsure of her surroundings.

"This is such a pleasant room, Coralee," Ginny said, smiling at her. "Why don't we just sit here a moment and visit? Ellery and Fairlee always have plenty to say to each other."

Coralee looked shy, even pained as she forced herself to return the smile, but she put the pillow on the edge of the table and sat down at her regular place. Ginny, she saw, took her mama's chair. Cora studied the oak surface of the table in front of her. There was a sticky place she had missed, a puddle of dried orange juice the size of a nickel. She laid her hand over it.

"Ellery and Fairlee do get on," she said suddenly, as if their attachment had just occurred to her. "Fairlee likes young'ns. Maybe he oughta had hisself some."

The thought made Cora smile broadly, and for the first time she looked straight at Ginny's face. What she saw were startling blue eyes in a small face circled by a frizz of reddish hair that had escaped from combs buried near her crown. She wanted to touch the curls, to know if they were soft or springy, but she kept her hands over the sticky spill on the table and waited for Ginny to speak.

"I don't know about that," Ginny began, and Coralee had to push her mind to remember what they were talking about. Children, it was. Fairlee should have had babies. Well, first he should have had a wife, she decided, and laughed out loud.

"What?" Ginny was looking at her quizzically.

"Fairlee and babies," Coralee cackled. "Fairlee and a wife!" Then she frowned as she remembered. Fairlee had been in love once. He'd courted that Withers girl when she was in high school and he was a year or so out, already working on the roads and making good money. Fairlee's pay was nothing to sneeze at. Of course, sometimes it was all they had, because later on, after Papa quit at the lumber mill, he didn't do enough farming to keep them going. He sold little bits of land now and then. Sold off timber, too. Raised a few cows. Once they'd made money off cabbages, planted every flat acre they could clear in cabbages. She'd liked that. She loved to stand back from the field so the cabbages looked like separate scalloped balls of blue-green velvet in meticulous rows of ochre dirt. Two years running they lost the crop to drought, and Pa gave up on them. Over Cora's protests he let the fields lie fallow, moaning and groaning to himself that no matter what a man did on a farm, there was always more heartache than money in it. As time passed, Papa got more and more outdone by the world, left more and more of the decisions to Fairlee. Pa had acted old all his life.

But that wasn't why Fairlee didn't marry. That Withers girl just wasn't the right one—she never could settle on one beau, and after a year or two of mooning around, Fairlee gave up on her. Maybe he'd marry this Ginny— it wasn't too late. But what would that mean? Coralee's mind raced, shoving thoughts this way and that. She pinched her forehead, trying to clear a track she could concentrate on. If Fairlee got married, would this woman and her girl come down here to live or would Fairlee go up to the house she'd built? She knew he loved that house, because he'd spent all spring and summer bragging on it like it was something he was doing himself.

So he would go up there, and where would she and Pa be? Down here, that's where. By herself, because Pa wasn't company at all unless you wanted a quarrel. Talking to him was the same as spitting in the wind; it came back on you. The loneliness of this picture she'd imagined spread through her, seeped into her heart, where it caused a squeezing ache she thought she'd cry out with. "God help me, he's not a-marrying nobody," she said, so fiercely she startled herself.

"I wouldn't think so," Ginny said mildly. What could

Coralee be thinking? she wondered. "Of course, I'm not the right person to discuss marriage with, I don't suppose. I wasn't very happy in mine and certainly don't intend to give it another try anytime soon."

There. Coralee's frown eased away, her shoulders relaxed. Her hands slipped into her lap. "You make cloth," she said. "Is it all like this?" She nodded at the pillow.

"Oh, no, that's just one pattern. I make many other designs for pillows. I also weave tablecloths, blankets, runners, place mats, scarves and shawls, and cloth for clothing like vests and jackets, cotton tops and skirts for women. I wish I could make more clothing, but I'm a lousy seamstress. Most of it is handwork, of course. Maybe you could help me, Coralee! I could bring the fabric and a pattern down to you and you could help me put an outfit together. Would you do that?"

The stillness in the room rubbed against them like scratchy cloth.

"I just make edges," Coralee said finally.

"I'll need that, too. I have to spend so much time tying off fringe. You could do that part as well."

"I stay busy every minute," Coralee said, although it wasn't true. Some days she spent hours with her jewelry box emptied out on her bed, trying on things and then arranging them again in the compartments. It was a game to her, and like all games it got boring. After a while the stones seemed lusterless. Sometimes she even remembered they were cheap—Fairlee didn't think she knew that, but she did. Most of the time it didn't matter, though. Colored glass was pretty enough. One day long ago she had put on all the jewelry she had at one time—three or four rings on each finger. Necklaces made bright confusion around her neck. Bracelets encrusted her wrists. She sparkled all over, even her head, where she clipped earbobs to her hair in a circle.

"Just look at you," her mama had said as she paused in her weary shuffle past Coralee's open door at just the moment when light ignited the glass and made Coralee a brilliant, shimmery display of color. "You're my precious jewel." Mama was sick then, near death but still doggedly maneuvering the stairs, unwilling to imprison herself in her room or bed. Her body was a prison enough, incarcerating a heart that beat fitfully. Her lips and toes and fingertips were always blue, Coralee remembered, and sometimes she gasped soundlessly for breath, but she never complained, never stopped moving or trying to eat a sliver of toast or a spoonful of egg custard. She died in the hallway, fell into the banister as she went down so that in the coffin she looked not only thin and old and dead but battered as well. A black bruise no liquid tint could hide spilled out of her white hair, across her temple and down her cheekbone.

"It's where she fell," Pa had said over and over again gruffly to the mourners who trooped past the casket. He seemed to need to explain that he hadn't struck her himself. Why did he need to do that? Coralee wondered now. What did he have to blame himself for?

"Cora," Ginny said, breaking through the grating memory of her mother's death. "It was just an idea I had about the clothes. It's not important."

"I'll help you," Coralee said impatiently, although she

knew Ginny couldn't know the flight her mind had taken, so deep into the furry past. Why was it this strange woman in her kitchen reminded her of Mama when nobody in her own family did?

Mama needed me, she thought suddenly, and this woman needs me too. Everybody else treated her like a baby, even Fairlee; but not Mama. Mama always respected the kind of help Cora was to her. She always said her thank-you like she knew all Coralee did was for love, not duty.

"You just call me up when you're coming and I'll be ready."

"Oh, thank you, Cora." Ginny put out her hand and Coralee took it awkwardly, aware of the sticky place she'd acquired on her palm. Ginny's hand felt strong, like a man's hand, but gentle.

"Well then," Ginny said, smiling as she got up. "I'll collect my daughter and get back to work. I'll call you, though, in a day or two."

"That's Mama's chair," Coralee said shyly, "where you were sitting."

"Oh, I'm sorry!" Ginny lifted it carefully back into place against the table. "You should have told me."

"It's no matter," Coralee said. "Mama's been gone twenty years." But she felt tears welling behind her eyes. Deep in her head they stung her with memories, and she twisted her head away from Ginny.

"I lost my mother, too," Ginny said softly. "I thought I'd never forgive her, but I have."

"What did she do to you?" Cora's tears sunk inward, burning her chest.

"She died," Ginny said. "She left without my saying good-bye or telling her I loved her. Without any of that."

"I took care of Mama," Cora said. "She was bad sick but she died with her clothes on. I didn't say good-bye either. When she fell right there in the hall, I thought it was a chair tipped over, that's how unawares I was."

They looked at each other a long moment. Ginny saw a flushed face, broad and open to her, damp eyes self-consciously holding hers. "We will know each other," she said silently, focusing all her energy on the words, willing their meaning to reach the woman next to her.

"Ellery!" she called then, swinging through the door into the hall. "Time to go!" She was not surprised to find Coralee coming behind her, through the dark hall toward the light.

24

Rob was sick to his stomach the entire first week of school. He awoke panicked by his clock radio's staticky alarm and lay there trembling in the dark while nausea lurched and rumbled in his stomach. The room, now strewn with his belongings, felt alien to him—there was no streetlamp to cast light on his familiar disarray—and he slapped at the alarm as if to stave off an unidentified assailant.

It was the sour taste of vomit in his throat that forced

him out of bed every morning. Once he barely made it down to the bathroom before a retch tore into his mouth. The dry heaves that followed made his chest ache all day. His breastbone felt like he'd been pounded in a fight.

Between six and seven thirty he moved methodically through his chores—getting showered and dressed, forcing down a bowl of cold cereal, helping Fairlee over the edge of the tub, returning ten minutes later to help him out, disappearing again while he dried himself. Back to help with underwear, pants, socks, shoes. Fairlee was cheerful through it all and only the first day showed any embarrassment at their shared predicament.

"I reckon this will take some getting used to," he'd said good-naturedly. "You doing for a baby and me being one."

"You'll be taking care of yourself in no time," Rob had answered, trying to be pleasant. None of this was Fairlee's fault.

He drove the truck to school, and it grumbled and stalled along the dirt road until he reached the highway, where he could practice shifting gears smoothly, making the old engine race under his feet. The next time Ellery Collier rode with him, he'd know what he was doing.

He saw her at school—he'd managed to get into the same history class—but she didn't encourage him to talk to her. It was easy enough for him to oblige. He just shut himself down, ignoring everybody. He knew how to be anonymous and would have been except that he shared lunch period with Travis, who stayed after him like a pit bulldog holding on to a shirttail.

"You eating that pig slop?" he'd called across the cafeteria the first day while Rob waited in line with his tray. Travis was sitting with a beefy entourage Rob figured were his football buddies. "Come on over here and I'll give you a ham biscuit and a cold tater. Now that's eating!" He emptied his milk carton in one long gulp.

The other boys moved over to make room for someone Travis liked. They introduced themselves. One of them, a giant with a fresh Mohawk, even offered Rob his hand. They wanted to know what sport he played in New Jersey.

"A little basketball," Rob said, not wanting to admit he hadn't even tried out for the junior varsity.

"He's feisty," Travis added, since everybody on the Tyler High School team was over six feet. "Quick, son. Real quick." He slapped the table a solid lick. "Wait till you see him on the court. Whoa!"

"I haven't decided if I'll try out," Rob protested. "There's not much point since I'm leaving as soon as my uncle gets well." He saw his explanation was inconsequential to them. Nobody cared if he played or not.

"We're going to beat the shit outa Lakeland come Friday," one of the boys said. "We're gonna kick their ass all over the field."

"They got Woodrow," Travis reminded them.

"Yeah, that's one nigger who can clean your cleats." The lineman across from Rob shook his head. His arms bulged out of his ragged-sleeved sweatshirt. ALABAMA was faded across his chest.

"We can stop him. Ain't nobody we can't stop."

"Hellfire, Jack. First you got to catch him!"

"Coach Myers wants to use a four-four defense," Travis said.

"Shit, man, I don't see how a four-four will stop him. What we need is a little contract on that nigger." The Mohawk snickered.

"Don't look at me!" Travis threw up his hands in protest. "I'm the quarterback, the glamor boy. I'm the cheerleaders' dream."

"Leanna was after you before she knew what a football was."

"Listen, Travis, if that son of a bitch is out of the game, all them recruiters gonna be looking at you, man," the lineman said.

"I hear he's already being scouted by twenty schools."

"Yeah, Mr. Blackass Woodrow's going to the big time," Jack said, rolling his eyes in disgust.

Rob hunkered between them, eating his spaghetti. Redneck racists, every one of them. He didn't say anything.

Later that day he noticed there were no more than one or two black students in any of his classes. One was in his English section, and that afternoon she showed a surprising amount of spunk. After studying the syllabus, she raised her hand to question the absence of black writers from their reading assignments. "Where is Phillis Wheatley?" she wanted to know. "Du Bois and Dunbar? Langston Hughes?"

"American literature can't meet everyone's expectations and interests," the teacher said pleasantly. "This is a survey course. Remember, however, there is a mini-course in black studies offered in the winter."

"But nobody takes it," the girl protested.

"Nevertheless, it is available. Also, *Native Son* is on the supplementary reading list for this class," the woman intoned, speaking now to the group. "Any of you who would like to read it for a book report may do so."

"Black people make up ten percent of the American population," the girl continued quietly, but Rob could see she was weakening. Her hands rattled the syllabus slightly.

"And hardly a fraction of a percent of this school," Ms. Masters said, smiling. "Please see me after class, dear."

So the girl relented, cut down by politeness. Rob knew what would happen. Taken out of the forum of the classroom, the issue would die; the other students would go unaffected. Still, she had tried. The girl must have felt his empathy, because as the teacher continued her droning commentary on the weekly class requirements, she glanced at him, a quick, piercing look meant to identify an ally. He offered a brief, blank smile in return and looked away. He wasn't getting involved. It wasn't his fight.

He sat across the room from Ellery in history but at an angle from which he could see her out of the corner of his eye. She slouched in her seat through most of the class looking disinterested but taking frequent quick notes in a thick spiral notebook. Maybe she was writing something else. Halfway through the third class she startled him by lifting her hand and asking Mr. Hardison to reiterate a previous point. Not only did Mr. Hardison reiterate, he elaborated, charged up by a student's unexpected interest. From elaboration he moved expansively afield, an aside that lasted the rest of the hour while Ellery's pencil rested on her desk and she punctuated Mr. Hardison's enthusiasm with obligatory nods of approval. The rest of the class slept.

"What was that all about?" Rob asked, catching up with her in the hall.

"I was tired. When I get tired of taking notes, I just get the teacher off the subject." She slid a book into her locker and slammed the door shut. "Everybody knows Mr. Hardison's thing is the Civil War. You ask him something that he can even remotely associate with the war and he's off."

"And you get Brownie points for inspiring the old coot."

"I hardly need Brownie points," Ellery snapped, and breezed away as if she owned the hall.

"She makes straight A's," Leanna said from behind him. She was carrying her books against her chest, and a purse made like a monkey dangled off her shoulder.

"Where did you get that?" Rob wanted to know.

"Isn't it the cutest thing? Travis says it's going to attack me one of these days. He's just jealous. He doesn't want anything snuggling me but him." She giggled and then took Rob by the arm, leading him down the hall as she talked. "You're coming to the game Friday night, aren't you? Please do! Travis would never say so but it would really make him feel good if you'd come. He likes you, you know, and not just because someday you'll be related by marriage. He told me just the other night he thought we ought to get together again. You bring Ellery, and we'll meet you at the dance afterward."

"I'll think about it," Rob said, withdrawing his arm. "Ellery and I aren't attached at the hip."

"Don't you wish!" Leanna laughed, undeterred by his lack of enthusiasm. "Look, Rob, she's by herself here. I don't think she had a date all last year. I admit she hasn't tried very hard, but can you blame her? If I had to leave all my friends and my school and Travis and go live somewhere else, I'd just die." She stopped. "Well, your situation is different! You've got family here and besides, it's just temporary. This is the only place Ellery has to live."

To get away from his cousin, Rob said, "I'll ask her." He figured she'd refuse.

25

She didn't. Instead, she created an outfit from the stuff they'd bought at the thrift shop, put three coats of mascara on her lashes, rimmed both eyes and mouth with a thin line of black and painted her lips the color of ripe cherries. Before pulling an old fedora down on her forehead, she powdered her tan to make her face conspicuously pale.

"Good grief," Ginny said under her breath.

"Good grief what?" Ellery paused on the stairs to give her mother the full effect.

"Nothing." Ginny turned back to the yarn she was measuring around the pegs of the warping frame.

"No, go ahead. Tell me." Ellery stormed down. "You can't just say 'good grief' and let it go. It means you don't like something. That's the expression you get."

"You know what it is." Ginny was still winding, but she'd lost count, so she paused, then stopped altogether.

"No, I don't. Tell me."

"You do know." Ginny put down the yarn. They were facing each other, the space between them a void, a black hole neither would step toward. "You're baiting me, Ellery. You want an excuse to leave here mad so you can do whatever you please."

"You started this. I didn't!" Ellery fired back. "I was just on my way out. You want me to go out, don't you? You're after me all the time about making friends and putting forth an effort. So I'm doing that. I'm obeying orders, but that's not enough, is it? What is it this time, Mother? What's wrong with me now?"

Ginny sighed, facing the abyss. She might as well plunge in. "You used to coordinate things. You used to show such a flair for clothes, a talent even. I can't believe you'd leave the house looking like that."

A blast from the horn of Fairlee's truck broke between them.

"Just watch me, Mother," Ellery said, and was gone.

26

It was still light at eight thirty when Ginny turned the Jeep around in the yard and headed down the mountain to the Dicksons'. She was surprised by the urgency she felt to hear another voice. All her life she had thought of herself as a loner, but lately she'd wanted someone to talk to, especially during the twilight hours that emptied slowly into the lonely stretch of night. She was apt to cook something fattening between seven and nine and then have regrets in the morning when there was a layer cake nobody would eat or cookies to go stale. Her limited income—her weaving was just beginning to sell in profitable quantities—prevented her from buying many books, and she'd canceled all her magazine subscriptions and book club memberships when she'd left Charlotte. She particularly missed reading a news magazine. Occasionally giving in to her curiosity about what was happening in the world, she purchased an edition at the grocery-store checkout. In case I get invited to a party, she would say to herself, smiling, for she was glad to have escaped Ted's idea of a social life—cocktail parties at the city club, brunches on sultry summer lawns, frenetic Christmas gatherings that resulted in oily fingerprints on her good silk dress and a weepy ache behind her eyes from being trapped in crowded smoky rooms.

She didn't miss it, even though all day she'd wished she had someone to talk to. I need a friend, she thought as she swung the Jeep down the lane, and it looks like Coralee Dickson is it.

The house, set against the flank of her own mountain, was trapped in gloom with only a pale-yellow glow through the long front windows to separate it from the shadows.

"Anybody home?" she called from the front porch. She could hear a television on in the living room, then a scurrying bumbling racket through the screened window. The door opened abruptly, casting her in warm light.

"It's that woman again," old Mr. Dickson announced over his shoulder.

Ginny could see into the room now. Fairlee was on the sofa, his walker next to him. "Hello!" she called around Mr. Dickson, who wobbled in her path, holding on to the edge of the door. "It's Ginny, Fairlee."

"Let her by, Papa," Fairlee said, pulling the walker to him.

"Don't get up." Ginny sailed defiantly around the old man, who slammed the door after her and went muttering back to his rocker.

The television was a small color set perched on an end table in front of the fireplace.

"It's that boy's mess," Grandpa griped to her, sinking into his chair. The rocker creaked loudly, tossing him backward. "He comes from up north bringing all this here junk. I told 'em I'd never see one of them dad-blame things in this house. But here it comes!" His attention was already on the screen, where Luke and Beau Duke were outrunning a police car. "A bunch of dang fools. Just look at 'em."

Fairlee grinned and motioned to Ginny to sit on the sofa beside him. "He's taken to it like a fox to chickens," he whispered. "One day he was in here watching them stories, all that kissing and mooning about, and I think he took to that, too. One thing for sure, he's never seen anything like it."

"I can believe that." Ginny laughed. "I came to see how you're doing. I know Rob's at the ball game, because he came by for Ellery."

"I hope that's all right with you," Fairlee said. "Rob's

a good boy at heart, but I get the feeling he's not much for showing it."

"I could say the same about Ellery," Ginny sighed.

"Now, she's all right. You ask me, I'd say she's as sweet as honey and pretty as a picture."

"You didn't see her tonight," Ginny said. "Appropriate only for a Halloween party."

"Aw, Ginny, let her be. I bet you had you some getups when you were a girl."

"As a matter of fact, I did." Ginny laughed.

"You see there. She's her mother's daughter all right."

"That's what I'm afraid of. Is Coralee here?" She was certain the scurrying had been Coralee's disappearance.

"In the kitchen, I reckon. Or upstairs. Go call to her if you want to."

Ginny found her in the kitchen.

"I heard it was you," Coralee said shyly, "so I thought I'd make us some lemonade. You'll drink some, won't you?"

"I'd love it. There's nothing better on a warm evening. I don't know when I've had a lemonade that wasn't made with a mix," she went on, hoping this small talk would alleviate Coralee's nervousness.

"Before you know it, it's winter," Cora said, bearing down on the halved lemon, her small agile fingers kneading the rind to loosen every drop of juice. "We got this old snowplow that Fairlee rigs up to the front of the truck. By first snowfall he oughta be able to clear your road if'n it's not too deep. One time we had twelve inches over a night. It all froze up, then eight more fell. Nothing moved in this valley for days and days. Somewhere down yonder on the road the power went out, and they were a week getting it fixed. I had firewood though. Fairlee saw to that. You know how the Indians tell if there's going to be a bad winter? Amount of wood on a white man's porch! From the looks of ours you'da thought a blizzard. And Lord-a-mercy that's what we got. It was pretty falling, I can tell you, and pretty a-laying, and if'n you've got wood and plenty food laid by, you can just sit warm and enjoy it."

She stopped and sugared the lemon juice in the pitcher, ran tapwater over it. The spoon clicked against the glass as she stirred. Her face twisted abruptly, eyes wide as if she were seeing a spook.

"It's the wind you got to watch out for," she said, then moaned suddenly as if she'd been struck from behind. "The wind won't let you be once it's got you. Sometimes it blows through here like it's battling and feuding with every man-made thing, like it's bound and determined to swoop you up and carry you off somewheres. It sucks at this old house, pulling it this-a-way and that, working up under the roof. You can hear it! You can feel it right in your bones. It's a-coming, it's a-coming."

Coralee set a glass of lemonade in front of Ginny, who jerked away from the movement, startled to find herself safe in the kitchen. She had been caught up in the whirring, mournful tone of Cora's rising voice, and she swallowed the lemonade quickly to quench the dry, prickly feeling in her throat. She felt as if she'd been walking against a stiff, hot breeze.

"I reckon I'll take some to Fairlee and Papa," Coralee said. "Papa gets mighty dry watching that television set. He ain't done nothing else since Davis sent it here, and after all that fussing and carrying on he did. Why, he used to go over to Rosalie's sometimes, and he'd come back fit to be tied 'cause they were all sitting around looking at the television and not paying him no mind. Papa never could take the littlest amount of neglect. Mama waited on him hand and foot, and now I reckon I do." She was pouring the other lemonades while she talked, her back to Ginny.

"I guess there's always something that needs doing," Ginny said, thinking of Ellery, although she was watching Coralee, the way she stood now holding the tray of glasses as if it were a gigantic burden tugging her out of herself, sapping all her energy.

"I just thought I'd reach the time when I didn't have to take care of nothing but me," Coralee said. "I want that feeling one day before I die." She smiled nervously, thinking she'd stepped too far from pleasantries and didn't know how to redeem herself. "Course," she said, "I'm not planning to die anytime soon. I'm taking care of that. Can't nothing get in here 'cept what I let in."

"Let me help you," Ginny said, rising to take the tray. They looked at each other over it. Four hands grasped the edges. Coralee let go.

"We'll watch the television if you can stay awhile," she said, pushing open the door into the hall. "Afore long we can see what's happening to them folks in Dallas. They've got trouble in every direction."

"Makes for good entertainment," Ginny said, following her down the hall.

"Huh," Coralee said, "just goes to show what folks with a lot of money and no sense will do."

117

27

Ellery and Rob had been wandering around the gym for thirty minutes before Leanna and Travis showed up. Leanna was still in her cheerleader's uniform, a short full red skirt and a sleeveless white vest with a red-and-black T sewn on it. Travis was ruddy faced and damp from the shower. He held Leanna so tightly their walk was clumsy, like two drunks stumbling into each other.

"Look at that outfit," Travis roared, grinning at them. "What did you do, Ellery, join one of those gangs?"

"I'm thinking about it," Ellery shouted over the music.

"I think she looks terrific," Rob said. "Sorry about the game. How's your cornerback doing?"

"He got his bell rung, that's for sure." Travis laughed. "Shouldn't of tried to stop Woodrow by himself. He's all right, though. A slight concussion, the doc said. Sent him home with his mama." His hand fell carelessly over Leanna's breast. "We gonna dance or what?"

They turned onto the dance floor and were locked in the dim, moving light.

"I guess we could dance," Rob said.

"If you want."

They moved forward without touching, then turned to each other. "I've never been much of a dancer," Rob said.

"You want me to lead?" Ellery asked.

"No," Rob said, pulling her to him. "And I wish you'd take off that ridiculous hat. There's a great face under there somewhere."

She plopped the hat on the back of Rob's head. Her shoulder fitted neatly under his, and her hair brushing his neck sent a shiver through him. His hands moved easily across her back, pressing her against him as they rocked slowly in place.

"Rob," she said into his chest while the music circled them, closing in around their heads.

"Hmm?"

"I can't breathe."

He pulled back, abandoning her at arm's length, his face hot, throat burning with quick fury.

"Well," she said stubbornly, "my nose was pushed into your sweater. I can't stand not breathing like that. I get panicky."

"Damn it, Ellery, does everything have to suit you?"

"You could ask yourself the same thing. At school you act like I don't exist, and then when you need something, like a date, you sure don't hesitate to call me."

"When I need a date? I don't need a date! I don't need any of this! I asked you because—"

"Because Leanna told you to. I'm supposed to keep you out of trouble, I suppose. Keep the Yankee cousin happy so he'll stay. Don't you think I know she's instigated every time we've been together except when Mom and I went to your house? And look what happened then. You weren't even civil."

"I wasn't civil? I seem to remember you were the one picking a fight. I wanted to talk to you that day. I really wanted to."

"So why didn't you?"

"I don't know." He looked away from her toward the

other dancing couples, who swayed easily to the music, the soft light moving across them. "I don't know why I do anything, Ellery." The dancers went blurry, as if the lights' intensity had changed.

"I've got the same problem," Ellery said softly. "I keep on doing it, though. I never learn."

He could hardly hear her over the deejay's sound system, so he moved closer. Her eyes were damp, too.

"Me too."

"Do you think two mixed-up people could dance without suffocating each other?" he asked, rushing over the words because he was already taking her hand.

"I guess it's worth a try."

They clung to each other for a moment, then he released her a little, giving her room. "This is the best I've felt in months," he said into her hair. And it was true.

28

In his room he turned on the stereo, bouncing Santana's drums at Woodstock off the walls. It was the oldest album he had, and hearing it, he always wished he had been there. But then he was always wishing he were someplace else. He switched on his headphones and fell across the bed. The music bombarded his brain, and yet he was thinking about Ellery, about how he'd kissed her good night as gently as he could, not wanting to frighten her or demand too much.

She'd ducked into the house anyway, leaving him on

the dimly lit porch wondering where he was. Literally. What is happening? he'd asked himself, jumping off the porch and climbing into the truck. "What is this thing called love?" He mouthed the words going home because he could hear the tune in his head.

It had to be one of the old songs his mother hummed. She was always humming around the house, occasionally breaking into song in her crackly, off-key voice. The sound of her singing used to nettle him. How could she be happy, he would wonder, when he was so miserable?

Of course he knew he'd brought her plenty of misery. He had been the cause of all the contention between his parents. He'd interrupted their comfortable lives with his chronic hostility, had sent them into sporadic tizzies of anger and remorse.

"I'm doing okay," he said aloud, although he couldn't hear himself over the music. Being with Ellery had left him feeling light-headed, even slightly crazy. Suddenly, he wanted to sing something, a song he didn't even know, had never heard. He was bursting with it, but no matter how he coaxed his brain in search of them, he couldn't find the words.

29

Ellery set the needle on the second band of Puccini arias and waited for Eileen Farrell's voice to break into the silence of her room. It was Cio-Cio-San singing of how someday a ship would enter the harbor, how she would wait on a hill and see in the distance a man coming, her own true love so long away at sea. She would not come when he called to her, prolonging the moments of anticipation before she would be in his arms. This would all happen, she sang, because she was waiting for him.

Tears came to Ellery's eyes as she listened to the soaring, hopeful voice. She knew better than Cio-Cio-San. She wasn't gullible anymore. Would never be complacent or tricked into believing anything was permanent. She had thought she'd live her whole life in Charlotte, had believed her parents would love each other forever. She had thought she'd always be the center of that little universe, but she had been wrong. It had been a lie that had lured her into trust.

She fell across her bed, letting the music pour over her. All this will happen, Cio-Cio-San sang, I promise you.

"But it didn't happen that way, Butterfly," Ellery whispered into her pillow. "He was a fraud all along."

30

On Labor Day they took Fairlee's advice and packed a picnic, which they lugged up the mountain to where a smooth shelf of rock jutted out of a grassy knoll overlooking the cove. They spread one of Coralee's old quilts under a wind-warped dogwood and plopped down on it,

Ellery on her stomach, her cheek against her folded arm.

"Aren't you going to look at the view?" Rob asked, hugging his knees. The sky was clear and crisply blue without the hazy cast he'd come to expect. He watched a few wispy clouds scudding across the horizon on the wind. An autumn sky, Ginny had called it when Rob had stopped to get Ellery.

"It looks solid, like paper, doesn't it? I feel as though I could reach up and crinkle it," she'd said.

"Oh, Mother," Ellery had groaned, jumping over the steps into the yard. "That's the *artiste* in her talking, and it's such a bore!" she'd complained to Rob.

But Ginny had grinned at them, undaunted by Ellery's impatience. "I think I'll tag along," she had said playfully. "It's a great day to touch the sky."

"Do you think you could tear yourself away?" Ellery had asked Rob, because he was staring foolishly at Ginny, who was stretching her arms upward so her flowing sleeves slid up her arms. Rob thought she was beautiful now that he'd gotten used to her looks—the carelessly kept hair that reminded him of museum paintings of European beauties he'd seen in New York, her expansive physical movements, as if she were about to leap away; the soft Indian cottons that made up her wardrobe except when she was in jeans and T-shirts decorated with slogans he'd never seen on his own mother: ADAM WAS A ROUGH DRAFT; ARMS ARE FOR HUGS; MERRY ME.

"I'm ready anytime," he'd said, hoisting the picnic basket off the porch. All week he'd thought about Ellery, had spent wakeful nights touching her in the ragged silence of his room while he knew she slept on the edge of the mountain above him, out of reach but waiting, too, he felt, for today to come, a day they could spend together without the infringement of family or school. It was such a relief to be free of lectures he couldn't concentrate on or buzzers that forced him through the halls of hooting rednecks, girls clustered on the fringes of mob movement, lockers clanging. There was no place no talk at school, no hiding places.

"You're not going to look?" he asked Ellery again, because she hadn't moved.

"No, but I suppose you're going to try to touch the sky," she said into the quilt. "Sometimes I can't believe Mom. She's truly unreal."

"I like her," Rob said.

"Well, I don't." Ellery rolled over, her arm now across her face and blocking her eyes.

"Nobody likes their parents. You're not supposed to." Rob was quiet, watching the sky but seeing his house in Montclair. They would be spending the day separately until dinnertime when, with steaks sizzling on their plates and foil-wrapped potatoes scored and buttered, they would sit at the patio table in the shadow of their suburban house and acknowledge the end of summer. It was the same meal every year—the same efficiency, the same perfection. That was what he resented most—the shape he was supposed to fit into, the average American middle-class family he was expected to complete.

"I was getting good at keeping my distance," he said now to Ellery. "Must have done an excellent job, because I'm definitely out of Dad's way now."

"I haven't seen my father in a long time," Ellery said

softly, still in hiding. "We talk on the phone sometimes, but I guess we're kind of avoiding each other, sort of like people who go through a disaster together and don't want to be reminded. Like as much as I want to go back to Charlotte right now, I know it would bother me to see all the places I used to love, like my old school, all the restaurants and shops we used to go to, and the studio where I went for my flute lessons.

"Sometimes I can see myself in all those places. I study myself doing all the things I used to do, trying to figure out where I went wrong. What did I do that was so terrible?" She paused as if she expected Rob to have an answer.

"Daddy used to take me to school, and a lot of times I didn't hug him good-bye. I was in a hurry to be with my friends. Sometimes I didn't even wave to him, just left him sitting there in the car watching me run away. I never spent much time with him, either. I was always practicing my flute, hanging out with my friends, reading and listening to music in my room. Sometimes when I practiced in the living room, I'd see him fold his paper and close his eyes, but when I finished something really hard, like Handel's Vivace, he never applauded or said anything. He just went back to his paper."

"You didn't do anything wrong, Ellery," Rob said, dropping on one elbow beside her. She was in his shadow. "Your parents messed up, not you."

"How can you know that?" Ellery moved her arm so she could look at him. He was leaning toward her, and she could see the fine tips of his eyelashes, the chapped ridges on his lips. "I've been so lonely here, Rob. I know

125

I haven't tried, but I couldn't make myself. I feel like there's a big rock against my chest and I can't budge it."

He waited a long moment while the wind lifted, trembling the leaves above them. Then he brushed his hand across her shirt, barely touching but feeling beneath the hard buttons and smooth cloth a shuddering surge of coolness, the stone's jagged surface. She didn't move, and so he relaxed his hand on her breast, thumb heavy at the bone where she held her breath. His fingers moved against her, crossing her neck, into the collar of her shirt, out again, down to her waist, beneath skin and cloth. He could feel the fluttering muscles at her stomach, the low sighing breath pushing upward. He pulled his hand away, curling his fingers into a fist.

"Here it is," he said, and she opened her eyes to see his hand hurled upward, out across the bluest sky she had ever looked into. "And now it's gone. No more stones holding us down. No more wishing things were different. We've got each other now."

It seemed right that she should reach skyward and bring his face to hers.

31

Nothing went okay for very long. He knew that, had a history to prove it. He tried to study, tried to concentrate in class, but he felt drowsy most of the time, floating in some dreamy place that had soft worn edges like the quilt Coralee had lent him. In algebra he was far ahead of the class, so he did the problems thoughtlessly, relying on instinct to get him through. In English he memorized the vocabulary words minutes before the tests, skimmed through the sermons and diaries assigned from the colonial period. His art class, designed, according to the mimeographed catalogue, to give him "a lifelong appreciation of painting and sculpture from antiquity to modern times," was actually the flipping of slides through a projector while the colors glowed on a screen that slid down from the ceiling of the auditorium. In the dark he let his grogginess envelop him, although he woke himself periodically, alerted by the click of the carousel moving and the bright square of light that appeared when a slot came up empty. Maybe he was getting it subliminally. At night he dreamed of marble breasts, smooth necks turned seductively away from him, thighs that glistened in moonlight.

Only watching Ellery in history class was he alert. He looked at her blatantly, starved by afternoon for the sight of her, willing her by his stare to glance in his direction. Sometimes she did, but mostly she took copious notes, her pen scurrying over the page of her notebook. Her moving wrist was beautiful to him. Now and then she would stop and stretch, slip backward in the desk with her head thrown back and her long black-clad legs stretched into the aisle and crossed at the ankles. Every day she wore her black high-top sneakers, and he wished he'd been with her when she bought them. He wished he'd been with her every moment of his life. By the end of the third week he'd had a test in every subject, had passed them all by the skin of his teeth. Being in love was a lot like being stoned.

On Thursday during lunch Travis asked him for a ride home that afternoon. "I had alternator trouble this morning, so I left the car in the shop and the guy said he needs to keep it at least until tomorrow. Practice is going to be short today, so I should be ready to go by four thirty."

"That's fine," Rob said. "I've got to get a prescription filled and pick up some groceries anyway. Then I'll come by for you. And take your time, Travis. You wouldn't believe what I'd do to keep from going home."

"You ought to be playing football, buddy." Travis laughed. "We'd keep you busy."

"That's where I draw the line, just short of getting killed or permanently maimed," Rob said.

It was almost five when Travis pushed through the side door of the gym, carrying his book bag and a soft-drink can. He crushed the can and dropped it into the trash before getting into the truck.

"Thanks, buddy," he said. "I guess Harley or Butch could of come get me but they'd be pissed about it. They've got more work than they can do right now."

Rob backed the truck out of the parking place and turned through the gate to the road. "I suppose the Christmas tree business keeps them busy," he said.

"Yeah, but they got themselves another crop. You don't think we make a living on cabbages and Christmas trees, do you?"

"I don't know."

128

"My grandpa made whiskey back in the old days, ran it all over six counties till the revenuers came and shut everybody down. Course that didn't stop Daddy later on. He just made it on a smaller scale. Daddy's white lightning was so smooth, you could of fed it to a baby. You ask your Uncle Fairlee or your grandpa. They used to buy from Daddy." Travis grinned and slapped the seat between them. "Now Daddy's got another business. Actually Butch and Harley got the idea, and Daddy went along with it. I mean, you got to make a living somehow and this land is poor. You don't know how poor till you try to live off it."

"My dad left here after high school," Rob said. "I guess that was the reason."

"Yeah, well, I'm leaving, too. I'm going to get an education, get some kind of career going, I don't care if cannabis does pay for it."

"You grow grass?"

"What do you think I've been talking about? You can't smoke it unless somebody grows it."

"I'll be damned, Travis."

"This land up here might not be good for much, but it's perfect for grass. On top of that, it's easier to hide than most places. Butch and Harley even took an airplane ride and marked on a map where the best spots would be. I reckon Daddy doesn't even know where every patch is. Neither do I. I keep away from it."

"Maybe you shouldn't be telling me all this," Rob said.

"Maybe not," Travis replied. "Nobody else knows, not even Leanna. She wouldn't understand and it would worry her to death. But I know you smoke the stuff.

You remember you said something about it that day we went tubing. Scared me witless. You know, sometimes the government sends people down here just to narc, and I've always got that in the back of my mind. Butch and Harley say there's nothing to worry about. They're real careful. They've got everything all worked out. I just never figured Butch and Harley were too smart themselves."

Rob tried to concentrate on driving.

"Turn left right here. The house is about a half a mile in."

The lane was rough, and they splattered through a spring that ran across it.

"On a calm night you can hear a vehicle digging out of that stream," Travis said. "The acoustics out here are fantastic. Of course, nothing's going to stop the narcs if they have reason to come looking, unless it's a firefight."

"You're kidding." Rob shifted down to first to pull the old truck up the steep yard in front of a freshly painted farmhouse.

"I wish. There've been two shoot-outs in this county already and no telling how many pounds of grass burned. Those narcs must get some kind of a good high, breathing two hundred thousand dollars' worth of smoke. The air's got to be pure gold."

"Two hundred thousand dollars' worth! Are you going to college or do you plan to buy one?"

"Daddy's planning a real nice retirement, that's for sure. But Butch and Harley will stay at it as long as they can. How much is enough, anyway? It's hard work, though.

You've got to hide the plants so good you can hardly get at them yourself. And there's the worry of it."

They sat staring at the house. The place looked deserted.

"Well, you want to come in?" Travis asked. "Looks like nobody's home. We could have a Dr Pepper or something."

"I guess I should get these groceries on to Coralee." Rob waited for Travis to grab his book bag from the floorboard and open the door.

"Well, thanks for the ride." The door snapped open. "Listen, Rob, maybe I shouldn't of told you. You know it's got to stay between us, don't you? You can't tell Ellery or anybody."

"I understand. Don't worry, Travis." Rob put his hand on his arm. "Hey, man, it's between us."

Travis gave him a tight smile. "I reckon I've been needing to tell somebody. It's the worry of it, you know."

"Gotcha. No problem." Rob raced the motor lightly.

"See you tomorrow then." Travis shut the door. He still stood close to the truck, as if he wanted to postpone Rob's leaving.

"See you," Rob called, pulling the truck away.

On the way home he slung around the curves, hanging in gear, squealing tires, slapping the clutch. On one of the turns he heard the grocery bags falling, but he didn't slow down.

32

Ginny took courage and went down to Coralee's with six yards of cloth and some shawls to be fringed. She found her loading the dryer in a little room off the kitchen, which must have once been the pantry.

"You should be hanging that wash on the line on a day like today," Ginny said. "It's gorgeous out."

"Man on the television said it was going to rain," Coralee said, stuffing the sheets in.

In New England maybe, Ginny thought but held her tongue. Living with Ellery had shown her how meager the return on nagging could be.

"I brought some cloth," she said, spreading the yardage out on the kitchen table. It was tweed, the color of toast. "And I have a pattern of sorts. I was hoping we could fit it to me. That way, if it doesn't sell, I can wear it myself."

Coralee touched the cloth. "I might ruin it," she said. "It's too pretty to practice on."

"If we ruin it, we'll have learned something. I can make some more cloth, Cora. Let's just see what happens."

The pattern was for a skirt softly gathered on an elastic waist and a collarless loose-fitting jacket with big sleeves and shoulder pads.

"It looks like something from the thirties." Coralee laughed.

"That's the fashion these days," Ginny said. "Everything comes around again, doesn't it?"

"I reckon it does." Coralee was unfolding the pattern and studying the pieces.

"It's mostly hand sewing," Ginny continued. "A machine would pull the threads. Listen, Coralee, Ellery and I are going to a craft fair in Asheville this weekend. Why don't you come with us? You could see a lot of different kinds of handwoven clothing plus some beautiful wood-carving and pottery. It's a wonderful show."

"I can't. I can't do that." Coralee's mouth twisted, flying around the words.

"Of course you can. You'd be with me all the time." Ginny watched the face, the terrors skirmishing behind her eyes, the anxious burrowing of her forehead and cheeks as she fought with herself. "I know you don't go outside, Coralee. Ellery told me you haven't gone out in a long time. I think you have a condition called agoraphobia—that's the fear of open spaces. A lot of people have it and they get over it. It takes time but they do it and you can too. I know you don't want to be cooped up in the house all the time. Fairlee says you used to love the garden and going into town on Saturdays and going to church. You have to miss all those things."

"I can't," Coralee said, as if all she could hear was her own voice.

"Then we could just go out on the porch. I'll go with you. We can just stand there a minute. You need fresh air and sunshine, Coralee."

"No."

"Well, will you think about it? Promise me you'll think about it. I could come every day if you'd let me. Just for a few minutes. You can learn to go into the yard, Cora, I know you can. You could sit on the porch again."

"I've got to stay safe," Coralee said stubbornly. Her voice was hard, a taut ribbon of bitter fury.

"I thought that, too," Ginny said. "I married because of it. I did everything I was told because of it. But in the long run being safe meant being in prison. It took a long time, but I came out of it. I guess I thought for years somebody had to open the door for me. I was waiting for that. But the truth is, the door was locked from the inside. Nobody could open it but me."

"I'm afraid. Sometimes when I'm lying in the bed, my breathing stops I'm so scared," Coralee said. "I think I'm scared of dying more than anything."

"Maybe so," Ginny said, "but my problem was that I was afraid to live."

33

They left home intending to go to Simmonsville to the football game, but when Rob saw a church sign that announced HOLY FAMILY IN THE VALLEY, THREE MILES, he turned off there.

"Where are we going?" Ellery wanted to know.

"You don't really want to go to the game, do you?"

"Leanna's expecting us, Rob. She may tell your aunt Rosalie if we don't show up."

"Leanna's not that dumb," Rob said.

"I know, but she's not real subtle, either."

Rob smiled in the dark. "Let's risk it."

Their headlights blazed a path through the deserted cove until they came to a tiny natural-pine building nestled among some oaks.

"It looks like a doll church!" Ellery said. "Just look, Rob. Oh, I'd love to see it in the daylight."

"We'll come one Sunday," Rob offered. He hadn't missed the weekly ritual or the liturgy he could say by heart, and yet seeing the little church in the white beam of their lights, he thought he could hear the *Agnus Dei*. "O Lamb of God, that takest away the sins of the world" whispered in his head.

He cut the lights and the church was invisible. There were no stars, no movement in the trees. He breathed heavily, listening to the night.

"What is it, Rob?"

"Nothing. I was just thinking."

"About what?"

"You." The *Agnus Dei* drifted away from him. "I spend twenty-four hours a day thinking about you."

"You do not."

"I don't even sleep at night."

"Don't tell me that. I don't want you thinking about me all the time."

"I can't help it."

"You ought to be thinking about your schoolwork."

"You take precedence."

"We can't afford to get serious, Rob. You're leaving at Thanksgiving, remember?"

"I thought we were already serious. I thought Labor Day up on the mountain meant something to you."

"It did."

"So show me." He was touching her neck, running his finger along her jaw. There was no light anywhere.

She moved into his arms. It was like coming out of the cold. "I've been thinking about you, too," she said.

"And hopefully about this," he added, moving his lips over her cheek, across her temple and forehead. "And this." He breathed across her eyelids as he brought her face up with his hands. "And this." The words became a kiss, soft at first and then more urgent, swallowing her mouth in his. The darkness was close, holding them in a warm furry cocoon.

"This was all I could think about all week," Rob whispered into her hair. "Some nights I thought I'd die from wanting you."

"Oh, Rob." Ellery moved away, flattening her shoulders to the back of the seat.

He couldn't see her face. "What is it?"

"I don't know." Her voice came from far away, a tiny thread of sound crossing the darkness.

"Yes, you do. Why did you pull away?"

"You scare me." She hesitated. "This scares me. What happened up on the mountain—it just happened, you know. It seemed right at the time."

"But now you're sorry? Is that it?"

"I didn't say that."

"You have to know I care about you," Rob said. "I didn't plan what happened any more than you did. I didn't take you up there expecting to get laid."

"I know that, Rob. It was spontaneous, but this isn't like that."

"So it's okay if it's spontaneous but not okay if I've been thinking about it?"

"That's not what I mean. It's just that you expect something now. Why else are we here? I thought we were going to the game."

"We'll go then." Rob turned the key and pumped the accelerator so the Jeep roared.

"No," Ellery said, pushing his hand from the key. She turned off the ignition and the engine grumbled into silence. "We've spent most of our time together arguing about stupid things. Now I think we'd better talk."

"I don't see what there is to talk about. We had sex. I enjoyed it. I thought you did too." He turned toward her. "Listen, Ellery, maybe we should just go on to the game."

"You have a girlfriend in Montclair, don't you?"

Rob looked out at the dense space beyond the Jeep. At the black center was the little church.

"Don't you?"

"All right. There's a girl I hang out with, but she doesn't mean anything to me. We have fun, that's all."

"Maybe that's what you want now. Maybe I'm just a diversion from your misery."

"I wish you'd stop harping on how miserable I'm supposed to be. I'm adjusting, for God's sake." Rob slammed his fist on the wheel.

"That's the point. I don't want to be part of the adjustment."

"You're not!" He was rubbing his aching fingers. "Damn it, Ellery, I love you, so I want to have sex with you. It's as simple as that."

137

"But you don't even know me! What about how I feel and what I want?" Ellery waited in the dark, barely breathing.

"I obviously don't know anything about what you want," Rob said, his voice leaden.

"I don't mean to hurt you," Ellery said finally. Her voice had a tremor she tried to swallow. "I just don't think we should do anything we can't talk about."

"But it's already happened. We can't go back and start over." Rob turned toward her again and drew a sharp breath, trying to mask his impatience. "I've got protection, if that's what you're worried about."

"That's important, but it's not everything. I think we need to talk about our feelings," she began tentatively.

"That's easy enough. According to you, all I feel is horny."

"Rob!" She slumped on the seat and stared out the window. "If you're not going to try to understand what I mean, we may as well forget it." He was quiet, so she went on: "I just don't feel like I know myself very well right now, so how can I be sure about anything? Most of the time I feel so awkward, you know, like I don't belong in my own skin. I get so frustrated at everything, I could just scream and there's no reason for it. I just hate myself.

"Then sometimes I feel really fantastic. Once this summer I was alone in my room—Vivaldi was on the stereo, one of *The Four Seasons*—and this feeling came over me, this perfect sensation of knowing myself and liking myself too. All the things wrong with me were okay. I was okay. I could actually see it in the mirror like those photographs that show heat. There was a light all around me like an aura. I moved my arms and the aura stayed. I danced around the room watching myself in the mirror and that glow was still there. It was there for minutes, all warm and rosy around me. It was the best I've ever felt in my life."

"I felt that way stoned once," Rob said. He rested his hand on her thigh, making contact.

"It's not the same thing," Ellery said, but she didn't move away.

"I need you, Ellery." Her thigh was solid under his hand. Pressing down, he felt the bone.

"You need somebody. I just happen to be here."

"Is that what you really think?"

"I think we got involved before we knew what we were doing."

"Speak for yourself. I always know what I'm doing."

"You don't have to be like this, you know." She sighed. The dark outside the window looked impenetrable, like a wall they'd have to push through. "You could tell me how you really feel. I'd listen, Rob."

"I feel great."

Ellery shifted on the seat and his hand fell away from her thigh.

"Okay, it's not so great," he said. "Actually, it's a drag. At least, it was until last weekend. See, you inspire positive thinking—among other things."

Ellery shrugged. "Well, that's really terrific after I've spent a lot of time and money on a negative image."

"To keep people away?"

"To keep myself together. But I don't feel very together now." She bowed her head. Her locked hands in her lap ached and she released her fingers, which moved restlessly in the dark as if feeling for an exit.

Rob could feel her slipping away. In her mind, she was already gone.

"We can go slow," he said, reaching for her. "I mean, one thing doesn't necessarily lead to another." He was touching her neck just below her ear and he felt her shiver, one slow tremor like the fluttery motion of a sprite. "We can stop anytime—I can stop."

Ellery's hands were motionless again, locked together to avoid him. "I read the letters of Sylvia Plath last year and there was one line I've remembered ever since." She paused, knowing he was finally hearing her. " 'You have seen me through that black night when the only word I knew was NO,' " she said softly.

The darkness collected around the words, holding the sounds in the space between them like a shield.

"I guess you want to go to the game," Rob said, moving his hand to the wheel. It was cool where he clutched it. "Or would you rather go home?"

"I think it would be better if I went home," Ellery said.

He reversed the Jeep, casting a quick white beam of light across the little church. An ache knitted in his chest, a tight ball of hurt he couldn't let go of. He knew he was driving too fast, but nobody stopped him.

34

At Ellery's house he traded the Jeep for Fairlee's truck and spun out of the turnaround, spitting gravel against the porch. Where could he go now? Everybody he knew from school was at the game. In fact, everybody in town would be there. There was nothing else to do on a Friday night, but he didn't want to go all the way to Simmonsville in the truck. He wasn't even sure how to get there. He'd depended on Ellery to know the way.

"So I'll find something to do," he answered himself as he turned the truck toward town. If nothing else, he had the money to buy a bottle at Bert's. A pint of vodka ought to do the trick. He might even pick up a six-pack of beer, depending on how much service charge Bert expected. No matter what the county government did, they weren't going to stop a man who really wanted a drink.

"I don't know what you're talking about, boy," Bert said, leaning over the counter of the snack bar in the middle of his deserted service station.

"Does this clear up your understanding?" Rob asked, peeling a twenty-dollar bill out of his wallet.

"What's your name, boy?" Bert asked, never looking at the money on the counter.

"Rob Dickson. I'm staying out at Fairlee Dickson's for a few months. He's my uncle."

"Fairlee Dickson? Used to work for the highway department?" Bert said, making a connection in his head. "Well, I still don't know nothing about no hard liquor.

This county's as dry as a corn cob." He eyed Rob while slipping the twenty off the counter and into his pocket. "Now the john's out back if you're wanting it. Here's the key to it. Bring the key back, you hear."

The key had GMC engraved on it. A rusting Chevy, its tire rims resting on concrete blocks, sat in the dark just beyond the lighted entrance to the rest rooms. Rob stuck the key in the trunk lock and turned it. The lid popped open, but there was no light inside. He put his hand in hesitantly, feeling for a bottle. There was a box of pints in paper bags and he gripped one and shut the trunk.

"Here's the key," he said to Bert, holding the pint under his jacket.

"I've never seen you before, boy," Bert said, and turned back to his little television set.

Rob parked the truck at the bottom of the lane, where he could see the lights from the house. The bottle was bourbon, a cheap brand from the smell of it. He'd never drunk whiskey, and at first it was hot going down, singeing his throat and churning angrily in his stomach. It tasted terrible. After a while it got better and the fire cooled to glowing coals in his gut. He couldn't feel much of anything. Once his numbed lips didn't connect with the bottle at all and he felt the spill of whiskey soaking through his shirt. It gave him the urge to urinate, and he got out of the truck and peed against a tire.

Just like a dog, he giggled to himself, grabbing hold of the doorjamb to pull himself back in. I am a dog. The idea sent him into a gale of choking laughter and he sputtered and snorted breathlessly. I am a hound dog.

He began to howl, but the sound was crackly and hollow. I am dog tired, he thought, and grinned, recognizing his joke.

He shook the bottle, listening for a slosh of liquid. The bottle was almost empty, and he drained it on his tongue. He couldn't feel the trickle, didn't even know when to swallow. He gagged helplessly, curling himself around the empty bottle. The dark was spinning. He could see it filling up with colors. Ellery was flying in the colors. She had gigantic psychedelic wings and she dipped toward him, tipping the swirling colors in his face. He tried to watch her, even to reach up and pull her down to him, but the colors blinded him with their brightness. Ellery hung there in the air above him for a moment, then few upward, crossing the sun, higher and higher until she was lost in its fiery light. No! He could feel a protest coming, spewing up out of his gut. Come back!

It was the earliest stream of light striking the truck that woke him. His first movement flooded him with nausea, and he leaned out of the truck, retching and heaving while vomit surged upward, choking him with its bitter, hot taste. Minutes passed before he was able to lift his head and see where he was.

He was afraid to drive the truck, even the quarter of a mile to the house. He felt half blind; besides, they would hear him. He had to squint to focus on anything farther away than his own hand. He left the truck there and stumbled down the rutty lane, his arms waving for balance like a man on a tightrope. Once he thought the house was moving instead of him.

The kitchen door was unlocked, the light in the hall

still on. They hadn't waited up for him. Maybe nobody even knew he'd been out all night. He climbed the stairs carefully, pulling up on the railing and putting each bare foot down slowly to ease around the creaks. In his room he fell across the bed exhausted, his head still swimming and unable to grasp a single thought long enough to get the significance of it. He felt heavy, almost paralyzed.

Ellery, he remembered suddenly when, for an instant, her image pierced the rushing movement in his head. Now he knew what his sadness was.

35

He awoke soaked to the skin with sweat, his head a lead ball attached to a limp frame that fought wearily against movement. He had to force himself to turn over on the rumpled bed, and even then he couldn't open his eyes— they were glued shut. He forced his hand to touch his face and rub across his eyelids. His hand felt like sandpaper.

"Well," a voice came at him out of the thick stuffy space above his head, "I'm not a bit surprised."

He recognized the tone, had heard it in his father's voice, knew where it came from now. "I'm sick, Aunt Rosalie," he moaned, holding his hand tight across his eyes.

"I don't doubt that," Rosalie huffed. "That's what a hangover is. It's sick and well deserved, too. Now you get up from there! You smell like a brewery." She was tugging at the bedspread, trying to roll him off with it.

"This bedspread's going to have to be washed, and don't you expect me to do it. Coralee either. You can wash it yourself." She gave up on moving him. "Here it is, going on eleven o'clock in the morning, and Fairlee had a doctor's appointment at ten fifteen. I made it specifically on Saturday so you wouldn't have a problem with school, and now he's missed it. He's not even washed. He's down there in yesterday's pants Coralee finally helped him into when she couldn't rouse you."

She was at him again, had a firm grip on his shin, squeezing. He tried to pull his leg away but it wouldn't move.

"Coralee thought you were dead. She was screaming at me on the telephone about how you're up here on the bed with your clothes on! I told your daddy he better not be dumping his problems on me, and now look, I've got everything on me again, you included. I ought to call Davis right this minute and tell him what's what. He thinks he can leave a spoiled brat down here and that takes care of his responsibility. Well, he can think again!"

"Damn it, get outa here, Rosalie!" Rob groaned, pulling the pillow over his face. It would serve her right if he suffocated and she had a corpse on her hands as well.

"Don't you talk to me like that, Rob Dickson!" she cried, ripping the pillow away from him. "Open your eyes right this minute!"

He forced his eyelids to make a slit. The glare in the room pierced the center of his skull. Rosalie was a giant pink frond swaying in front of him. He couldn't stop her from moving.

"I'm going to throw up!" The floor careened up to him as he turned off the bed, caught crazily on his feet, and sprinted down the stairs to the bathroom.

"What is it?" he could hear Coralee asking. "Is he bad sick?"

"He's drunk, that's what," Rosalie said. "I knew this wasn't going to work out. What can you expect from somebody brought up like that? Davis and Carrie might have book learning but there's not a lick of common sense between them. Never has been. All Davis could ever think about was getting away from here. Didn't matter where, as long as it was someplace different. I'd tell him, here's the place to live, this is where your roots are. But he'd just start going on about advantages and the good life, whatever that might be. I reckon we've got an example of all that right here in the bathroom, puking."

Rob's stomach bounced into his throat, settled again. His head was swimming but he felt better. He flushed the toilet and splashed cold water on his face and hair. When he opened the door, the two women were standing there waiting for him.

"You look terrible," Coralee said.

"He feels terrible, too, and he deserves every bit of it," Rosalie fumed. "Now I've got to call the doctor's office and apologize for Fairlee's not showing up. I should of come out here and got him myself. And what about the groceries? They didn't have a drop of milk for breakfast. The washing powder is out. There's nothing in the kitchen but junk food. I know you've been spending the grocery money on potato chips and cookies and Lord knows what all! Don't tell me you haven't."

Rob straightened himself up from the doorjamb and took in a hard, rattling breath. "Rosalie, I don't give a damn what you think about anything."

"Rob!" Coralee tried to get close to him but he moved back from her. He could smell himself. The sickening odor on his clothing mixed with Rosalie's hair spray and the odd, musty scent of the hallway.

"Leave this to me, Cora," Rosalie said, bristling as if she'd been struck. "You never could take care of anything."

"There you go!" Rob said. "I can't do anything right. Daddy can't. Now Coralee can't. Just you, Rosalie. You're the perfect one. You've always done everything you were supposed to do. Well, you make me sick. If I hadn't just thrown up, you'd make me. Now get outa here! I'll call the doctor. I'll get the groceries. I'll do every goddamn thing you can think of but I don't intend to put up with you. So you can take your fat butt home, Rosalie, and you call Dad if you want to. Nothing would suit me better than getting on a plane tomorrow. Now you just think about that!"

He slammed the bathroom door and turned on the shower. In seconds the room was steamed up, the mirror fogged over. He disappeared in it.

When he came out of the bathroom, Rosalie had gone and Coralee and Fairlee were waiting for him in the kitchen. "I thought you might need a little something to eat," Fairlee said, grinning at him. "Drink some of this tea Coralee made. It's made outa herbs and you ain't gonna like it, but it'll stay on your stomach better'n anything I know of. Then you can put a piece of toast with it and see how you do. Come on, taste of it."

The tea was bitter and smelled dusty, like spiderwebs, but its warmth soothed his raw places and it didn't churn in his stomach. He sat down at the table with it.

"It's okay," he said because they were both watching him.

"I knew it!" Fairlee laughed. "Don't think you're the first to tie one on in this house, boy! I had me a few nights on the town myself. What I want to know is, where's Ellery? Rosalie says the truck's down at the end of the lane, just barely off the road to hear her tell it, and it's empty. You took Ellery home, didn't you?"

"Of course I did." He didn't want to think about last night unless there was a chance he'd gotten it all wrong. Sometimes he did that. He got mad before he had time to think. Hurts came easier to him than reasoning did. He knew that. "We decided not to go to the game, so she was home early."

"It was a little spat what caused all this," Coralee said. She was buttering him a piece of toast. "I told Rosalie, Rob wouldn't get stinking drunk for no reason." She put the plate in front of him. "Shush. Papa's coming and he don't know a thing about it."

"Can't find the truck." Grandpa was quarreling to himself when he came in from the back porch. "I done walked clear around this place and the truck's gone, Fairlee. Somebody's come in here and robbed us blind. You get the sheriff on that telephone, boy, and get him to looking. Somebody's riding around in that truck, having them a big time."

"We won't robbed, Papa," Coralee said and then hushed, not knowing exactly how to lie.

148

"Rob had a little trouble with the truck last night," Fairlee continued for her, "so he left it down at the end of the lane. He'll go down there and see if he can start it up directly."

"Harump," Grandpa grunted. "Can't drive that thing, can you, boy? City slicker like that, he just knows about fast cars. I seen 'em on the TV. Little tiny things you got to hunker down and crawl into. I bet you got one of them. Anything what takes money, you got it. That's Davis' way. Too big for his britches the day he was born."

"I'm going to get the truck," Rob said grimly. Standing up, he felt a flood of dizziness.

"You didn't touch that toast," Coralee reminded him. "You oughta put something in your stomach."

"That's right, boy," Fairlee said. "The truck can wait."

"Will all of you just leave me alone!" Rob slammed out of the screen door and off the porch. It was afternoon by the sun. Half of a Saturday lost to him. So what, when he had three months to waste?

He felt better walking. The tea had settled his stomach; now his swollen head was shrinking to normal size and his breathing was easier. He threw the empty pint into the woods and got into the truck. It cranked on the first try. He was lucky somebody hadn't stolen it in broad daylight. He chugged up the lane toward the house. He would call Ellery. She was the only thing going for him and he wouldn't give her up, not this easily. He had never fought for anything before—had never wanted anything as much as he wanted to be with her. So he'd get her back. He went straight to the telephone, but there was no answer.

36

Leanna went with Ellery and Ginny to the craft fair. "We'll meet at the gate at six o'clock and have dinner before we go home," Ginny said. "Have fun, girls." And she was off to talk to the weavers whose booths were mingled with the other craftspeople's on the coliseum floor.

"Lord, look at all this stuff!" Leanna said. They were ambling down the first aisle while the music from a dulcimer drifted above their heads. "I looked for you at the game last night." They stopped in front of a pottery display and Ellery picked up a mug to test its weight. She touched the scarlet glaze for a moment and put the mug down carefully.

"We didn't go. We just talked awhile and then he took me home."

"You had a fight, didn't you? I can tell. Lord, Ellery, I know all the signs. Travis and I used to argue a lot more than we do now. I'd just get sick, I mean physically ill, when we had a fight. I decided it wasn't worth it, so I just started giving in. Agreeing with him, you know. He says it does me good. I like to get my own way, that's the truth. I got it from Mama. Now I just go along about the little things—like what show we're going to see and stuff like that."

"And what about the big things?" Ellery wanted to know.

"Oh, you mean about sex and all that? Look at this!" Leanna was touching a handwoven vest banded in ribbon. "I hope your mama sees these so she can make

150

some." They moved on. "Well, we've had it. Sex, I mean. After all, we've been going together since the sixth grade. By the tenth—that's four years—there was nothing left to do. It sorta happened naturally. Not that I wasn't scared to death somebody would find out. I went all the way to Simmonsville to the clinic there to get a diaphragm, and I use it too. I'm faithful. So it all worked out."

"You're in love with Travis?"

Leanna stopped in the aisle and looked at Ellery. Bright satin windsocks swung over her head. "I guess I am," she said seriously. "Of course, I tell him I am. It gets easy to say, you know, and I mean it, I really do, but sometimes I don't know. I mean, what if this isn't it? Travis wants us to get married. He says it will make college easier. We want to go to the same school anyway." She toyed with a streamer on a windsock. "He says two can live cheaper than one. He's got in his head how we'll have this cute little apartment instead of living in the dorm. He says he's spent enough time in locker rooms not to care about living with a bunch of guys, but I don't know. I was sort of looking forward to being with girls, talking and all like we're doing. I think it would be fun for a while. But I'd miss Travis. I'll probably miss him this very night. It's the first Saturday night in years we haven't been together. He wasn't real excited about my coming, but I didn't let him stop me. I have to do things on my own sometimes." She frowned, riffling through the streamers to make them flutter.

"I've never gone steady," Ellery said, "but I guess I envied some of the kids back at home who did."

"Travis and I have known each other all our lives, and
151

two years ago he gave me this pre-engagement ring—that's what it means. Mama wouldn't mind if I got married. Right now she wants me to stay home and commute thirty miles to college, but if I was married she wouldn't say that. I told her I was going to live at school if I had to hold down three jobs to do it. Sissy got married right out of high school and my brothers stayed right there at home until they got married. Mama holds on to us like that. She reads those romance books but she's not wanting any tall, dark stranger to come around. She likes the kind where the girl wakes up one day and sees the guy she's known all her life is the perfect man for her. I don't know. I used to read those books, too, but it got so boring, always knowing what was going to happen. I don't think I want a life like that."

"Just one long happy ending," Ellery said, walking on. "I could live with that."

"But you've done things. You've lived more than one place. You've had experiences."

"Yeah, great. I'm the product of a broken home." Ellery stopped in front of a jewelry booth and studied the silver rings in the case.

"Your mama's crazy about you, and it looks to me like Rob is, too."

"My life sucks."

"Ellery, it does not!"

"Oh, come off it, Leanna. My dad's in Charlotte having a ball and my mother's out in the woods being a forty-year-old hippie. I hate school. I hate Tyler Mills. I feel absolutely, positively alone."

"You've got me."

"And you've got Travis."

"He doesn't take the place of friends, Ellery." They left the ring case, moving on to a display of woodcarvings—human faces released from blocks of walnut, a wildcat with a gleaming maple coat, cream-colored ducks with buckeye feathers.

"Did you know there's an island somewhere in the Caribbean where the women have a separate language?" Ellery asked her. "They talk to each other in it and nobody else knows what they're saying."

"Hey, that sounds neat. I wish we could do that." Leanna ran her finger down the cat's back.

"I think you have to have a history together to do it. A language goes way back. You can't just invent it all at once."

"We could start, though," Leanna said, urging Ellery back into the aisle. People were milling around them carrying packages and pushing strollers. "We could start with a code. Like, if I say, 'You want to go to the ladies' room?' you'll know I have something to tell you."

"Girls have been doing that for years."

"So, you see, we've already got a secret language."

"It's not the same, Leanna," Ellery said impatiently.

"You just don't want to do it," Leanna complained, fingering an enamel brooch.

"Okay. I don't want to do it. I don't want to bother. Come on, we're blocking traffic."

They turned the corner into the next aisle. "Then we'll never learn to talk to each other," Leanna said. "Not about important things."

"Don't worry about it," Ellery said, taking her arm.

153

"We'll do what we've always done. We'll talk around the guys. They don't listen anyway."

"I guess you're right," Leanna said. A man was playing "Wildwood Flower" on a hammered dulcimer in the next booth. The tune sparkled around them. "But Ellery, another language would be wonderful, wouldn't it?"

37

Rob dialed the number over and over again through the afternoon and evening, dreamed dialing in his sleep, heard Ellery answer, a breathless voice saying "I love you, Rob, I love you. Come." In his sleep he ran across the ridge, panting, his noisy breath chuffling in his chest, racing toward her forgiveness, toward open arms ready to comfort him. The front door was open, the stairs so minor an obstacle he thought he flew slightly above them, into her room where she waited. She was wearing something long and loose and white, a gown like a princess would sleep in, like Juliet would wear, both innocent and seductive as if she weren't sure what he expected or wanted. Before he reached her, he woke up.

It was nine o'clock, later than he'd intended to sleep, even though it was Sunday. He went downstairs to the bathroom, then stopped at the phone on his way to get dressed. "She's out running, Rob," Ginny said. "We were late getting back from the craft show last night, so we slept in."

"So did I," Rob said. "Will you tell her I called?"

He waited near the phone until noon, went to the dinner table still expecting it to ring. Coralee had been watching a healing service on television.

"I should get on one of them programs." Fairlee chuckled. "Get myself healed in a jiffy."

"You don't believe," Coralee said solemnly. "I know that and the preacher would too. You've got to believe to make it work. You've got to have a show of faith."

"It's the Lord what heals," Grandpa said, "and he's done disappointed me several times. Look at what happened to your mama. Don't think I didn't pray. Got on my knees right regular over that woman and all for naught. The Lord took her, and I'll be damned if I see the point to it yet."

"There's things beyond our understanding, Papa," Coralee said.

"I got baptized, didn't I?" Grandpa grumbled on. "Raised this family thataway. Saw to it all you young'ns got dipped in the Little Tennessee. I done everything the Lord ever called on me to do, but I lost your mama and saw Davis get joined up with heathens, so what good did it do me?"

"We're not heathens," Rob said. "We're Episcopalians. There were Episcopalians before there were Baptists."

"Boy, you ain't got a lick of sense," Grandpa argued. "There's Baptists right in the Bible. You don't see nobody getting sprinkled in there, do you? Jesus hisself got immersed in the river. Right there was the start of the Baptists."

"Religion and the Civil War," Rob muttered, mashing peas with his fork. "Dad warned me."

"Say what about the war?" Grandpa yelled. "You don't know no more about the war than you do about salvation. I told your daddy, I said, 'You go up there and live with them Yankees, and 'fore long you'll be one, even if you carry the names of Jefferson Davis and Robert E. Lee.' Everybody in this family's got Lee in their name. I saw to it, but that ain't no protection in New Jersey. Davis don't care nothing about where he come from. This here family was in the war, boy, and got hurt by it. My grandpappy lost everything he had, his good eye included. His brother Jessie got hit in the mouth, bullet took his tongue right out so's he couldn't even yell out his pain. He couldn't never tell what it was like at Shiloh 'cause he couldn't write more'n just his name. Spent the rest of his life dumb. But he tried to protect what belonged to him. That's what it was all about, boy! Protecting yourself. Protecting the people from the government. Some folks in this valley just throwed theirselves away, siding with the North. They thought blacks ought to be running around loose. They thought slavery was a bad thing. Hellfire, them niggers needed taking care of from all I could tell."

"I'm not going to listen to this!" Rob pushed back from the table. "You make me sick, all of you. How can you sit here day after day listening to this ignorant old coot! Nobody ever argues with him, so he goes along believing every stupid thing he thinks of. Why don't you tell him to shut up?" He had focused on Fairlee. "Why don't you get Coralee out of this house before she gets any crazier? Why don't you do something? I don't see how you put up with all this shit!"

"Rob!" It was Coralee who got her breath first.

"Don't talk to me, Coralee. I'm sick of all of you. I'd as soon be sent to hell as stuck out here with you bunch of crazies."

He was out the door and heading for the truck before he realized he didn't have anywhere to go. He couldn't go to Ellery's and there was nothing to do in town. Travis. He'd go there. He had fifty dollars. He'd buy that much pot. What else did he have to spend his money on? He had expected Ellery to call him by now. So she didn't want to see him. So what? There were other girls. The world was full of girls. There was Marsha back in Montclair. He'd be there in less than three months. Meanwhile he'd buy himself some good times. Good times came cheap if you had a weekly payoff from your dear old guilty dad. Fifty dollars a week folded between the pages of a note typed on college stationery from his mother or scrawled under his dad's corporate letterhead. "We know you can do it. We're proud of you." Proud of what? The fact that he hadn't run away or flunked out yet? Well, give me time, folks, he said to himself, revving the truck. I'm just getting started. You ain't seen nothing yet.

There were two trucks and two cars, one of them Travis', parked beside the Williamses' house. Travis came to the door and stepped out on the porch. "They're watching the Redskins game," he said, closing the door behind him. "What happened Friday night? We didn't see you and Ellery at the game."

"We got held up and didn't make it."

"That's what I told Leanna, but you know how she is. I could hardly get her interested in any post-game activities, she was so worked up." Travis grinned. "I managed, though."

"We had a fight," Rob said.

"Good grief, man, you haven't known each other long enough to have a real fight. That takes some working up to."

"Not with Ellery and me."

"I guess you're right. You're both egging for one most of the time, it seems to me. You oughta just relax. Go with the flow, buddy."

"That's why I'm here," Rob said. "I need some grass."

"Come on," Travis said, leading him off the porch. They leaned against the side of the truck. "Listen, Rob," Travis said quietly, "I don't deal."

"I know that."

"I shouldn't of told you. If Butch or Harley find out I did, I'm dead, man."

"I haven't told anybody and I don't intend to," Rob said, "but I need some stuff, Travis. Just a couple of joints if that's all you can do."

"Oh, man," Travis shook his head. "You are so messed up. I can't believe this."

"I can't stay here without it, Travis. I mean it. I've been thinking about splitting."

"Well, maybe you ought to."

"But I can make it if I can smoke. What harm can it do, a little feel-good now and then?"

"All right. A couple of joints is all, though. After that you'll have to get it somewhere else. I'll have to lift it off Butch. He's the only one of us who does the stuff. It'll be tomorrow before I can get it."

"Okay. Tomorrow. At school," Rob said.

"Aw, hell, man. In the parking lot or something. We've got to be real careful."

"I know. I'm not stupid, Travis," Rob said, climbing into the truck.

"You can't prove it by me," Travis replied, and headed for the house.

38

On his way home he met Ginny in the Jeep, so instead of turning down the Dicksons' lane, he went up the mountain to Ellery. He'd done a deal with Travis. Maybe face to face he'd have a chance with Ellery, too. He could hear music coming from the upstairs windows, a crystal soprano voice hanging above the valley. He knocked on the door but no one came. Finally he went around to the side of the house and yelled up toward Ellery's window. The music softened after a moment and he saw her at the screen.

"Hi," he called up, feeling like a fool. Maybe he'd expected Juliet instead of this girl with ragged hair and purple fingernails. Well, he was no Romeo himself. "I tried to call you this morning, but your mom said you were running, so I thought I'd just come over."

"I'm writing a paper for American lit," Ellery said.

"I'll only stay a minute. I just want to talk to you." He was begging, but he didn't care.

"Just for a few minutes, Rob," Ellery said. "I really do have to finish this paper today. Try the door. I think it's unlocked."

He crossed the porch into the house, zigzagged between the looms, then sprinted up the stairs before she could change her mind. Her door was open.

He'd never seen her room before, had expected something austere, almost temporary, but the room looked like his sister's, full of the junk girls collected. Oddly shaped decorated boxes, books, baskets of makeup and cassette tapes, figurines and stuffed animals, records in a painted fruit crate. On the wall above the bed was an oil painting of a young girl, full of splashy colors and light. Ellery was at her desk so he sat down on the bed. The music coming from the stereo was violins, a painfully haunting melody.

"What's that?" he asked, picking up the jacket. Placido Domingo was the only name he recognized.

"It's the Intermezzo from *Cavalleria Rusticana*," Ellery said, still writing.

"That due tomorrow?" Rob asked, nodding toward the papers on her desk. "I'm glad I didn't get in that section."

"It's my favorite class."

A chorus was singing, their voices perfectly blended.

"What's happening now?" Rob asked. "My Italian's pretty rusty."

"You really want to know?" Ellery put down her pencil and turned toward him in her chair. "They're leaving church, so they're singing about going home and having the rest of the day free."

They listened for a moment, then Ellery picked up her pencil.

"What's your paper about?" Rob asked before she could start working again.

"Anne Bradstreet. There's not much information about her, so I'm really having to dig into her own writing."

"You're going to make the rest of the class look bad," Rob said.

Ellery shrugged. "Who cares? I want to get into a good college. I'm thinking about myself here."

"What's happening now?" Rob asked, because he recognized a word. Domingo was singing something about his mother.

"He has to fight a duel, and he's asking his mother to bless him as if he were going off to do something honorable, like fight in a war."

"Why's he fighting a duel?"

"He deserted one woman and is having an affair with another. It's her husband he has the duel with. He's not much of a hero."

"So what's that?" Rob asked when a scream pierced the room.

"He just got killed," Ellery said.

"Good God." Rob lay back on the bed, his head on a stuffed bear.

"It's beautiful music," Ellery said, "but I don't think the story's all that tragic. He got what was coming to him."

"Are all operas tragic?" Rob asked, glad to finally have her attention.

"Most of them. At least, all my favorites are. Aida and her lover get buried alive; Gilda dies in a sack. Tosca thinks she's saved her lover from the firing squad, but the bullets turn out to be real, so he dies and she jumps off a parapet. Madame Butterfly kills herself too, but with a sword because she's Japanese. The heroines in *La Boheme* and *La Traviata* die of consumption. Otello smothers Desdemona."

"And you get into that stuff? No wonder you're a pessimist." Rob grinned.

"Maybe so," Ellery replied. "I've learned not to expect much from people." The stereo had turned itself off, and she got up to change the record. "What do you want to hear?" she asked, her back to him. She was wearing nylon running shorts and a loose T-shirt.

"Anything except death scenes," he said, and saw her choose a recording of flute solos.

"Poulenc's Sonata for Flute and Piano," she said. "I'm trying to learn it." Instead of going back to her desk, she sat down on the edge of the bed beside him.

"I tried to call you all day yesterday," Rob said.

"We went to the craft show in Asheville. I thought I told you."

"Maybe you did. I got so hammered Friday night, I could barely remember my name."

"You got drunk? Oh, Rob." Ellery played with a loose thread on the bedspread.

"Then Rosalie showed up yesterday morning fit to be tied and accused me of everything she could think of."

162

"Like what?"

"I didn't get Fairlee to the doctor, for one thing. The groceries were low. The usual stuff. She's just a bitch, Ellery. I'll never do anything to suit her." She was close enough for him to put his hand on her knee. She didn't move away. "I'm sorry about Friday, Ellery."

She put her hand over his, curling his fingers away from her knee so they were holding hands instead.

"We could go somewhere tonight," Rob said. "To the movies maybe."

"I've got this paper to write, Rob. And I need to practice my flute. We're finally getting to play something in concert band that I need to practice."

"And you want to practice?"

"Sure. I love to learn something new."

"I love you," Rob said. He was afraid she'd pull her fingers away but she didn't.

"You expect too much, Rob," she said. "I used to be that way and I got hurt. I don't want that to happen to either of us."

"But we could be good together, Ellery. Look, I'm here asking you about operas, for God's sake. I'm trying."

She smiled. "I know. But maybe it wasn't meant to be."

"How can you say that?" He reached for her shoulder with his free hand and pulled her down beside him on the bed. "We'll take it slow from now on. I promise. I'll never hurt you, Ellery."

"We've had one argument and you got drunk."

"We won't have any more arguments." He touched her cheek.

"Of course we will." She lay perfectly still.

"Okay, so then we'll get to make up. We're making up now, aren't we?" He kissed her cheek, moved onto his side so he could reach her mouth. She let him kiss her, returned the kiss tentatively, as if she were ready to pull back at any moment. "It'll be all right. You'll see," he said.

The music was like a cushion they could float on. He leaned forward, covering her body with his. He could feel her heartbeat—or was it his own? Their drumming was louder than the music. "I could spend the rest of my life here with you," he whispered.

"We'd starve," Ellery said, but she hugged him to her for a moment. "Nobody can live on love." He nestled against her neck, kissed her ear, the soft flesh under her jaw. "Besides, Mom will be home in a few minutes."

Her breath shuddering up against him made him shiver. "We'll hear her coming," he said.

"If we're on the porch, we'll see her coming," Ellery said. She dropped her arms to her sides and slid from under him. "Come on. Up."

He dragged himself off the bed and watched her running a comb through her hair at the mirror. "You look terrific." He put his arms around her waist, hugging her back against his chest. "Everything's okay now, isn't it?"

"I don't know, Rob. Is it?" It was then they heard the Jeep coming.

39

"I got Coralee out on the front porch!" Ginny said after Rob left.

"I don't believe it. How?" Ellery asked.

"I'm not sure exactly. I went down to try on the skirt and jacket she's making out of that wheat-colored cloth. She's doing a beautiful job with it. I wanted to try it on, so we went up to her room—it's the dreariest little room, Ellery—nothing's been changed in it for fifty years, I'm sure. She has a narrow little white iron bed and a dresser somebody did a poor job of painting so it's terribly chipped. There's probably a beautiful piece of wood under there. Anyway, I tried on the suit and then she wanted Fairlee to see it, so we went down, but he was on the porch. She called him in but I said no, I'd come out. And then I just took her hand. I think she pulled back a little right at the door, but I didn't give in and there she was. She didn't move a step away from the wall, but at least she was outside. Fairlee noticed, of course, but he had the good sense not to say anything. He just admired the suit, and then I took her hand again and we went in. She was out there two minutes, three at the most, but it's a start. I know it seemed like an eternity to her."

"That's great, Mom," Ellery said.

"I think so too," Ginny said and put her arm around her daughter's shoulder. It was the first time they'd touched in a long time, and she was surprised at how solid Ellery felt, how firmly separate and complete. Ellery didn't move away.

"What's for supper?" she asked, slipping her arm around her mother's waist. Ginny felt too thin to her, almost fragile. Maybe somehow they were finally equalizing. Maybe the time was coming when they could fit together again.

"BLT's," Ginny said. "This is the absolute end of the tomatoes, I promise. Do you think you can eat another one?"

"Sure. Anything to keep from cooking."

"Maybe we could go to the movies tonight. See something mindless," Ginny said. "We haven't done anything like that in a long time."

"Rob already asked me," Ellery said, "but I told him no. I've got a paper due tomorrow and I want to practice the new music."

"I guess I'm getting the same answer he got." Ginny squeezed Ellery's shoulder and let her go.

"Another time, Mom."

After supper Ginny went back to her loom. She was weaving a piece of blue wool for Coralee to make into a dress. There was no design to follow, and she fell into the rhythm easily, watching contentedly as the cloth formed in front of her. She heard the practice runs of the flute, the familiar scales and trills Ellery used to warm her fingers and fix her lip. Then the music began. It wasn't the new music she started with but a cantabile of sustained notes as pure and mournful as a keening cry.

Outside in the rapidly falling night, Rob was running across the ridge, down into the swag, up again toward the Collier house. He could see the lights a long way off like moving, flickering beacons through the trees. Then he heard the flute calling to him as a trail of melody wafted into the dusk.

He wanted to run right to the sound, follow it as the children had followed the Pied Piper. But he knew better than to show up under Ellery's window again.

"You expect too much," she had said, warning him that she could not provide all he needed, was no solace for him in the night. The pressure in his chest bore down, squeezing his heart as he ran on. Skirting the flute's tender melody, he willed himself to hear only his own breathing, the hard pounding of his feet. But it was the flute's song that haunted him while he flailed restlessly in his father's bed that night. He had no defense against its loneliness.

40

He hung around the lockers between classes the next morning, hoping for a glimpse of Ellery, and between fourth and fifth periods he finally saw her coming down the hall. She was wearing baggy fatigue pants and a camouflage jacket, no makeup, her hair brushed back from her face. Would he ever be able to define her or was she a chameleon, complete with built-in disguises? Even her looks kept him off balance, made him suspicious of new tactics, subversive strategies.

"Hi," he said, leaning against her locker until he saw

she was passing with no intention of using the locker or stopping for him. He trailed her, his heart pounding.

"I thought about you last night," he said over her shoulder.

"Oh, Rob. Not again." She kept moving.

"Okay, okay, not like that. I thought about our hanging out together. Just having fun. That's what I was getting at yesterday."

"You were talking about love," Ellery said, shifting her books from one arm to the other. She was still walking.

"That's what guys always say. It's just friendly."

She stopped, turning on him so abruptly he had to slam on brakes to keep from running her down.

"Come off it," she sighed. "At least let's tell the truth here."

"I'll buy that. The truth. What is it exactly?"

"I can't handle this. I feel like we're on a roller coaster and I want to get off, Rob. You're here for a few months and you want me to change my life. Well, I can't afford it. It's not that I don't like you. I do. But I just can't handle it. I don't think we should see each other."

"But we can't do that. We have a class together," Rob argued. His legs trembled and a clammy sweat rose out of his chest.

"I don't think we ought to date," Ellery said. "At least not for a while."

"I don't understand these southern expressions. How long's 'a while'?" Rob asked, trying to lighten his voice. "The rest of this week? Okay, we won't see each other the rest of the week. Until Sunday? We'll go on a picnic Sunday. That's plenty of time."

"I don't know," Ellery said wearily. "You wear me out. You make me hurt you and I don't want to."

"Come on, a picnic on Sunday. I'll fix everything. I'll borrow Coralee's quilt."

"I can't, Rob."

"Of course you can. You don't want to. That's it, isn't it? You really just don't want to." He was sweating but she looked cool, untouched. He wanted to hit her, to make sure she was really there, could actually feel something.

"Okay, have it your own way. I don't want to. Satisfied?" She moved away, the buzzer blasting above their heads. Before he turned away, he saw her slumping against the wall, her head bent, arms hugging her books at her chest. He hoped she felt terrible.

41

After lunch he cornered Travis outside the cafeteria. "You got it?" he asked, stepping between Travis and his buddies.

"Not here, man," Travis groaned. "I'll talk to you in the parking lot before practice. You better chill out, Rob. You look like hell walked over."

All through history class he slouched in his desk and stared at his textbook although it was turned to the wrong section. When the buzzer sounded, he was the first to slam his book shut, the first out the door. In the men's room he splashed water on his face, then leaned dripping against the wall, breathing in the hazy residue of smoke left over from the lunch break. The bathroom smelled like hemp.

Art class turned out to be a lab period—no slides he could ignore. Instead the teacher handed out sheets of artist paper and black pencils with instructions to draw a flowing line, to find form in the movement of arm and hand, to become part of the form itself. He didn't know what she was talking about, but he gripped the pencil heavily, bore down on the paper and created madness in one continuous line like the picture a child makes in the midst of a temper tantrum. At the end of the hour, when he passed her desk to turn in the drawing, his hand was trembling as if he'd been handling an axe.

He waited beside Fairlee's truck. The sky had turned cloudy, queued up for a squall. When the rain started to fall in big splashing drops, he got into the cab and leaned his head against the steering wheel. At home he'd be in his car by now. He'd have Marsha with him. They'd be heading for the arcade or to hang out at the record store where her sister worked. She'd put any tape they wanted to hear on the store machine. Sometimes Marsha would put one of the demo tapes into her pocketbook. "It's used anyway," she would say, slapping it into his tape deck so they could ride around listening, their shoulders moving to music, not even caring where they went.

He came to when Travis opened the truck door and got in, then pulled a sandwich bag out of his practice jersey. "Here," he said, dropping the bag on the seat between them. "Enjoy, if that's what you do with it."

He started to get out, then turned back. "If anything happens, I don't know anything, Rob. I hardly know you at all. You're just Leanna's Yankee cousin. Right?"

"You worry too much." Rob grinned. "I owe you one, Travis."

"Just don't ask me again. This is a one-shot deal." He ran for the locker room, his cleats clomping on the wet pavement.

Rob found matches in Fairlee's glove compartment. It was raining steadily now, a rhythmic pounding on the roof. The windows fogged up. He locked the doors and breathed in the first curl of smoke. His body shuddered with it. God, those boys knew what they were doing. This was the best dope he'd ever had. "Better than you, Ellery Collier," he said aloud, and sank into himself, willing the calm to gather in his head, to ooze like thick warm syrup into his fingertips, his toes, his stomach. He was surprised how fast the joint went.

The rain had slackened a little. He rolled down the window enough to dangle his hand out. The rain felt warm even though it had been chilly in the morning. He pressed the roach out in the ashtray and put it back in the bag. His head was swimming and his eyes itched slightly. You're not buzzed, he thought to himself. What you need, boy, is a cloud right in the center of your brain, a soft foamy cloud you can sleep in. He hadn't slept all night. He could still feel his raw nerves, could remember the silent hurtful encounters with Fairlee and Cora, the tomblike house being slowly swallowed by the dark. I can't go back there, he thought.

He remembered the other joint. Travis had promised

two. He would do it now. When would he ever need it more? The match crackled in the thick air. He sucked in, held the smoke, felt it spiraling down, loose in his chest.

Like an angel, he thought, feeling a soft buzz behind his eyes. He pulled again, pressing his lips tight to the warmth. It was like kissing an angel.

42

He spun out on the curve he'd been warned about. "It don't look like much till you get in it," Fairlee had told him on their first trip into town to the doctor, "but it's a mean one. That twenty-mile-an-hour sign ain't there just for show." A long time ago, Fairlee had worked in the sign department, had tested curves himself. "We'd try 'em in a logging truck," he remembered. "Whatever speed was just below a jackknife, that's what we marked 'em. Now it's more scientific like. They do studies and all, but there ain't no better test I know of than a loaded logger."

Now Rob tested his face for blood. His lip was bleeding where his mouth had hit the wheel. He crammed part of a napkin between his lip and gum. He could feel the swelling, his mouth turning inside out so he couldn't control his spit. His nose burned, ears seemed full of liquid. He shook his head like a wet dog, but the fog centered in his brain didn't clear.

"I am stoned," he said aloud. "Sh-h-h, we can't tell that." The air blowing up his throat stung. He could smell gasoline although the truck was dead, stalled where the front tire had dug into the ditch. He turned off the switch and leaned back against the seat. He had to think. The rain was slow and steady, a deep mist on the windshield.

He'd walk to town, he decided after a few minutes. He'd get a wrecker to pull the truck out, go on home like nothing had happened. He slid out of the truck, catching himself on the muddy bank. The truck was tilted into the ditch, one front wheel sunk in the mud, the other hanging in the air, inches above the bank. He slammed the door shut, remembered he'd left the keys in the ignition, tried to reach the door handle, couldn't, considered how nobody could go anywhere in the truck anyway, began walking.

Within minutes he was soaked through with the cold drizzly rain. He felt it seeping beneath his skin, enervating him with soggy weariness. Maybe he shouldn't be doing this. Maybe he should wait at the truck. Eventually Travis had to come by on his way home from football practice. Or maybe he should be going in the other direction, toward the house. Go tell Fairlee the truth, use the phone to call a wrecker. He couldn't remember any houses between here and Fairlee's except Ellery's, and he wasn't about to climb that mountain. Didn't want to see her anyway. He'd go back to the truck. Travis would take care of everything. Maybe even get one of his brother's trucks to pull him out. Who said he couldn't think stoned?

He had to remember which way the truck was. He leaned against the speed-limit sign to figure it out. Walking, he had seen the back of the sign. So now he should see the front of it. No, that wasn't right. He had seen the yellow diamond from the truck, had read it while his foot pressed down on the accelerator. The truck had to be past the sign. That was it. He would walk away from the back of the sign.

He had rounded the curve, could see the abandoned truck through the rain and was thinking how clever he was to find it when he noticed the blue circling light of a patrol car stopped beyond the truck.

The patrolman shot a beam of light into his face, then leaned back into the cab, flashing the light over the seat and floorboard.

"This your truck, son?" the policeman asked. He was wearing gray raingear, was tight and dry.

"No sir," Rob said, standing away from the truck. He thought he might fall under the weight of the rain.

"Fairlee Dickson," the patrolman read, shining his light on the registration card Fairlee kept above the sun visor. "You know him?"

"Yes sir." There was a dry white buzz in Rob's head like a warning signal. Don't say anything, he heard in the buzz.

"You all right, boy?"

"Yes sir."

"No injuries?"

"No sir."

"Well, you're drenched, aren't you?"

"Yes sir."

"I think you better get in the car," the patrolman said from behind the beam of light. "This truck's not going anywhere, but I think we better ride on back to town."

43

He called Ginny from the sheriff's office. He'd have to be half dead, and crazy too, before he called Rosalie, and who else was there? Well, crazy he wasn't. Stoned maybe, but not crazy. He didn't think he'd said anything wrong, hadn't confessed to anything. Even in the patrol car he'd been lucid enough to know he was wrestling with the enemy. The patrolman had found the roach bag on the floorboard. He knew who the truck belonged to, knew who Rob was from his driver's license. He probably knew Rob had been driving the truck and suspected he was high, but Rob hadn't admitted anything, hadn't signed his name anywhere. Now he thought of Ginny Collier. He hoped he could depend on her not to lecture him.

He waited in the brightly lit station holding the towel someone had given him tight around his shoulders. He was cold down to his bones and his face throbbed. He knew his puffy lip and muddy clothes made him look comical, like a derelict.

One of the deputies, a young man with a thick mustache and a stocky muscular build, brought him a cup of coffee along with the summons. "You hold on to these papers," he said. "Your court date is on there. I know you're high," he said congenially as he settled in the chair beside Rob. "Hell, I used to do some grass myself before I got into law en-force-ment." He gave Rob a cagey smile that stayed half hidden in his mustache.

"I bet you can get some good stuff up there in New Jersey. Get it shipped in from South America. I reckon you brought some down with you," he went on. "Course, we got the best you can grow right here. Sinsemilla can get fourteen feet high right in this county. I've seen it."

Rob sipped his coffee. The heat stung his raw lip.

"Yes sirree. You're in the cultivation center of the United States right here in these mountains," the deputy said, rubbing his broad hand against his thigh. He was almost touching Rob. "But I reckon you know that. A smart boy like you don't need me telling him nothing."

Rob didn't answer. It seemed like hours since he'd called Ginny. He wrapped both hands around the Styrofoam cup but it didn't warm him any.

"Folks is harvesting right now. Bringing in the crop, you see, just like it was regular tobacco. Drying it out and everything."

"I don't know anything about it," Rob said.

"I believe you, boy," the man said. He stood up and shook his pant legs down over his thick calves. "I'll be seeing you around. Now that's something you can believe yourself."

Ginny finally arrived, puddling water off her raincoat, her damp hair curling around her flushed face. "Are you all right?" she asked, bending over him. She touched his hair, lifted his chin gently to examine his lip.

He nodded, willing himself not to cry. He was glad it wasn't his own mother who had come to bail him out. Ginny let her hand linger on his cheek. "You wait here. I'll have you out in a minute."

He watched her signing his bond at the desk, guaranteeing he wouldn't go anywhere, promising five hundred dollars if he did. She trusted him more than he trusted himself. He got up, feeling heavy headed and dopey. He hoped he wouldn't fall down on the way to the Jeep, could get home without throwing up. The coffee was bitter in his mouth and stank on his breath.

"Let's go," Ginny said, taking his arm. She felt warm and strong against him.

"Thanks, Mrs. Collier. I don't know what I would have done—" he started.

"Right now let's just get out of here before anybody figures out I'm not related to you," she whispered. "You can thank me later."

Neither one of them said a word during the ride home.

"I'll do the talking," Ginny said when she stopped the Jeep beside the Dicksons' back porch. "You're in no shape. Anyway, I don't think you know what kind of trouble you're in."

She pushed him up the steps and through the kitchen door. Fairlee and Coralee were there waiting as if an alarm signal had gone off in their heads when they heard the Jeep coming.

"Oh, my Lord, what happened?" Coralee cried, seeing Rob damp and bedraggled in front of Ginny.

"There was a little accident," Ginny said. "Rob skidded on that bad curve and the truck's in the ditch. A patrolman came by and took him down to the sheriff's department. He called me because he knew you didn't have any way to go get him."

"You all right, son?" Fairlee asked. His voice seemed choked.

"Just a busted lip," Rob said, trying to smile. "About the same condition as the truck, Fairlee." He was afraid to keep standing, but he couldn't seem to move.

"Come sit down, honey," Coralee said, pulling out a kitchen chair. "You look all shook up."

"He is," Ginny said. "Look, Fairlee, I think I better tell you what I know, because Rob needs some food and a good night's sleep before he can do much explaining." She sighed and put her hand on Rob's shoulder. "He's been charged with possession of marijuana and driving under the influence of narcotics. I signed his bond."

Coralee was shaking and Ginny moved to her. "It's going to be all right, Cora. He's safe. That's the important thing." She was talking to Fairlee now. "He's going to need a lawyer. Maybe you should call Jason Burnette. He handled my closing and my divorce. I think he'd be helpful." She sighed. "The truck has to be pulled out of the ditch, but that can wait till tomorrow. Maybe you should get it checked out before Rob drives it again. I'll give him a ride to school tomorrow."

"I can get a ride with Travis," Rob said. He didn't want to see Ellery.

"I'll do just like you say, Ginny," Fairlee said. "Jason Burnette. I'll call him tomorrow."

"Good. I'd better go, then," Ginny said. "It's already suppertime. Rob, walk out on the porch with me."

He got up stiffly and followed her outside. The rain had stopped but the air was cold. He couldn't draw a deep breath.

"It's about Ellery, isn't it?" he asked quickly. "I've never smoked around her, Mrs. Collier. I swear. This is the first time since I've been here."

"I believe you, Rob," Ginny said. "But she's vulnerable. You have to know that. She's had a hard time adjusting to a lot of things, and I don't think she's the right person to help you with this."

"We've already decided not to see each other," Rob said.

"Oh, Rob, I'm sorry. I didn't know that. Well, now I feel like an idiot bringing it up at all." She smiled and squeezed his hand. "I know you mean a lot to her, Rob, no matter what's happened between you. I just want you to handle this trouble on your own. I think you need to do that."

"I understand. Thanks for everything, Mrs. Collier." His bones ached with cold.

"Now, go get a hot shower and have some supper." She left him on the porch, and he watched the lights disappear up the lane before he turned back to the kitchen. The supper was laid out, the family waiting.

He wanted to take a shower, but instead he sat down at his place and piled his plate with Coralee's cooking. The emptiness in his stomach was the only kind he was sure he could conquer.

44

He awoke before dawn, watched the day slowly float through his room, coming in shallow and cool like light on water. He got up before he needed to, took a shower, ate breakfast out of a cereal box. He didn't want to call Travis for a ride, didn't want his trouble exposed. What could Travis say except "I told you so"?

After helping Fairlee clean up, he started out walking. He was sure he could hitch a ride once he was on the highway. The road was soggy, the sky clear. A wind swept down the valley, cool and crisp, bringing autumn with it. When he reached the curve, the truck was still there, looking ready for the junkyard. He stopped to pick up his books. They were strewn on the floor, felt damp when he clutched them under his arm. After he rounded the curve, he heard a car coming and Travis pulled over in front of him.

"What happened?" he called. "I saw the truck last night, and I didn't know whether to phone the house or the hospital. Finally I called Ellery and her mom said you were all right. Why didn't you call me, man?"

"Nothing to tell," Rob said. "You're sure you want to show up at school with me? I got charged with possession. Cop found two roaches in the bag."

"Aw, man—" Travis stopped. "What'd you tell them?"

"Nothing. This deputy kept after me about where I got it. He thinks I brought it from home."

"Don't bank on it." Travis squealed back onto the road. "You got a lawyer?"

"Fairlee's talking to somebody Ellery's mom knows. Burnette, I think his name is."

"Good," Travis said. "He's young and I hear he's smart. If you're lucky he won't be prejudiced against grass."

"You can put me out before we get there," Rob said.

"Will you stop with that? Nobody's going to think anything about my giving you a ride to school. What does Ellery say about all this?"

"I don't know. We're not seeing each other anymore," Rob said.

"Cheer up, boy! Could be worse," Travis said, slapping Rob's knee soundly. "Listen, Rob, don't say anything to the lawyer or to anybody that you don't have to. I know guys who thought they could talk their way out of something like this, and it didn't work out that way."

"Quit worrying, Travis. It was definitely out-of-town pot."

They pulled into a parking space. "Let me know if you need a ride home," Travis said. "And Rob, don't let the situation with Ellery get you down. When this other mess is over, you can work it out. Look at Leanna and me, all these years together. You better believe we've had our ups and downs."

"Ellery's not Leanna," Rob said.

"Now that's the truth." Travis laughed. "And you, old buddy, just ain't got my style."

Fairlee called Rob at school to tell him the truck could be picked up at a body shop on the edge of town. "And you've got an appointment with this Burnette fellow at four o'clock," he said. "His office is right there on Main Street. You can't miss it." He paused and Rob thought for a moment the line had gone dead. "Rob, we're going to work this out," he said finally. "You just do what the lawyer tells you and I'll take care of the rest."

"Have you called Dad?" Rob asked.

"No sir, I haven't and I don't intend to do that unless we have to. I think we can handle this, son, just between ourselves. What do you say?"

"Thanks, Fairlee," Rob said.

"Well, don't thank me yet. You go show Mr. Burnette them papers and find out if he can keep you outa jail."

Rob heard a click on the line, then dropped the receiver on the hook in the secretary's office and stood there waiting as if he needed someone to tell him what to do next.

"Do you need a hall pass?" the secretary asked him. "What class are you supposed to be in now?"

"History," he mumbled, hoping that was true. The fact was he didn't know where he should be.

45

Jason Burnette's office was empty—no one waiting in the small cluttered waiting room full of plants and a collection of Goodwill chairs that ran from modern metal to ornate antique. The secretary's desk was neat, the phone silent, but there was a light on in the corridor.

"Hello!" Rob called. "Mr. Burnette!"

He could hear a chair squeaking, the dry slap of a book closing, and then Jason Burnette appeared around the corner. "Sorry, Rob—you are Rob, right? Fran had to leave early today and I promised her I'd be on the lookout for you." He offered his hand. He was wearing jeans and hiking boots, a green chamois shirt and gold-rimmed glasses. His handshake was firm and he pulled Rob slightly forward, leading him into the office.

"Sit," he said, going behind his desk and plopping into the squeaky chair, "and show me what you've got there."

Rob laid the folded papers on the desk and sat down in a narrow straightback chair.

"Not there," Burnette said, using the papers to wave him out of the chair. "That's where the guilty sit. They seem to think they have a straight chair coming. Sit here." The other chair was upholstered on seat and back and had smooth oak arms.

"Now," the lawyer said, satisfied with their arrangement, "give me a minute to read this." He read quickly, humming, groaning, agreeing as his eyes moved down the page.

How can he function in court without a poker face, Rob wondered, because Jason Burnette was grimacing over the page, writing a quick note on his yellow pad, his pencil stabbing as he punctuated.

"Now, Rob," he said, his pencil making a border of fierce black dots on the paper, "I'm going to ask you a few questions about yesterday."

Rob nodded, waiting.

"Did anybody see the accident?"

"Not that I know of," Rob said.

"Nobody arrived on the scene immediately?"

"No sir."

"Did anybody see you in the truck?"

"No sir."

"You weren't in the truck when Mr. Carlson arrived? I see here he's the patrolman who made the arrest."

"No sir."

"Where were you then? How'd he find you?"

"I started walking back to town to get a wrecker to pull the truck out. Then I decided just to wait in the cab. It was raining. When I got back to the truck, the patrolman was there."

"Did he search you?"

"At the station. I was wet."

"Find anything?"

"No sir."

"You're charged with possession."

"Yes sir. He found two roaches maybe a half an inch long in a plastic bag. It was in the truck."

Jason Burnette smiled at his paper. "Anybody see you smoking?"

"No sir."

"Has anybody seen you smoking in this county?"

"No sir."

"Do you have a record anywhere?"

"I got a speeding ticket in New Jersey last year. And a ticket for running a stop sign. A bunch of us were taken in for causing a disturbance in the park last spring, but they let us go after an hour. I think that's it." Rob paused. "Once I got picked up for shoplifting, but there was nothing on me. Nobody knows about that."

"I take it you like to walk right on the edge."

"I guess so," Rob said.

"A lot of people do." Jason Burnette frowned. "I'm supposed to catch them when they fall off. Sometimes I can. Sometimes I can't." He stared straight at Rob, the rims of his glasses flickering in the lamplight. "I'll see what I can do. You understand we have to go to court on this in three weeks. That's September thirtieth, at nine o'clock. A lot depends on who the judge is—we've got one who throws the book at drug cases. The other two are more lenient."

"What does that mean?" Rob asked. A weird dry sensation was climbing his throat, like he'd breathed in a nasty chemical.

"You could get up to six months for driving under the influence," Burnette said. "That's what generally happens when there's a serious injury or another vehicle involved. Ninety days for simple possession. A fine. Probation. Right on down to a dismissal. I guess you're interested in staying out of jail?"

"Yes sir."

"Well, give me a few days to check out the evidence. I'm not promising anything, but I'll have to say that after you got yourself into this mess, you did some things right, or maybe it was just plain dumb luck." He stood up. "I've got to walk over some property before it gets dark. Have a boundary dispute on my hands. That's why I'm dressed like this—I don't want you to think I'll come to court in Levi's. You've got enough to worry about. You need a lift somewhere?"

"I have to pick up the truck at Parker's Body Shop," Rob said.

"I'm going that way. Come on."

Burnette snapped off the light, and they went down the hall and out the front door to an old Mercedes. "I bought it in Germany while I was stationed there in the Air Force. That was between college and law school."

"It's a fantastic car," Rob said, rubbing his hand over the leather dashboard.

"It is," Burnette agreed, listening to the engine purr. "And I'm glad I've got it. I'd sure never get one on what I'm making here."

"Maybe you should go up north. Lawyers in Montclair drive new Mercedes," Rob said.

"No thanks," Burnette laughed. "I wouldn't trade peace of mind for a Rolls Royce. I like being my own boss. I like living around people who have all their immediate family within hollering distance. I've learned a lot in the three years I've lived here. I don't worry as much, don't work fourteen hours a day. I laugh a lot more. Well, here it is."

The body shop was a big concrete block building with a sign above the triple doors that read PARKER TIRE AND BODY SHOP—WE FIX ANYTHING BUT A BROKEN HEART. The truck was parked in front of one of the openings.

"That's it," Rob said. "Thanks for the lift—and for everything."

"I'll call you if we need to talk again. Otherwise, you

show up at the courthouse about eight thirty on the thirtieth."

"About the fees," Rob said as he pushed the door open.

"Your uncle's taking care of that," Burnette said. "You mean a lot to him, Rob. He's concerned about you, and not just because of this."

"See you the thirtieth," Rob said, and shut the door.

The Mercedes pulled away, leaving him standing there in the open lot. The truck looked just the same to him, like yesterday had never happened. Flat tires and dented fenders can be repaired, Rob thought. He wished everything was so easy.

46

Rob drove cautiously through town, mindful of the speed limit and the cars backing out along Main Street. He idled the engine patiently at two stoplights and gave a timely signal when he turned left to go past the high-school football field. He stopped the truck beside the fence for a few minutes to watch the bodies rolling and tumbling in their spaceman garb. The white helmets glinted in the late afternoon light. Padded shoulders banged fiercely into each other.

He found Travis, recognized the stance, the shifting movement backward as he twisted his body upward, his arm controlled, centered as if it shot straight out of his chest. He released the ball in a powerful arch and it sailed into the dusk, a spinning bullet over the enemy's heads. Rob leaned against the truck to watch a couple of plays, postponing the journey home. He dreaded seeing Fairlee and Coralee, although he knew they must be waiting for him, anxious to hear what the lawyer had said. They wanted to see him safe.

The coach blew his whistle, a shrill piercing blast that drifted skyward. Rob could almost see the blaze of sound it made in the purple haze. Travis bounded toward the fence, struggling out of his helmet as he came.

"I see you got the truck," he said, panting against the fence. "What did Burnette say?"

"No promises but he thinks he can help me. I'm not supposed to worry for the next three weeks," Rob said sarcastically.

"That's when you go to court?" Travis rattled the fence and let it go. "I sure as the devil hope you can stay outa trouble that long."

"I'm planning on it," Rob said.

"That's good." Travis sighed and rubbed his hand in his sweaty hair. "But sometimes trouble has a way of following a person, just like a dog goes sniffing around. You watch out, you hear, so you don't step back in something that stinks. I'll see you tomorrow," he called, heading for the locker room.

Rob got back into the truck, made a complete stop at the intersection back onto the highway and headed slowly home.

At first he thought he was dreaming the blue light that flashed into his vision about a mile outside the town limits. He pulled over and waited in the cab. It was the deputy from yesterday, his thick hand gripping the window rim.

"I thought I recognized this vehicle," he said, unlatching the door so he could see inside.

"What did I do?" Rob asked, looking straight ahead, away from the sharp beam of the deputy's flashlight as it searched the cab.

"You come on out here and we'll talk about it," the deputy said. He stepped back a pace, his other hand firmly on the black holster at his waist.

Rob jumped out of the truck but didn't move away from it.

"This thing run all right?" the deputy asked, slapping the fender. "Seems to me it might be a road hazard, you were going so slow."

"You stopped me for driving five miles below the speed limit?" Rob asked. The skin down his back sizzled like heat and cold had suddenly met on his spine, but he struggled to control his voice, to keep his tone flat and noncommittal. Trouble's a dog sniffing, Travis had said. Maybe Deputy Gatewood was what he'd meant.

"Driving too slow is just as bad as driving too fast," the deputy said, smiling through his bushy mustache. "You ought to know that, boy. I betcha in New Jersey you boys just knock somebody that ain't moving along right off the road. Let me see here a minute." He sprang into the cab, ran his hand around the steering column, under the dashboard, across the seat, flashed the light onto the floorboard. "Don't see no reason this vehicle goes so slow," he said, and climbed down, still grinning.

"You get on home now," he ordered, and waited while Rob got back into the cab. He slammed the door shut. "You know, that marijuana that came in with you, it was mighty pure. Now I think on it, I wouldn't be surprised to find out it was some of North Carolina's finest. No sirree, I wouldn't be surprised one little bit."

Rob cranked the truck, put on his blinker, moved carefully back onto the road. The blue light faded behind him while he watched where he was going, concentrating on the double yellow line. He wanted it to mesmerize him so he didn't have to think beyond calming the churning panic in his chest. How could he endure three weeks of this?

At the Dicksons' Coralee had the steaming bowls of supper on the table and was washing up the cooking pots when he came in the back door.

"He's here!" she cried, wiping her red hands on her apron. "Law, we've been so worried, Rob. Fairlee's just beside himself, and Papa, well, he knows about it. We thought to keep it from him but Ginny was here today and we were talking about it on the porch, not knowing he was standing right in here. He heard every word about your having an appointment with a lawyer and all, so we had to tell him. He's rankled, that's for sure. One thing this family's always steered clear of is trouble with the law."

Fairlee pushed into the kitchen, his walker banging on the door. He looked old, like he'd aged years during this long day. "You saw Burnette?" he asked.

Rob nodded. "He thinks he can help. He said not to worry." Rob wanted to smile but he couldn't. His face felt frozen. "I'd better wash up." He went past Fairlee into the dark hall, felt for the switch in the bathroom and looked at himself in the stark white cast of the light. His lip was trembling. His eyelids twitched, swelling around tears. But he couldn't cry. He was too empty, too used up. He ran water in the sink, sloshed it onto his face, let it drip off his chin and hands. He didn't feel anything.

47

"Did you see Rob today?" Ginny asked Ellery while they were doing the supper dishes. The meal had been one of uneasy silence, steeped in the tensions of a troubled day.

"Yes." Ellery lifted a cup out of the drain and shook the water off before wrapping it in a dish towel to dry it.

"How is he?"

"I saw him. I didn't say I talked to him." Ellery's fist was in the bowl of the cup.

"His lip was swollen last night," Ginny went on. "I probably should suggest he see a dentist. You can loosen a tooth and not know it until it starts to discolor."

"I think he can take care of himself," Ellery said stiffly. She looked down at the edges of the plates in the drain. They glinted like blades.

"I've never seen a seventeen-year-old yet who could,"

Ginny said. Her hands, laced with soap, moved up out of the water. "He told me you aren't dating anymore, Ellery."

Ellery didn't answer. The plate was slick in her hand.

"I know you like him," Ginny said.

"I like a lot of people."

"Name five." Ginny ran water over a saucer and stuck it in a slot in the drain.

"All right, Mother." Ellery made deliberate drying circles on the plate. "I like him. But it didn't work out."

"Oh, Ellery." Ginny paused while Ellery turned away from her and leaned her forehead against the side of the refrigerator. "Do you want to talk about it?"

"I wish—"

"You wish what, honey?"

"I wish I were home. Everything would be different there," she said painfully.

"I'm sure there are lots of kids here you'd like, Ellery, if you just tried to get to know them. Rob Dickson's not the only person in the world, you know."

Ellery swung back to her mother, flinging the dish towel over the remaining dishes. "I never said he was! Oh, what's the point? I can't talk to you, Mother. Can't you see that? Everything I say gets translated into what you want it to mean! You want me to tell you how I feel about Rob, but if I said I love him, you would think: 'Oh no, she doesn't. She thinks it's love, but of course seventeen-year-olds don't feel things like that.' "

"I would not!"

"It's just how you think about my being miserable

here. I say it's the pits, and in the next breath you say I'm adjusting.''

"But you *are* adjusting!'' Ginny dropped the sponge into the soapy water. "I'm just trying to understand you, Ellery, and to help you clarify your own thinking.''

"Maybe that's what you intend, Mother, but you end up manipulating. You take my words and make them yours. I want my words back. I want my feelings back. They belong to me!''

Ginny let out a heavy sigh. "I don't know how to talk to you. That's obvious. You're so volatile. Everything becomes a challenge. I'm not trying to challenge you, sweetheart.''

"But you are, Mother. Don't you understand? You've got the power.''

"Then why do I feel so helpless?'' Ginny asked.

"I guess it's because you can't get into my head anymore,'' Ellery said calmly. "I can't let you. I thought we were beginning to get along. I want us to, but now I think I need to love you a little less than you want me to.''

"And I should love you less, too? How could I do that?''

"Well, care a little less then. Just let me fall back a little. Think things out for myself. We're not an even match right now.''

"I didn't know this was a battle,'' Ginny said sadly.

"Well, it is.''

"Where are you going?'' Ginny asked, because Ellery had taken the keys from the hook next to the back door.

"Down to the Dicksons'."

"I don't think you should, Ellery. Let Rob take care of this himself."

"I'm not going to rescue him, Mother. I'm not into saving people like you are."

"I told him I didn't want him seeing you, not until after this mess he's in is cleared up."

"You told him that? How could you, Mother? You had no right!"

"He needs his family now, Ellery. He needs to find his own resources."

"It's because he does drugs now and then, right? You think little Ellery can't handle it!"

"I think he's in serious trouble, and I don't want you in it with him."

"I'm just going to talk to him. I was really hateful to him yesterday."

"Go then," Ginny said, turning back to the sink. The water was flat and milky. She turned on the faucet so she couldn't hear the rumbling Jeep and her daughter disappearing into the night.

48

He knew she'd been standing there a long time by the way she leaned on her elbow against the doorframe, her other hand deep in the pocket of her jeans jacket.

She'd been watching him flip through a magazine, his head and arms hanging over the edge of the bed, his bare feet crossed in the air. He rolled onto his side, drawing up.

"You've got it loud enough," Ellery said, coming in to adjust the volume on the stereo. The Grateful Dead's guitars whined to a whisper.

"What are you doing here?" Rob asked. He sat up and pushed the sports magazine under the bed with his foot.

"I came to see you," Ellery said. She was leaning against the dresser now. He could see her back in the mirror. In its wavy reflection, her strong shoulders rippled with an illusion of softness.

"Well, now you've seen me. I'm not damaged—no broken bones, no lacerations."

"Mom said you cut your lip."

"It's healing already. Everything's fine."

"I'm sorry about yesterday," Ellery said.

"Everything's cool. You needn't worry."

"You have to go to court," Ellery said. "Oh, Rob. I wish none of this had happened."

"It's not your problem."

"I care what happens to you," Ellery said. "You know I do."

"What I know is that by Thanksgiving—if I'm not in jail—I'll be in New Jersey. I'll be back with Marsha where I belong. Did I ever tell you about Marsha? She keeps a buzz. Once she drove ninety-five miles an hour on the highway and she couldn't even see."

"I know you want to hurt me," Ellery said.

"Why should I want to do that? I don't care about you one way or the other. You were a diversion, sweetheart, just like you said."

"Oh, Rob," she said softly, and something turned in him.

"Crank up the Dead before you go," he said, flopping back on his stomach. The bed moaned under him. He felt her movement, felt the untraversable distance between them, knew on his skin when she was gone. He closed his eyes. How could he look at his dreary life without her in it?

49

"What do you think will happen to Rob?" Coralee was on the back porch just inches away from Ginny, who stood on the top step. They could hear the truck coming up the lane. He was in second gear now, holding back. The engine shuddered.

"Jason Burnette will do everything he can," Ginny said. "I had a long talk with him early in the summer when he came up to see the house. He's very bright and personable, and he seems to have a way with young people."

"I think you like him!" Coralee giggled. "Does he have a wife?"

"Not that I know of. But you know I don't want to

get married, Coralee. I think you do, though, the way you keep bringing it up. The fact is, he's too young for either of us." Ginny laughed at Coralee's embarrassed grin and took her hand. "Let's walk out and meet Rob," she suggested.

"I can't do that!" Coralee cried, but she didn't pull away. "I used to have asters and mums along there." She was pointing toward the fence on the other side of the lane. "Purple and gold and bronze ones that bloomed in the fall. They were the prettiest things."

"I suppose it's too late to plant them now," Ginny said.

"Law, yes. I used to set them out in August. I planted everything by the signs, you know. Mama and Papa believed in it—well, I do, too. I've seen the truth of it. We mostly planted on Fridays. One time Papa planted potatoes in the light of the moon—he'd get all full of hisself sometimes and just go ahead on a tangent—I bet there weren't fifty potatoes what made. We had to buy them down the road, but Pa never did tell. Everybody knows you plant potatoes in the dark of the moon. Well, here he is."

Rob was getting out of the truck.

"Look who's here to see us," Coralee called, patting Ginny's shoulder.

Rob nodded to Ginny, then stopped in his tracks when he realized Coralee was outside. "What's happening?" he asked.

"Ginny's been helping me," Coralee said shyly.

"She comes out on the porch every day now," Ginny said. "It's you doing it yourself, Coralee."

"This is just how far I can go," Coralee said, holding steady as Rob approached.

"That's geat, Coralee. It really is," Rob said, not stopping on the porch. "See you, Mrs. Collier." He went through the kitchen, and they heard him bounding up the stairs to his room.

"The doctor says next week maybe Fairlee can start using a special cane, one of those with three feet on it. This morning he got hisself in and out of the bathtub. Another few weeks and he'll be driving again," Coralee said.

"And Rob can take off," Ginny added.

"I reckon he will." Coralee sighed. "The truth is that boy's been the cause of considerable upset around here."

"I don't doubt that," Ginny said. "I've got a teenager at home I can't get along with either. Ellery thinks so much. She takes everything so seriously. I want her to learn to make decisions on her own and to take care of herself, but I wish she could relax and enjoy herself more." Ginny gave Coralee a sad smile. "I didn't make a decision all my own until I was almost forty. I went from cleaning my room at home to cleaning a dormitory room to keeping house. You don't grow up that way— you just get better at cleaning. Now I'm trying to do what I need to do for myself, but it's hard. I don't have much experience in it."

"That's like me," Coralee said.

"Exactly," Ginny answered. "We're both learning."

50

Rob moved in a dream world where nothing was quite real. There was nothing he could touch. It amazed him that he lived through days of not touching anyone, not speaking to anyone. He was deaf at school, mute. Several times Leanna called after him in the corridor but he pretended not to hear. Sometimes he had no choice but to sit in the vicinity of Travis and his friends in the cafeteria, and once Travis motioned to him to join them but he didn't. He carried a paperback copy of Emily Dickinson's poems among his books and pulled it out constantly, as if it were a weapon against intrusion. Mostly he looked at the pages—the exclamation marks, the dashes that held the words apart like knife cuts.

Over and over again he saw individual words—death, soul, heaven—but he rarely read anything until one day when his eyes focused on the word Madness. He knew about madness, and he forced his mind to concentrate on the words surrounding it.

Much Madness is divinest Sense—
To a discerning Eye—
Much Sense—the starkest Madness—
'Tis the Majority
In this, as All, prevail—
Assent—and you are sane—
Demur—you're straightway dangerous—
And handled with a Chain—

The truth of it frightened him and he shut the book, but the words were in his head now, had bored in like a drilling insect. He was dangerous. The chain was real.

A beige sheriff's-department car was waiting for him at the top of the lane to the Dicksons'. He saw it before he turned in and thought briefly of driving past, but what good would it do? He pulled over and waited. It was Gatewood.

"Well now, we got SBI crawling all over us, boy," Gatewood said, ducking his head through the open window. "We got Drug Enforcement Administration people down here say they ain't leaving till they find something. I keep telling them the marijuana crop's done been harvested, but they want to see some action."

Rob didn't say anything.

"Just two weeks and you're in court, Dickson," Gatewood continued, turning his head to spit a trail of tobacco juice on the ground. "Got yourself a lawyer?" There was a brown rim on his lip. He brushed down on his mustache and got it.

"Yes sir. Jason Burnette."

"Well, that's mighty fine. Burnette's good, he's real good. But he'd have to be God Almighty to get you outa this one, boy. Yes sirree, ain't nobody around here that good. Only one thing I can think of what'll do you right. You could help us out a little. Give us a location or something like that."

"I don't know what you're talking about," Rob said.

"That Williams boy? You know him, don't you?"

"Travis dates my cousin," Rob said. "That's all I know about him."

200

"They got a lot of land up there. Places a man can't hardly get to. Used to be stills up there—probably some working right now—but we got something else bothering us besides rotgut. Got this other itch needs scratching."

Rob could hear a car coming, and he turned his head away while Travis passed.

"I need to get home," Rob said.

Gatewood spit again, then thumped the side of the truck with his knuckles. "You think on it, boy, and you do it right quick like. Else you might find yourself with plenty of thinking time."

That night he dreamed he was in solitary confinement, a dank cell of shadowy light, a barred door. He pushed his arms between the bars, but no matter how far he reached, he couldn't touch anything.

51

Every day Rob felt more and more incarcerated, as if a key inside himself had carefully turned to lock in his panic and keep other feelings out. At school he managed to slip unnoticed into his classes and to get through each hour without calling attention to himself. Once he knew his way around the building, it was easy enough to duck into the library or the deserted auditorium during lunch. He wasn't hungry, anyway.

After days of turning his back on Leanna and Travis,

they had given up on him. No one else seemed to notice him at all. Ellery ignored him, too, although no matter how he tried to ignore her, he would find himself watching for her in the corridor or parking lot. In his head, there was this sensory beam he couldn't control. In history class, she was a gray fuzzy blur on the edge of his vision. He spent part of every hour convincing himself she looked moody and hostile, even absurd in her punk clothes; he couldn't imagine why he'd ever liked the way she looked. There was something cold and hard about her. He could see that now. No wonder her dad had given her up. She was impossible. Anybody could see that.

Wandering around in the library during a lunch break, he discovered a record collection. They were mostly old classical recordings, probably the neglected remains of a music teacher's enthusiastic spending spree. He checked out *Tosca*.

At home he put Act I on the turntable and looked for a libretto Ellery had told him always accompanied opera recordings. There wasn't one, just a story sheet which he read while the music played. The plot turned out to be an awkwardly developed political tale about a painter trying to protect his friend who had escaped from prison. Maybe he'd have had better luck, Rob thought, if he hadn't had a temperamental girlfriend, Tosca, to mess everything up.

Rob changed the record eagerly, wanting to hear the voice of the villainous chief of police, Scarpia, who intended to capture the escapee, eliminate the artist, and have his way with Tosca in the bargain.

At first he thought the banging came from the music, then he knew it was at his door. "What's that cater-wauling?" Grandpa roared from the hall. "All the time a racket! He's shut hisself up in there, listening to that mess!"

"Leave him be, Pa," Cora was saying. "He can listen to what he wants to."

"You mind your own self, sister!" Grandpa pounded on the door again, making the old lock rattle. "You come on outa there, boy, and eat your supper 'fore it's ruint."

"I'm coming!" Rob yelled back, but then turned up the volume full blast until he was sure the old man and Coralee had gone away.

He made certain he was late for supper and then picked at his food. Every afternoon now he was stopping by Ennis' for a burger and fries to compensate for missing lunch, and his stomach felt heavy with indigestible grease and old chili.

"How about a beer?" Fairlee asked him one evening in the hall as Rob was about to disappear up the stairs.

"Okay," Rob agreed, and he brought two cans from the kitchen out to the front porch.

"You could go to the game this Friday night," Fairlee said when he'd settled in a porch rocker and snapped open his beer. "You can take the truck anytime."

"Thanks," Rob said, swilling the beer, "but I think I'll pass."

"I hate to see you holed up in that room, son." Fairlee's rocker creaked loudly and then settled into a soft clacking rhythm. "I told Davis this was going to be harder on you than anybody, but he wasn't of a mind to listen.

Course, about then I was thinking you and Ellery might just get to enjoying yourselves. She's like most women I know of, part angel and part—well, I reckon you know what I'm on about. Don't think I didn't see how you two started out tussling. That's a battle of wills, boy, and if I recollect, it's right much fun."

"The fun's over, Fairlee," Rob said, getting up from the swing. "And so's the beer. Thanks." The aluminum popped as he bent the can between his hands. "I'm going in now. I've got a history quiz tomorrow."

Upstairs in his father's room, he turned on the third act of *Tosca* to listen, as he had every night that week, to Cavaradossi sing his song of farewell. The melody was now as familiar as the empty space in his chest, and he lay immobile on the bed waiting for the shots from the firing squad to blast the gloomy light slowly closing in around him. Only then did he turn his face into his pillow and sink into dopey sleep. When he awoke later in the darkened room, it was the red lights from his stereo that reminded him of where he was. They glowed in the night like a banshee's eyes.

52

Leanna called him about the raid. She cried on the phone, telling him how the sheriff's car and two trucks had pulled up in Travis' yard and men got out, some in uniforms with guns, some carrying machetes and dressed for hiking.

"They just about scared his mama to death," Leanna said. "Thank the good Lord Travis wasn't there. He was at school. Wasn't a soul at home but poor Mrs. Williams, and there they were showing her a search warrant, just about accusing her of being in the marijuana business. I can't believe it! Travis wouldn't be involved in anything illegal. I know him, Rob! Don't you think I'd know about something like that?"

"Did they find anything?" Rob asked. He felt his breathing stop, was standing there in the hall without one sensation of life. The receiver banged against his face. It was trembling in his hand.

"Well, of course not!" Leanna huffed. "What do you mean asking that? You might know all about marijuana, Rob, but Travis doesn't. He's an athlete. He takes care of himself. He doesn't need anything like that."

"How'd you hear about it?" Rob asked, to stop her ranting.

"Travis called me just a few minutes ago. He came home and found his mama all to pieces. Harley and Butch were nowhere to be found, and Mr. Williams was out working in the trees. That's how they make most of their living, you know. Christmas trees." She paused, having found herself drifting away from the issue at hand. "Travis just didn't want me to hear about it somewhere else."

"Did Travis tell you to call me?" Rob asked.

"Well, no," Leanna said. "But I thought you'd be interested. I thought you considered Travis your friend. You ought to care about what friends you've got, Rob.

I don't see people lined up waiting to get to know you, especially not with the trouble you're in."

"Thanks, Leanna," Rob said, and put down the receiver. He was still standing there when Coralee called him to supper.

The meal was silent except for the sudden bursts of thunder that clattered above them. "Late in the year for a thunderstorm," Fairlee said, stirring his coffee. "It's lightning off there somewhere. Bet we have us a little rain tonight."

"I'm going to set this oil lamp and these matches right here in the middle of the table," Coralee said anxiously. "Oh, I don't like storms."

"I suppose you think there are people who love them," Rob said.

"Mama used to have to drag your daddy in," Coralee said, ignoring the sarcasm in Rob's voice. "He'd want to stand on the porch in the worst storm you ever saw."

"Lightning struck a tree down on Barber's Creek one time. A big oak right next to a house got split wide open. Everything metal in that house got turned smut black and everybody's hair stood right on end, but that was all there was to it," Fairlee said.

Rob was barely listening, hearing instead the conversation with Leanna, going over and over in his head everything he'd said to the deputy, every word he'd uttered in the sheriff's office. Maybe he'd said something he couldn't remember. He'd been out of his mind. Or last week when he met Gatewood coming home, had he reacted to Travis' name without realizing it? Had he given himself away with a twitch of his cheek, his heavy grip on the steering wheel, the growling flipflop of his stomach?

"What ails you, boy?" Grandpa was asking him. The wheedling voice pierced his memory, made his mind go blank.

"Nothing," Rob muttered.

"Listen at that!" Coralee cried, because the wind was beginning to blow, bringing a gusty sheet of rain against the side of the house. Slowly, almost one drop at a time, it began pounding the tin roof, each ping a different metallic note.

"It's gonna be a doozie," Fairlee said.

"Did you do up the windows in the truck?" Grandpa asked. He was mopping chicken gravy with half a biscuit.

"Of course I did," Rob said. He hadn't eaten more than three bites. "Do you think I'd be sitting here if the windows were down in the truck?"

"Rob, don't," Fairlee cautioned.

"Don't what? All I ever hear is don't."

"Well, you went and got yourself in a heap of trouble anyhow," Grandpa complained. "Ain't ever been a Dickson in court, unless you're talking about that land dispute my pa had back before the Depression, and by God, he was on the side of the right. The judge said so. No Dickson never got hauled in by the scruff of his neck. Nary one of us got ourselves arrested!"

"All right. I'm the screwup," Rob said. "I admit it. I hit a wet spot and went in the ditch. I'm going straight to hell for it!"

"Rob!" Coralee was shaking, her hands gripping the edge of the table.

"Don't nobody get arrested for going in the ditch unless they was liquored up. I ain't no fool, boy!" Grandpa roared.

Rob pushed away from his plate.

"Where're you going?" Coralee asked him. "You didn't eat a thing."

"I've got to get out of here," Rob said.

"But it's pouring down rain," Coralee protested. "Fairlee, talk to him."

"Pa don't mean nothing," Fairlee said quietly. "He just gets riled up and don't know what to do with it."

"There's something I've got to do," Rob said. He was taking his jacket off the hat rack in the corner.

"Can't it wait, son?" Fairlee asked, still calm. "She's going to be in a swivet every minute you're gone."

"You and Coralee don't give a damn about me," Rob said. "And neither does he. He's worrying about what people will think. You've all been holding your breaths till you're rid of me. Well, I'm going."

"No, you ain't." Grandpa was up now, his bony frame shaking and weaving. "I ain't gonna let you. This is my house and ain't no kin of mine going out of it into a lightning storm like this."

"You can't stop me," Rob said, and before the old man could get to him, was gone.

He wanted to go to the Williamses' but he couldn't. Maybe Butch and Harley knew that Travis had given him the lousy joints. Maybe they were after him already for narcing, would gun him down or tear his face off. He knew what happened to squealers in the city.

He thought momentarily of Ellery, then closed his

208

mind against her. She didn't want his trouble. That was over. Over, over, over, the windshield wipers moaned to him.

He drove toward town, saw the valley in a white flash of lightning as bright as day. The grass and trees were blue in the light, the road a glossy silver in front of him. He went through town, considered stopping at Bert's, rejected the idea. He was more afraid of being drunk than of being sober. Now that's a switch, he thought, squinting through the wind-wet glass.

A few miles outside town the headlights caught the edge of the sign he and Ellery had followed to the little church, and he turned down the road with relief and stopped in the gravel parking lot, his lights shining on the face of the little building. He turned off the truck, then the lights. The dark made the rain seem closer. A flash of lightning lit up the sky and Rob counted the seconds, remembering what his dad had once told him about measuring the distance of a storm by the seconds between lightning and thunder. On the third count the thunder rumbled, the old truck shivering in its wake.

He sat there a long time waiting for the lightning to illuminate the little church, watching each flash as if it were a fireworks show. His jacket was wet from his run to the truck, and he took it off and spread it on the seat to dry. He thought about turning on the heater but he didn't want to waste the gas. Besides, he knew about carbon-monoxide poisoning. He wasn't that hopeless, not yet anyway.

He leaned back on the seat, listening to the rain. To-morrow he would know if Travis blamed him. He would know if he was a traitor or a friend. It wouldn't matter that he hadn't meant to do anything wrong. He could have ruined Travis' life, changed Leanna's future forever. Without intending to, he would have hurt people he really liked.

His heart felt tangled in his chest, clogged with regret, but the rain lulled him, soothing the exhaustion his anger always brought. Watching for the lightning, he fell asleep.

53

It was after midnight when he awoke. The storm was over and the rain had slackened to a heavy silent mist. Rob wiped off the inside of the windshield with his shirt sleeve, then turned on the wipers and the lights. The church was still there. No harm had come to either of them.

He started the truck, which sputtered and coughed, then rumbled warmly as it dried itself out. Rob's shoes were damp where the rain had swept into the seams of the old truck. He felt like a sponge, swollen and heavy with water. There was a broken tree limb across the stone walkway to the church, and he thought about getting out and moving it but he didn't have the energy. Somebody else will do it, he thought. Somebody who belongs here.

He headed home, splattering through the deep puddles, his tires spinning spray into the thick air. The sky was absolutely black until he reached town. He passed through the rosy glow of the streetlamps and under the flashing yellow caution lights. In the artificial light the storefronts looked like cutout cardboard boxes; they seemed to sag inward, their ragged awnings holding pockets of water. None of the windows were lit. It's a ghost town, Rob thought. Nothing that happens here is real. If I never see this place again, I won't have lost a thing.

When he turned up the lane out of the solid blackness of the valley, he knew something was wrong. The yellow porch light glared down on the empty rockers, and the lamps in the windows sent light so brightly outward that the house seemed to float on a misty cloud, shimmering above the gound. He parked the truck near the back porch, sprinted across the muddy yard and entered the kitchen in a burst of wet, shaky energy.

"What is it?" he asked Fairlee, who leaned on his walker at the kitchen window.

"It's Pa. He's gone," Fairlee said, looking out at the night.

"What do you mean, gone?"

"Seems like he went looking for you. I tried to get it in his head that you had the truck and you were safe somewhere, but nothing short of hog-tying him would have stopped him. I thought he'd gone on up to bed, but after a while Coralee went to see him and he wasn't in the house. He's out there."

Coralee flew into the kitchen, her face twisted in a grimace of dread and worry. She slid one of the gaudy rings up and down on her finger, scraping her knuckle

211

raw. "You didn't see him on the road? Where could he be, Fairlee?" Her hands moved shakily around her face until they found her hair and began to tug. She stood there crying and pulling at her hair. "He's dead. I know he is. Old folks and babies wander off all the time up here and nobody finds them till it's too late."

"Cora, just get ahold of yourself," Fairlee said, putting his arm around her to hold her still for a moment. "Don't go thinking the worst. He could be in the barn or somewhere like that."

"It's because of you," Coralee said to Rob, shaking free of her brother. "Ever since the day you came, you've been goading him, that or ignoring him, one. I know he's cantankerous—why, I've lived with him all my life. I've seen him when all I could do was shake my head and get outa his way. But he's my papa and he's your grandpa. It's not right to treat him like nothing, just because he's the way he is."

"I'm going to look for him," Rob said, turning back to the door.

"Now wait a minute, son. Don't go off half-cocked," Fairlee said. "Coralee, go get that rubberized poncho I had when I was working. This here's the best flashlight we've got." He nodded to a big one with a handle on the kitchen table. "Check the barn first, because he could be somewhere right here in the yard. Then go back down the road a ways. You could of missed him just because you didn't know to look. Then go the other way, toward the Williams place."

Coralee was dropping the poncho over Rob's head. It felt heavy and he slumped under it.

"He can't of gone far, not in this weather," Fairlee went on. "If you don't find him right soon, come on back and we'll call Rosalie and the sheriff. He won't do nothing before day, though."

"I'll find him," Rob said. He was already sweating under the rubber covering.

The barn was empty. He shone the light along the gray walls, into the mucky straw, among the abandoned, rusting tools, then latched the door and faced the night. His light jumped, bobbing along the hedge and across the wet grass as he looked for footprints. Nothing.

He got into the truck and turned slowly down the lane. The windows fogged up immediately, and he stopped to roll them both down. The mist flowed through the cab, cold on his face while his body sweated under the poncho. The truck balked and trembled as they chugged along through the mud. He turned down the dirt road, then onto the highway going toward town. The lonely stretch of road was dark and empty and he drove slowly, watching the edges where joe-pye weed and goldenrod had been battered along the fences. The ditch was rushing with muddy runoff from the storm. He drove past the curve where he'd spun out and pulled the truck over onto the soggy bank.

"Grandpa!" he yelled through cupped hands. The sound bounced back on him, motionless in the thick air. There was no wind to carry his voice. "Grandpa!" His voice had lost its resonance, was high-pitched and screechy like a child's scream. "Grandpa!"

The silence that answered him was crushing, and he leaned breathlessly against the truck, trying to fill his lungs even with the oily fumes that leaked from under the hood. The field beside him had already been plowed, the dry cornstalks stacked and tied. Beyond it, he remembered, there was a pasture scattered with outcroppings of rock amid the stubby grass. He shone his light across the field, caught the glint of washed stone, the hard bright eye of a cow left out in the storm. The cow answered his light with a low irritable moan and turned her head away.

Rob got back into the cab and turned the truck around, passed Ellery's road, then the road to the Dickson place, felt the slight incline pulling at the truck's innards as he drove toward Travis'. Beyond the Williamses' the mountains rose like the rippled sides of a pottery bowl. In the daylight he would have seen the colors, shades of brown, the black-green of the evergreens, the changing foliage of the locusts, maples and dogwoods, already brilliant on the higher slopes. Now the mountains formed a barricade to keep his grandfather in. There was no way an old man could have walked out of the valley in this direction.

It was raining again, a slow drizzle that made the old wipers squeak angrily as they argued with the glass. He went past the Williamses' lane, drove past open fields that rose gradually to meet the upward slope that had never been burned off and plowed. The forest was dense with a mesh of undergrowth clinging to its floor. The terrain was desolate, like land after a flood.

"Where is he?" Rob asked aloud, pounding his fist on the steering wheel. It was raining harder and the wipers slid easily now, a steady slap and click. "Damn this rain.

214

Why are you doing this to me?" he yelled toward the roof. The rain answered him with its steady drone.

He turned around in the road. What was the point? The old man had disappeared, walked off the face of the earth. He would have to go back and say so, admit that he was no finder of the lost, no rescuer from dark and lonely places. I won't do it, he said to himself. I'll drive around all night, I'll walk every inch of this valley, but I'll find him.

He wished he could go get Travis. Together they could find him. Travis knew the valley, knew tricks of survival. He'd know where to look. But Rob couldn't ask him. There was not a person in the world he could turn to, not one.

He turned down the Williamses' road anyway. It was one of the few places left to look before he headed back toward town. He stopped the truck and started out on foot. He could hear water, a quick gushing under the pounding rain. It was the stream that ran over the road where the Williamses had never put in a culvert or built a bridge. It was more than a trickle now. Water traveled down the shallow bed in a swirl of mud and debris from the side of the mountain. He flashed his light along the stream, starting where the water poured out of the woods, past the place where it cut noisily into the lane, then farther down where it fell through a chute of smooth rocks. His light struck the darkness, caught sparkles of rain in its beam, fell finally on a black mound, his grandfather's soggy coat. He was facedown, his chest against a rock, knees pulled tight as if he had tried to make himself disappear into the muddy earth.

"Grandpa!" Rob cried, but could barely hear himself over the rain and the rushing stream. He dropped the flashlight in the mud, retrieved it and half ran, half slid down the bank until he was leaning over the body, pulling at the drenched coat, looking into the bloody face, feeling the brittle lifelessness under his hands. He had never looked at death before, never felt it in his hands—not even a bird or a pet to be buried. His dad had done those things while Rob turned away, refusing to look, his own hurt trapped inside his chest, cold and untouchable. "Pa," he cried, holding the body to him, cradling it against the slippery surface of the poncho.

"Ah-h-h-h," came a moan on a breath so shallow Rob didn't feel it coming.

"Grandpa!" Rob cried, more frantic now. There was something he could do. "Grandpa, where are you hurt?"

But there was no answer, just the moan like a final exhalation, a painfully slow slipping away.

"You're going to be all right, Grandpa. I'm taking you to the hospital." Rob was trying to gather the body in his arms. He didn't know how to lift, didn't know if he should even try, and yet he was determined to do it. He fought his way out of the slick poncho and wrapped it around his grandfather, tried to raise him again, stumbled, caught the body finally over his shoulder, the long legs dragging in the mud, his weight pinned to Rob's chest. He got him into the truck and shut the door on him, got himself under the wheel, leaned the bloody cheek against his shoulder awkwardly, fought the gears to get the truck moving. They raced through the night, the slick road sailing up under them and disappearing as if it were a ribbon being curled. Finally he turned into the Dickson lane, laying on the horn as he came, pulled up close to the porch, saw Coralee and Fairlee at the door.

"I found him," he was yelling before they were out on the porch. "I've got him but he's hurt. I'm taking him to the hospital."

"I'm coming!" Coralee yelled back, and was off the porch and into the rain without a coat, her white arms flailing the air as she ran. She passed through the truck lights like a thin, unwieldy ghost, swung herself into the cab and pulled her daddy's body to her, holding his head at her breasts, her arms fast to the yellow poncho that shed water in a muddy puddle around them.

"I'll call you as soon as I know something," Rob called to Fairlee, who clung to his walker on the edge of the porch.

He waved them off and they were gone, the truck steaming exhaust into the rain, its red taillights piercing the dark like the fierce eyes of an animal suddenly gone mad. All the way to town Coralee crooned. It was a babbling song interspersed with pleas that God have mercy, that Papa not die in her arms, that Rob not kill them on the way. Her voice rose and sank like waves over Rob's head. It seemed to him they would never get there.

54

They waited in the deserted lobby until dawn, saw the haze rising as if it were a lacy coverlet being slowly lifted and shaken in the thin morning air. The mountains were there; then an orange ball oozing over their edge to turn the sky first pink, then lavender, then the cool, piercing shade of blue Rob had come to expect.

"What is it?" Coralee asked, seeing his back trembling as he leaned against the windowpane. His hands gripped the cold metal ledge.

"Just the dawn's early light," he said as pleasantly as he could. As tired as he was, he still remembered that Coralee had done a brave thing, was still doing it, as she huddled under his jacket on the vinyl sofa across the lobby. "We'll get some good news soon," he added. "I'm sure we will."

The doctor was coming down the hall toward them, rubbing his stubble of beard as he came, his sneakers squeaking on the polished floor.

"Well, here we are," he said before he got to them. "Your father's in his room now, Coralee. We've got him all plugged up—I.V.'s going, oxygen and so forth. All the things we doctors do to make folks look sicker than they are."

"He's going to get well, isn't he?" Coralee asked, coming off the sofa.

"The best I can tell," the doctor said. "You trot on down there to room 101 and see if he's asleep, let him know you're here, while I have a word with this young man."

Coralee hurried off, still wrapped in Rob's coat.

"How is he?" Rob asked, watching the doctor's demeanor change as he settled his hands in the pockets of his white coat.

"The X ray showed four broken ribs on the left side," he said quietly. "One of them punctured the left lung, so we have a collapse to deal with. He's running a slight temp. I'm giving him an antibiotic through the I.V. When's Fairlee coming?"

"I have to go get him," Rob said. "I brought Grandpa in the truck."

"Tell him I'll talk to him at noon. Rosalie too. I'm sure she'll want to be in on this. We've got to get the leaked air out of his chest cavity and get that lung inflated." The doctor stopped, extracted one hand from his pocket and ran it over his eyes and into his hair. "I think he'll make it, son, but I'm not one to make promises in a case like this. We've got his age to consider."

"I shouldn't have moved him," Rob said.

"There's no way of knowing for sure, but I'd say the damage was already done," the doctor said. He moved away quickly, heading back down the hall.

Rob followed him at a distance, moving unsteadily as if he expected his knees to buckle at any moment. He went into the room where Coralee was already curled in the lounge chair next to the bed, her head on the armrest, her legs tucked under her. He took his jacket from across her chest and replaced it with a spare blanket, folded a towel and slipped it under her head. From the corner of his eye he could see his grandfather while he did all this, although he couldn't yet bring himself to look directly.

"Ah-h-h," Grandpa moaned, forcing Rob to look. There was the needle taped to the thin wrist; the bandaged cheek; the prongs of the oxygen cannula in his nostrils, its pale-green tubing looped around his ears; the wrinkled neck, its folds of soft sallow flesh so vulnerable above the rim of the white hospital gown; the bony chest that seemed not to move at all. Two bottles half full of clear liquid were taped to the floor beside the bed, with a tube running from one of them up under the sheet. The liquid bubbled slightly.

Everything on the bed looked washed out: the wrinkleless covering, the ashen skin that sagged away from the sharp contours of the face, the hair that had dried unbrushed in tufts and spikes. Rob put his hand up to smooth the hair down. It felt coarse and brittle under his fingers. "You're going to get well," he said softly into his grandfather's ear. "You're safe now."

The old man's mouth twisted in his sleep. His eyes moved under thin purplish lids. His hand grappled with the sheet, trying to take hold of the smooth cloth. Rob put his hand over the kneading fingers and the struggling stopped, the mouth softened.

"I'm sorry, Grandpa," he said, pressing the knotty fingers under his. It was all he could say.

55

Rob called Fairlee from the pay phone in the lobby and gave him the doctor's message.

"I'll call Rosalie," Fairlee said. "What about telling your dad, Rob?"

"I'll phone him later," Rob answered, feeling a quick lurch of dread in his stomach. "Let's wait until the doctor checks on Grandpa at noon. I can come get you whenever you say."

"Never mind that. Rosalie can bring me in. How's Cora?"

"She's been really great. She's with him now, sleeping in the chair. They're both asleep."

"You go on to school if you want to," Fairlee said.

"I'll see. I'm not looking my best," Rob replied, eyeing his muddy jeans and sneakers.

"Well, you had yourself quite a night."

"We all did. I guess I owe everybody in the world an apology," Rob started.

"Just take care of yourself, Rob."

"Yes sir," he said, and hung up.

He got a cup of murky black coffee out of the machine in the lobby, took a few swallows and threw the rest out. His stomach ached as if he'd been throwing up and his throat felt scalded. He went into the bathroom and washed his face and hands, crinkled a piece of paper towel and rubbed his front teeth, brushed his fingers through his hair. What could he do now? The coffee in his empty stomach was making his heart race, an unexpected caffeine high. Here he was in drug central and all he could get was a lousy cup of coffee. At least he could have a sugar fix. He went back to the lobby, where he bought a Coke and a candy bar from the machines.

"The breakfast of champions," a voice said behind him, and he knew without turning that Gatewood was breathing down his neck.

"What are you doing here?" Rob asked wearily, snapping the can open. The liquid fizzed up and settled again.

"My job, boy. My job." Gatewood grinned, planting his feet in front of Rob as if he were preparing for a shoot-out. "A little town like this, we hear what's going on. Why, somebody comes into the emergency room in the middle of the night, we know about it! We come check it out, make sure everything's all right with everybody concerned."

"Grandpa's in 101 if you want to interrogate him," Rob said easily, sipping on the Coke.

"Medical report says broken ribs and a punctured lung. What'd you do, boy, beat up the old man?" Gatewood needled. "The drug business ain't enough for you, now is it? I knew that the first time I laid eyes on you. I recognize a troublemaker, somebody can't keep his nose clean. I know 'em when I see 'em."

"He went out in that storm last night. He fell. I found him," Rob said carefully. "That's all there is to it."

"Ain't nothing that simple, boy. Now I'm here to tell you, court ain't that simple. We got a good solid case against you come Monday. Course, you got time to figure something out. You got the weekend to work on your memory." He slapped the black gun belt that hung on

222

his thick hip. He was still grinning. "You have a good one, you hear?"

Rob dropped the Coke can into the trash and went down the hall to his grandfather's room. Without disturbing Coralee, he laid the candy bar on the bedside table with a couple of dollar bills so she could buy breakfast. Grandpa seemed lifeless under his sheet. Rob watched for a long moment to see the slight rise of a shallow breath. Then he slipped into his jacket and went down the hall and through the lobby to the truck.

He didn't know where he was going. Not to school. Sooner or later he'd have to face Travis, have to take whatever was coming to him, but not today. Monday he'd have to stand alone in the courtroom surrounded by strangers and hear the truth about himself. He was a druggie, a menace to society, a pariah, a disgrace to his family. There would be no one to defend him except a slick young lawyer whose job it was to search out loopholes, to buy time, to skirt the truth: You are not worthy of the world, Rob Dickson.

He drove through town with the dry buzzing ache of sleeplessness hanging like a curtain behind his eyes. Deep inside his brain there was a soft whirring, a pattern of thought rising like a water spout.

Words formed in his head, long-forgotten phrases that pulsed suddenly in his temples. "Your adversary the devil prowls around like a roaring lion, seeking some one to devour . . ." came to him in a rush of heat across his forehead but was immediately washed aside by other words. "Rend your heart, and not your garments." "We have erred, and strayed from thy ways like lost sheep. . . ."

The words came tumbling, filling him up with tears. "Defend us in the same with thy mighty power." He was speaking aloud now, catching the familiar sounds on his wet lips. He couldn't remember all of anything, only a scattering of phrases from hours spent restlessly on his knees, a tiny prayer book clutched between his hands. "Here we offer and present unto thee, O Lord, our selves, our souls and bodies . . . accept this our bounden duty and service, not weighing our merits but pardoning our offenses. . . ."

He knew where he was going. The road seemed to unfold in front of him; his foot on the pedal hardly seemed essential anymore. Something else carried him—something that had stretched through his life, holding him against all odds until this moment of need.

He turned in at the little church and jumped out of the truck. The broken branch had been moved, and he regretted not having done it himself. He pushed on the brass latch of the door and felt it give, felt the pressure under his hand melt away so he was suddenly looking straight at the cross, the gleaming brass catching the early light of this new day.

The church was even smaller than he had imagined, only eight rows deep with a center aisle that led up two steps to the freestanding altar beneath three high arched windows. The sun made bright patterns of light on the altar rail and on the tops of the trees as their leaves turned on a breath of wind outside. He put his hands on his knees, holding them steady. He couldn't kneel. He sat there a few moments, fighting back his tears, wrestling with the noisy racing of his pulse. He willed himself to pray. He clenched his jaw, bearing down on his memory to make a prayer come out of the fragments of liturgy stored in his brain. He was empty now, pitifully void of words.

There was a rustling near the altar, the thin creaking of old hinges, and a man appeared from the left through a narrow door that was invisible when it closed behind him. He was carrying brass candlesticks in his gloved hands, and he set them on the altar carefully, stepped back to eye their distance from the centered cross, moved forward again to smooth the scalloped altar linen before realizing he was not alone.

"Hello," he said with a smile. He was an elderly man wearing a flannel shirt, his thin gray hair waving slightly as it fell above his round tortoise-rimmed glasses. He pulled off the cotton gloves a finger at a time, still smiling at Rob. "Don't mind me," he said. "I'm just doing a little housekeeping in preparation for Sunday."

His hands were small and smooth. "I try to give the brass more than a lick and a promise in the fall, getting ready for Advent, you know." He came down the steps and into the aisle. "I'm Tom Fowler, the priest in charge of this little congregation of twenty souls. Faithful ones, I might add, or else I'd be out to pasture permanently, a situation my soul itself rebels against. I would not know how to stop being a priest." He stood patiently waiting, his eyes fixed on Rob's face.

"I was passing by . . ." Rob mumbled.

"Ah. Tourists do that. They see this quaint little church and they stop to have a look. Some say to me how precious it is. Cute, they say, but I never find it necessary to take them to task. I've found the aura takes care of that itself. This place has the power of a cathedral if you let it have its way. Sometimes those folks end up on their knees."

"Actually, I knew this church was here," Rob said. "I wanted someplace to be alone."

"Well, I'll leave you then," the priest said simply. "Just close the door behind you." He turned to go.

"Wait!" Rob said without meaning to. He took a deep breath while Tom Fowler turned back to him. "Maybe you could stay with me a few minutes, if you have time," he added.

The priest looked at him kindly. "I don't believe we've been properly introduced, young man."

"I'm Rob Dickson. I've made a mess of things—"

"Join the human race, Rob." Fowler sat down in the row in front of Rob and turned around to face him, resting his hands on the back of the pew. "Tell me about it. Maybe it won't sound as bad as you think."

"I'm not from around here," Rob began, then stopped to draw another shuddering breath. "I guess you could tell that the minute I opened my mouth."

Father Fowler nodded and waited.

"My parents sent me down from New Jersey to stay with my dad's family. I'm supposed to be helping them out, but I'm sure my parents were hoping it would work both ways."

"And I don't suppose it's been a satisfactory venture," the priest said. "You'd probably have to participate in that kind of reformation to make it work."

"Yeah, well, I haven't participated." Rob smiled a

little. "I met this girl two days after I arrived. We came here one time to park." He waited to see how his honesty would be received.

Father Fowler gave him an open, straightforward look. "My parishioners talk about putting up a fence. A gate with a lock. What foolishness! You wouldn't be here now if you and your friend hadn't taken advantage of our hospitality once before."

"It's over with her," Rob said, looking at his hands on his knees. His nails were still rimmed with dirt. "I was more serious than she was." He paused, hearing Ellery's voice in his head. "No, that's not how it was. She was the serious one. I didn't want to have to think. I wanted something to be easy."

"And she felt you were using her," the priest said gently.

"Then I got in trouble with the law," Rob continued shakily. He didn't want to make eye contact, but the man held him there. "A friend gave me two joints—marijuana—I begged him for it. And I had a wreck. I have to go to court Monday. There's a guy from the sheriff's office after me, trying to get me to tell him where the grass came from. He says it'll make things go easier for me in court, but I don't think so. I don't trust anybody, not even myself. Last night I had a fight with my grandfather and left the house. I drove out here and sat in the parking lot and watched the storm. When I got home, Grandpa had gone looking for me on foot. I found him, but now he's in the hospital with a punctured lung. He looked dead when I found him. I thought he was dead."
His voice had fallen to a whisper, but Tom Fowler seemed

to have heard every word. "Basic, everyday screwup," he said for a brave finish.

"And so you came to church," Fowler said. "What did you expect would happen here?"

The question caught Rob off guard and he looked down, following the straight lines of the velvet kneeling cushions with his eyes. "I guess I wanted to make it all go away," he said finally.

"Just like that?" the priest asked him softly. "Snap your fingers? A little hocus-pocus and everything's fixed? Is that really why you came, Rob? For some magic?"

Rob bristled, clenching his fists on his knees. "Doesn't the church believe in miracles?"

"There's a difference between magic and miracles. Magic is a trick. The magician knows how he does it. A miracle is an act of faith. We are part of miracles because we believe they are possible, not because we can make one."

"I just thought I ought to pray," Rob said helplessly. "I want to pray. But now that I'm here, I don't know how." He could see the priest's hands moving toward him. They seemed to float in the air until he felt their gentle pressure on his shoulders.

"Maybe you expect too much of yourself right now, son. Maybe you want some perfect words to say," Father Fowler said. "There aren't any. Oh, you can leaf through the Book of Common Prayer and find phrases as perfect as the human mind can create. But what you want, I suspect, is your own prayer. More than that, you want the courage to pray it."

Rob nodded, feeling the warm comfort of the hands on his shoulders.

"Maybe you should think about prayer as talking to the God in yourself, the holy place within," the priest suggested.

"That's the trouble," Rob said. "I don't think there is a holy place in me."

"Of course there is," Tom Fowler said simply. "You may have to struggle to get to it. Sometimes it's covered up with other things, like a treasure in a junk pile. Or it's corroded from lack of use. But it's there. I promise you that. Now I think I'll leave you to it." The hands moved away, but the warmth flowing into Rob's chest and back remained. The priest stood up and stepped into the aisle. "Just remember, Rob, there's nothing you can discover in yourself that God doesn't already know. There's nothing that He doesn't forgive. You would do well to forgive yourself."

Rob closed his eyes, and when he opened them again the priest was at the altar, his back to him as he turned the pages of the missal. He could hear the dry whisper of paper lifting and falling. He dropped to his knees, his forehead pressed painfully to the rounded edge of the pew, his hands clutched at his chest. The pages turned slowly, comforting him with their purposeful movement. Between their rustlings he could hear intercessions in his head, hesitant and stilted like the beginning of speech. He tried to say them, but they stuck in his throat, awkwardly formed pleadings phrased like childhood rhymes, but he kept trying, concentrating on their simplistic form, the bare elements of praise and thanksgiving he recalled from long ago. Gradually the words came easier, falling into place on his tongue. Then he felt his chest widening and he could breath deeply again. Each new breath brought words with it that mingled in the fragrant woodsy air of the silent little sanctuary.

He raised his head to see that Tom Fowler had disappeared. The altar sparkled, so white and golden it made him blink. He closed his eyes again, and in the lighted place that remained somewhere at his center, he prayed.

56

Entering the hospital, still dressed in his stiff, muddy clothes, unwashed and unfed, Rob met Ginny, her arm linked with Coralee, who looked wrinkled and forlorn in the cotton housedress and worn sneakers of the night before.

"I'm taking her home to get some food and a shower," Ginny said. "Fairlee and Rosalie are in with your grandfather now. You just missed the doctor." She hugged Coralee to her side. "I'll stay with you while you get a real sleep, Cora. A catnap in a chair is no substitute for a few hours in your own bed."

Coralee smiled wanly, letting herself be led.

"I'd stay out of Rosalie's way if I were you," Ginny

called to Rob as she swung through the glass door. "She's dug every detail out of the two of them, and she's really on her high horse."

"How is he?" Rob asked from the doorway of his grandfather's room. Rosalie had settled in the lounge chair, her lavender pant legs riding her shins, feet planted solidly as if they were being set in cement. Her polished nails clicked on the wooden curve of the armrest while she watched her father, who was motionless on the bed, his narrow form barely making a ridge under the tightly drawn sheet.

"We can expect him to recover to some extent, no thanks to you," Rosalie intoned, savoring the spite in her voice.

"Now Rosalie, what's done is done," Fairlee said. "It was no more Rob's fault than anybody else's." He was sitting in a straight chair, his walker in front of him like a barricade. "Rosalie forgets how Pa can get something in his craw and not get shut of it."

"I know exactly how he is," Rosalie retorted. She bent over to pull a tissue out of her pocketbook and patted under her eyes with it. "I know how Rob is, too. No child of mine would do such as that. Why, I'd whip him within a inch of his life."

Rob waited, willing the words churning on his tongue to dissolve. Your daughter is what you might call sexually active, Rosalie, and your future son-in-law is two breaths away from a felony charge. He didn't move. His mouth stayed dry, parched from hunger and twenty-four harried sleepless hours.

"These bottles down here on the floor," Fairlee said

congenially. "That's where that loose air is emptying out. Doc says when the bubbling stops, all the air'll be out of his chest. May take today and tomorrow, maybe longer, to do it. Then they'll force some air into that collapsed lung, and when it blows up, it'll more than likely seal the little hole he's got right against the chest wall. Presto, he'll be fine and dandy."

"If he doesn't get an infection," Rosalie said. "I swear you just hear what you want to hear, Fairlee. Dr. Cole said our papa might never be the same again. You were sitting right there when he said it."

"You asked him that, Rosalie!" Fairlee was getting riled now. His weary face turned pink and blustery, like a hot wind was blowing on him. "You ask the man if Pa's going to be just like new and what do you think he'll say? Don't nobody come out of here all that much better than they come in and that's a fact. The hospital is for serious sickness and there ain't no miracle cures I know of."

"Has he been awake?" Rob cut in.

"He has. He took a little water. He asked about what happened to him," Fairlee answered. "He wanted to see you, but I think it can wait till tomorrow. He needs his rest right now."

Grandpa moved his head enough to make his jaw drop. His mouth formed an oval as if he were howling. Rosalie stared at his open silent mouth for a moment, but when he didn't move again, she let him be.

"Did you call Davis yet?" she asked. "He ought to know about this."

"I'll call him at dinnertime."

232

"If you think it ought to wait that long," Rosalie said in a huff of disapproval. "I've called him all I intend to. He never pays me any mind."

57

When Rob heard his mother's voice—her quick hello as if she had picked up the phone mid stride, the clipped vowels when she identified herself: "Carrie Dickson here,"—the sound was both so dear and so foreign to him that he almost put the receiver down again.

I'm not ready. He leaned his head against the metal framing of the pay phone and waited, longing for a broken connection, the operator's apology that his call could not go through. Instead he heard an anonymous voice speaking between them like an interpreter: "Collect call from Rob Dickson. Will you accept?"

"Yes, operator." His mother's voice plummeted into his ear. "Rob? How are you, sweetheart?"

"I'm all right. Mom, I need to talk to Dad."

"What is it, Rob? I can tell there's something wrong."

"Is Dad there, Mom?"

He could hear her calling to Allison to find her father, and then she was back, her voice breathless and pulsing with alarm.

"Here he is now. I love you, Rob." There was a pause, then her whispery words caught on the wire and came zinging to him. "There's something wrong with him, Davis. Hurry."

His father's voice was so distant at first he had to strain to hear it. "Rob, how's it going, son? Did you get the check? I mailed it Tuesday, so you should have gotten it today. . . ." The voice was getting stronger.

"I haven't checked the mail," Rob interjected. "Dad, it's Grandpa. He's had an accident and he's in the hospital."

"How is he, Rob? What happened to him?"

"We had a bad thunderstorm last night and he went out in it," Rob began, although his throat was tightening, the words choking as he swallowed. "The truth is, we had an argument and I left in the truck. He went looking for me, Dad. He fell and broke some ribs and one of them punctured his lung. The doctor says he should be all right but his age is against him. There's a long list of complications he could get. Can you come, Dad?"

"I'll get a plane tomorrow morning, maybe even tonight," Davis said. "Tell them I'll be there tomorrow night at the latest. Tell Pa."

"Dad, it was all my fault." Rob was crying now. His body shook like a windup toy that had been left to run its course.

"You just hang on, son," Davis said. "I'm coming."

58

"I told you it was going to end up like this," Rosalie said, flying in through the kitchen door on a gust of midmorning heat. "I take it he's told you about getting arrested. Why, he didn't even have the decency to call me and let me know. It was all over the school, practically all over town before I found out about it. And what could I say? I'm the one always out there in the public eye. It falls to me to have an explanation where there's not one."

"Hello, Rosalie," Davis said from the kitchen table, where he and Rob were eating eggs and toast after his early-morning arrival. "Have some breakfast."

"I ate hours ago. I've been to the hospital. He looks bad, Davis. His color is perfectly terrible, and every breath he takes is sheer agony to him. I went out there to the desk and told them he needs something for pain, but Nan Kiser—you remember her, don't you? I know you do because she was in the class right behind yours—she said Dr. Cole didn't have anything stronger than aspirin on the chart. Something about not wanting to depress his lungs, whatever that means." She set her purse on the table and rummaged in it for a pen. "I'm here to make a grocery list so there'll be something to eat in this house over the weekend." She glared at Rob before peering into the refrigerator.

"I went last night," Rob said. He could see the full shelves over Rosalie's hunched shoulders and puffy hair.

"Well," she said, shutting the door with a thud.

"Sit here and have some coffee with us, Rosalie," Davis said. "Calm down a little. I never see you when you aren't upset about something."

"I know you think I'm crazy," Rosalie said, towering over them. She swung her pocketbook over her wrist. "I feel crazy. That's the truth. Maybe I am. I've gone through enough to be, I know that. Where's sister?"

"She's still asleep," Davis said.

"After all this time, I see she decided to go out," Rosalie said, then set her jaw as though Coralee's success had provided yet another irritation to her. "I've been worrying with her over that for years, telling her she ought to just stop that foolishness and get her courage up—that's what the rest of the world is doing—but she'd just bow up and not say a word. Now here all a sudden she's cured just like I told her she could be three years ago!"

"It didn't happen all at once," Rob said, carrying his plate to the sink. "Ginny Collier's been coming over every day helping her to walk out on the porch."

"So that's how it happened," Davis said.

"Ginny stays beside her, talking to her all the time while they walk. She's been a good friend to Coralee."

Rosalie conquered her stunned expression well enough to clutch her dangling pocketbook to her side and snort noisily. "Well, she's welcome to it," she said. "I certainly don't have time to come over here every morning and coax a grown woman out into her own yard!" She was gone in a flurry of agitation.

"Well, let's get back to it," Davis said when they'd heard her car door slam.

"There's nothing else to tell. You know everything."

"Except why you don't learn," Davis said bitterly. "How many chances do you think you're going to get? I'm telling you, son, I think you're running out."

"I know you're disappointed, Dad."

"I'm not talking about me, Rob. I'm talking about you. Aren't you disappointed?"

"I guess so," Rob said. He watched the water rising over the dishes. Grandpa could have drowned. Another couple of steps before he fell and he'd have been face-down in the overflowing stream. His dad would be here for a funeral. That's how close he'd come. Air bubbles slipped from between the plates in the sink and rose through the water. He watched them dissipate on the surface.

"Can you stay through Monday, Dad?" Rob asked.

"I plan to," Davis said. "Listen, son, I don't deny I'm mad as hell over this mess you've gotten yourself into. Part of me wants to throttle you and that's the truth. But I don't know what good it would do, so let's just see if we can get through this mess somehow or other. You'll have to take what's coming to you without complaint. I expect that of you. Everybody in this family expects that. But I'll be there with you. That's a promise."

59

They stood by the bed side by side, not touching but almost—that breadth away that provides the warmth of contact without the strictures, that holds the scent of aftershave and light sweat and hopefulness in its moist atmosphere. Together they looked down on the sleeping face turned slightly away from them, the green oxygen tube denting the old man's cheekbone where he pressed it against the pillow. His breaths were hard and quick, even in his sleep.

"Papa," Davis said softly, leaning toward the long thin ear, so fragile it appeared useless, unhearing. "Pa. It's Davis."

The head moved slightly and a grimace of pain shot across the old man's drawn lips before he even opened his eyes. His free hand waved in the air, searching for contact. Davis grasped the hand in his, held it, his own strong fingers hiding the veiny, spotted flesh.

"How are you, Pa?" Davis asked, bringing their joined hands to rest on the covers.

"Not worth a goddamn," Pa wheezed on a labored breath. He grimaced against it as if the strain of speaking pained him.

"The doctor says you're going to be all right," Davis said. "Rob and I just talked to him."

"He said that?" Grandpa pulled his hand away and brought it trembling to tug at the cannula. "Then he ain't never had one of these up his nose." He tried to smile. He was looking at Rob. "You all right, boy?" he whispered.

"Just worried about you," Rob said, swallowing on the choking lump in his throat. "I don't know what gets into me, Grandpa."

"Well, I do," the old man said, panting between the words. He paused, trying to gather the breath to go on. "It's what all younguns got in them. I had it in me and your daddy had it in him, if I remember correctly. We both growed out of it." He stopped again and closed his eyes, waiting for the pain in his chest to subside. "Well, we got a little bit left, I reckon."

"We'll let you sleep now, Papa," Davis said gently. "I'm here, though. Both of us are. We'll be around when you wake up."

"Come morning I'm going home," Grandpa said, this time loudly, as if he'd been saving up strength to say it.

"We'll see," Davis said, patting his shoulder. He ran his hand down his father's arm to his wrist, tracing the bone under his fingers. They stood watching the colorless face, the slight furrow across the brow that came with every shallow breath.

"When I was a boy I used to look at his hands," Davis said so softly Rob had to strain to hear. He moved slightly so their shoulders were touching. "I used to look at the torn nails, the permanent ridges of oil and dirt on his knuckles, the calluses, and I'd feel such contempt. I hated the work they did, that scratchy roughness when I couldn't avoid his touch, the way he had to force his fingers to hold a coffee cup by the handle or to do up buttons. I wanted a father with fine hands accustomed to leafing through the pages of books, like Mr. Turnage who taught history at the high school, or one with the touch of old

Doc Walters who played the piano when he made house calls because he couldn't pass a piano without seeing what it could do. I wanted a father like that."

Rob felt tears on his cheeks, but he didn't move to wipe them away.

"I was a grown man, a father myself, before I could admit my hands are exactly like his, but even then, I couldn't let go of that fear of being like him. I couldn't turn it around and use it. I still can't. I haven't been any better son to him than he was father to me, but I could have been. I had resources he didn't have. I had opportunities. I could have, at least, done better by you."

"Maybe someday you won't think you've done so bad," Rob said. He caught a tear on his lip, rubbed his tongue across it.

"I'd like to think two intelligent people could work our their differences, could learn how to talk to each other," Davis said.

"They probably could," Rob said, "if you could find two."

"I was thinking about you and me, you jerk," Davis said, a lightness in his voice he hadn't expected to find there. He let go of his father's limp hand and put his arm around his son's shoulders.

The contact they made was unnatural to them—only estrangement was familiar—and yet Rob did not move. There was no pulling back, no studied maneuvering that would give one of them advantage over the other. Rather the hand on Rob's shoulder provided an unexpected solidarity, an attachment as true as the blood tie between them. They both knew there was no escaping that.

60

The next morning they rode to the hospital together, Davis and Rob in the front, Fairlee and Coralee in the back of Davis' rented car, a solemn family outing. On the radio a local evangelist railed at them about their refusal to be saved. "A sinner's like a dog turning back to its own vomit," the man roared at them.

"For God's sake, turn that off," Davis said, and Rob pressed the button that sent the tuner traveling through patches of silence and scratchy static. He gave up and turned the switch off completely.

"That was Jim Abernathy." Fairlee chuckled. "He found the Lord a few years back when he got ahold of some bad whiskey and just about died. Went into shock and they had to start his heart up again. He claims he had a vision of the hereafter—both sides of it—and he came back filled with the spirit and ready to spread the word. First thing he did was cut a record called *I'm Grounded in the Lord* and made enough money to get hisself a fancy suit of clothes and buy a little bit of air time. Now he's making a fortune off folks that don't have a pot to pee in."

"Fairlee! Hush!" Cora giggled. "Davis, let's ride through downtown. I haven't seen it lately."

They rode slowly down the deserted main street, turned the corner and passed the Baptist Church, where the parking lot was full and quiet. Rosalie's car was parked there. "I might just get myself down here some Sunday," Coralee said. "I've been missing some real preaching."

They went on to the hospital. "After we visit with Papa, I'll take us all out to dinner," Davis said, helping Fairlee from the backseat.

Rob had Coralee by the arm. "Oh, I don't know about that," she said. "It'll cost a fortune and we've got plenty at home."

"We'll see," Davis said, not pushing her. He and Rob exchanged looks over the hood of the car. At least she hadn't crumbled.

Ginny was in Grandpa's room. "Hello," she said, getting up from the lounge chair. "We've been having a little chat. I hope I haven't worn you out, Mr. Dickson."

Grandpa lifted his hand and patted the air to tell her he wanted her to stay. His color was better and his eyes brighter, but he was careful in his movements as if he expected a flood of pain at any moment.

"Actually, I've been doing the talking," Ginny said, taking the hand that still hung in the air.

Rob was surprised to see someone touching his grandpa so easily. Ginny Collier is fearless, he thought with admiration. She acts on how she feels. He wanted to do that, too. He wanted to tell everybody in that room he cared about them, but he didn't know how.

"I do have to run along," Ginny said, resting Grandpa's hand on the sheet. "I'll see you another day."

Davis and Rob followed her out into the hall. "I'm Davis Dickson," he said. "I just wanted to thank you personally for all you've done for Coralee as well as for Rob. He told me you posted bond for him."

"I'm glad he felt he could call me." Ginny smiled. "How are you, Rob?"

"Getting by," Rob said. He knew she was thinking about tomorrow.

"Rob's lawyer is the best around," Ginny said to Davis. "I'm sure he wouldn't mind your calling him at home today if you'd like to."

"I think Rob has everything under control," Davis said easily. "I don't know what good I can do but just be here."

"Yes, well, good luck tomorrow." She squeezed Rob's arm gently. "I'm rooting for you. So is Ellery. She's been so worried about all of this, Rob."

His heart jumped. He could see her face in Ginny's, hear her voice. "Thanks," he said, unable to look into her eyes.

After Ginny left, he wandered up and down the hall restlessly, looking into his grandfather's room periodically to see his family sitting around the bed. They were talking to each other, and Grandpa, raised up in bed now, seemed to be enjoying their company. Rob couldn't join them; something held him back, the unfinished business of tomorrow. He was not one of them now, perhaps he would never be. Maybe this was proof that you never know what's worth having until you've lost it.

He got a soft drink out of the machine just to have

something to do. The can was icy cold, and he pressed it against his cheek, let it numb the ache of tension in his jaw. He was standing there in front of the machine when he felt a heavy grip on his shoulder, a bearing down of strength he knew could crush him. Gatewood, he thought, ready to bolt, but it was Travis.

Rob tried to duck. His natural instinct told him to avoid the blow, protect himself, but he didn't have the strength. The weight of Travis' hand paralyzed him.

"How's it going, man?" Travis asked. His grip softened, turned into support rather than pressure.

"What are you doing here?" Rob asked, still panicked although Travis was smiling at him.

"Leanna dragged me over after church. I told her I'm not going in there where somebody's hooked up to all that stuff, even if it is her granddaddy, so I'm waiting here while she speaks to him. Didn't you see her go by?"

"No." Rob snapped the top off the can and offered it to Travis, who shook his head.

"You drink it. You need something. You look like you've seen a ghost."

"I thought you were going to hit me," Rob said with a weak laugh.

"Worrying about the raid, huh? I know you didn't narc. I admit it was the first thought I had—I mean it made a neat fit, didn't it?—you getting arrested on drug charges and us getting raided two damn weeks later. But I knew you didn't do it. Hell, man, it looks like I trust you more than you trust yourself."

"Leanna said they didn't find anything," Rob said.

"Clean as a whistle, just because they didn't look quite

hard enough. There's some I know of myself still not harvested, but I'm not saying where, and God knows what those boys have got hid deeper in. It scared them, though, and Mama's mad as a hornet. She's as close to her boys as white on rice, and she'll have a fit you'll hear clear to New Jersey if one of them gets arrested."

"What are you-all talking about?" Leanna called, coming down the hall, her high heels clicking. She walked pigeon-toed, her hips swaying to give her balance.

"Just look at that girl." Travis sighed. "I go to church just so I can see her all fixed up like that." He looked back at Rob. "You broke a sweet thing's heart," he said. "I suppose you know that."

"And what about my heart?" Rob asked, then shrugged.

"That's what folks say when they want an excuse to quit trying."

"I'm trouble," Rob said.

"You sure are," Leanna agreed. "But seems like you're worth it." She linked her arm with Travis'. "Travis is eating dinner with us. Why don't you come too? Mama cooks enough to feed the entire football team when Travis comes."

"I don't think Rosalie would appreciate having me. There's not been a civil word between us since I got here."

"Oh, phoo, that's the way Mama talks to everybody," Leanna said. "I think I'll invite the whole family! Why, she boiled a ham and fried two chickens before she went to Sunday school this morning." Leanna was clicking back down the hall before Rob could stop her.

"I reckon you better bite the bullet and come." Travis

grinned. "I think all of you folks had. You don't want to get on that girl's bad side."

"And what about Rosalie?" Rob asked.

"Shoot, I got her figured a long time ago. The more she's got to complain about, the happier she is. Looks like this afternoon she's going to be one happy woman!"

61

There was no avoiding Monday. It crept into the room where Rob lay beside his father, seeking him out with bright burning eyes, extended claws ready for the throat. He turned against the fierce red face of his clock, moving closer to Davis, his head deep under the heavy pillow. But still his heart raced on toward morning; his mind skittered into the void, filling it up with the worst possibilities—six months in prison, his body battered in a jail-yard confrontation with some two-hundred-pound thug. He saw himself raped. Under the sheet he curled his body into the smallest space he could make, every muscle tense and aching.

His dad's breath caught abruptly, seemed to stop as if he were dreaming all that Rob imagined. The alarming silence pulled Rob out of his wide-awake nightmare and he was about to put his hand against the quietened chest when Davis sighed and turned himself on his side, rocking the old mattress so it whined under them.

Rob stretched out his full length, his feet pushed against the footboard. Everything is going to be all right, he reasoned. Grandpa's recovering, Dad's here. He closed his eyes, collecting all the darkness into one space, controlling it under his lids. "Keep watch, dear Lord, with those who work, or watch, or weep this night, and give your angels charge over those who sleep. . . ." The words drifted away from him. He couldn't hold on to anything anymore. He felt himself floating on the rim of sleep, then sinking, his body too heavy for buoyancy. He bobbed between waves of panic and grogginess, caught in an endless black curl.

Before day he went downstairs. The steps groaned under him as if the house were finally openly rebelling against his presence. He passed Fairlee's dark room, stopped by the open door to listen. The room was quiet, and all he could see were the shadows of shapes, all motionless; the household ghosts were at rest. Nothing looked real.

"Rob?" Fairlee's voice came out of the darkness.

"Yes sir."

"Can't sleep?" There was movement on the bed, the heaving of springs, the rustle of bedding pushed aside.

"No sir."

"Me either. Come on in here a minute." The bedside lamp clicked on and Fairlee was bathed in dim colorless light. He pulled himself up against the headboard and waited for Rob to sit down on the rumpled covers. "Thinking about morning, I reckon. Well, it'll be here directly. There's no stopping it that I know of. One thing I've found out over all these years is that what you worry about the most ain't necessarily what gets you."

"I see you're awake, though," Rob said.

"Now I didn't promise I could do what I say. Most of what we know, we don't make use of. Why, you knew better than what you've done. I know that. Rosalie and Pa can go on and on about Davis—some of that's because they always loved him too much and they like to hold on to what's theirs—but I know he's done right by you, as much as he was able."

"He did," Rob said, sudden tears welling up. "I'm the one, Fairlee." He forced a little smile. "I guess you'll be glad to see me gone."

"Now have I said a word like that? No sirree, I haven't. You're welcome here as long as you've got a mind to stay, Rob. Hasn't a Dickson ever been turned off this place and we're not about to start now."

"I might be in jail," Rob said.

"You let Mr. Burnette worry about that," Fairlee said. "Now try to get some sleep, son. You don't want to be dozing off in the courtroom."

"That's not likely." Rob laughed grimly. "Thanks, Uncle Fairlee."

"No need. Maybe now we can both get some shut-eye."

With the click of a switch the room was engulfed in darkness again, and Rob heard the bed settle. He went quietly to the kitchen. Fog clung to the windows, obstructing the beginning of day. He turned on the light over the table and sat down at his place. Except for the hum of the refrigerator there wasn't a sound, no movement except the anxious rumblings of his mind. He had heard of people's pasts appearing before them in a split second. My life flashed before my eyes, people said remembering the slow-motion swerve from the path of an oncoming car, or the seconds that an airplane spiraled downward before the engine caught and brought them level. They went backward, saw again their connection to life. They held on to that.

He leaned back in his chair to take in the room. He supposed it looked like millions of farmhouse kitchens modernized forty years ago. At least it tells you something about the people who've lived in it, he thought. He knew which drawer was full of the bits of string, rubber bands and bread-bag ties Coralee hoarded. He could close his eyes and know from which hook his grandfather's hat hung, which burner the kettle was on, what was in the refrigerator and pantry. He could smell the cinnamon from the stewed apples they'd had for supper, the slightly rancid odor of old grease, the soft rotting wood around the old enamel sink. He knew where everyone sat, could see them there, could imagine the grandmother he'd never known hovering around the table while her children and husband ate, could see her mashing food for her ailing in-laws, carrying the smallest child in her arms as she replenished bowls, wiped mouths. His father was that baby who snuggled at her breast. Then he was a toddler at the table, young Rosalie spooning food into his mouth while Grandpa roared to keep them all in order, causing more ruckus than he could squelch. Coralee was serving by then, piling food on Fairlee's plate because he had the appetite of a horse, growing like he was. Rob could imagine the table laden with dishes brought in by the neighbors, the hushed busyness that came with a death. The "solemnest of industries," Emily Dickinson had described it.

Rob felt his tears but didn't move to wipe them away. He seemed to be crying all the time now. It was another edge he walked on these days, an edge of regret, of wishfulness, of . . . what? It was love, he supposed.

Tomorrow—no, today—his future would be decided. It was too late to change that, any more than he could change anything that had happened in this room—the arguments, the laughter, the sadness, the singing. All of it fit together. Maybe it had all been necessary to bring him to this moment. And yet he didn't feel as alone as he once had. The Dicksons, generations of them whose names he didn't even know, were there. His mother was there. They surrounded him, held him against his own flailing. Sitting there in the silent kitchen, it occurred to him that perhaps they always had.

62

They crept through the fog, the car lights casting a narrow downward beam on the faded yellow line. The edge of the road and the rocky fields were hidden from them.

"Just like old times," Davis said grimly, then tried to loosen his voice. There was no point in adding to the misery they both felt. "I drove a school bus my junior and senior years of high school. Almost every morning it was a battle with the weather. The prettiest day you ever saw would look like hell at seven in the morning."

They climbed the three flights to the top of the courthouse, where the glassed-in foyer of the courtroom looked out on the town. Rob didn't look down but stared beyond to the range of foggy blue mountains, their peaks trapped in cloud. A person can get lost up there, Coralee had told him time and time again. And once they're lost, they stay that way.

"Good morning, Rob," Jason Burnette said from behind him. "You're looking fine," he added, acknowledging Rob's tweed sport jacket and tie.

"Hi." The sound of Burnette's voice brought Rob a warm flood of relief. He had forgotten that solid core of confidence Burnette projected. "This is my dad. Dad, Jason Burnette."

"Good to meet you," Jason said. "Looks like we're going to have an audience this morning—that's good for everybody's morale. Keeps the judge on his toes. This is an election year, you know. We did all right in the draw, Rob. Judge Tyson can be a generous man when his diverticulitis isn't acting up. I had a glimpse of him a few minutes ago and he looked pleasant enough for a Monday morning." He rubbed his palms together, smiling at them. "So let's talk a minute."

They followed him to the glass wall, where he peered down into the fog. "Lousy weather," he said. "One thing I haven't gotten used to is plowing through this cloud cover two thirds of the year. You're local, aren't you?" he asked Davis.

"I was twenty years ago," Davis said hesitantly. "I suppose in some ways I still am."

Burnette was studying the lobby, making sure nobody was listening.

"We'll see how it goes, but right now I'm not planning to put you on the stand, Rob," he said, getting down to business. "I can tell you this much. The solicitor will call the arresting officer. That will be Patrolman Carlson. I've cross-examined him several times in the past. He's a good witness." He smiled a little. "We're all good when we've got a good case. I'll tell you just what I told Rob," Burnette said to Davis. "Considering how much he did wrong getting into this mess, he did a helluva lot right."

"That's a relief," Davis said, massaging Rob's shoulder.

"There'll be several pleas in front of us," Burnette continued. "In fact, a couple of them are mine. It may be ten thirty or eleven before your case comes up, so you'll just have to sit there and wait it out. I spend a lot of valuable time waiting." He shrugged and smiled at the same time. "Now, Rob, no matter what happens, you stay cool. We're not out of the woods until the judge says we are. Your demeanor could affect that. Well, it's nine. You better get a seat."

The courtroom was old and dark, the walls covered with solid walnut paneling interspersed with tall narrow windows thinly curtained. The wine carpet was worn under the wooden auditorium chairs.

"Looks just like I remember it," Davis said over Rob's

252

shoulder, and Rob gave him a quizzical glance. "Our ninth-grade civics class spent a morning here. It made quite an impression on me."

The hinges on the old seats squawked as Rob and Davis settled themselves midway back in the spectators section. People came and went, taking seats, talking quietly in the aisle. The two rows within the railing on the left side were half full of men in suits. Rob saw Jason Burnette taking a place among them. On the opposite side men in uniforms were settling in the empty jury box. Patrolman Carlson was there, and Rob glanced at him often, watching his steady gaze, the way he sat ramrod straight in the chair.

Gatewood came loping down the aisle, slapping the backs of the row seats and leaning in to greet people. He passed the Dicksons without a word and spent a moment speaking to Carlson, his back to Rob. Finally he slumped into a seat farther down the row. Rob looked straight at him, and Gatewood met his stare with a two-finger salute, his mouth curled in a grin that could have just as easily been a sneer. Rob looked away when the bailiff announced the entrance of the judge.

He was short and round with a cherub's face beneath a shock of white hair. He looked harmless enough, but Rob knew appearances were deceiving. Anyone looking would have said that between Gatewood and Carlson, they would take their chances with Gatewood, but Rob knew the menace behind that eager grin and back-slapping style. The patrolman had at least been courteous.

Time moved slowly, dragging through motions and

pleas, inaudible conversations at the bench, actions the audience wasn't privy to. Every few minutes Rob's bladder felt full, but then the sensation would pass. He could feel his pulse in his neck, his arms, his ankles. All his extremities throbbed. Twice he blew his nose although he knew the feeling of moisture in his head was just his anxiety. Putting his handkerchief back into his pocket, he caught a glimpse of red hair across the room to the far right of him. He knew without looking Ginny Collier was there. He felt a quick rush of gratitude. Someone moved down the row behind him, put a firm hand on his shoulder. It was Travis with Leanna following him, excusing themselves as they stepped around knees and feet. He heard them settle in the seats in the middle of the row, and he turned around briefly to acknowledge their presence. Travis gave him a quick okay sign and Leanna smiled and jabbed her finger in the air, pointing across the room. He expected to find Rosalie, but it was Ellery he saw. She was beside Ginny, her face drawn and pale as if she were hurting somewhere. He felt a biting pain himself. This was why she didn't love him, wasn't it? She had understood his capacity to hurt people. She knew what havoc he could bring.

He heard his case called, left his place beside his dad and went to the attorneys' table when Burnette motioned to him although he was hardly aware of his movements. He hadn't known he could walk.

The solicitor was tall and thin. "A lean and hungry look" popped into Rob's mind from somewhere. Well, this was a drama, wasn't it? A courtroom scene, and today he was one of the players. He focused on the solicitor's bony profile, the hooked nose, pale receding forehead. A perfectly respectable villain, Rob thought. But no, I'm the villain, he remembered suddenly. I am on trial here.

He tried to follow the questioning, his mind weaving in and out of the answers Patrolman Carlson gave. Had any of that happened? Had he looked bleary-eyed, spoken thick tongued, walked unsteadily? He had been read his rights. He remembered that happening just as Carlson was recounting it. You have the right to remain silent. Carlson had said that and Rob had pressed his lips together, shut down his crazy swirling mind. He could remember the void in his skull, the smell of his wet clothes, the warmth of Ginny Collier's Jeep.

It was Jason Burnette's turn before Rob realized what was happening. He locked his thumbs into his damp palms and held his tight fists on his thighs. Concentrating on the tension in his hands, he could look at Carlson and the judge, could pretend to be hearing the questions Burnette was asking from beside him.

"Let's see, Patrolman Carlson, you first became involved in this case when you came upon a pickup truck in the ditch on Sparrow Creek Road?" Burnette said.

"Yes." Carlson was firm in his seat, his shoulders pressed to the back, head straight as if he were on guard.

"That was about five in the afternoon?"

"Yes."

This was all territory the solicitor had covered, but Rob struggled to pay attention.

"Now at that time no one was actually in the truck, were they?"

"No."

"And when you first arrived, no one was even near the truck, were they?"

"No."

"Not even the defendant?" Burnette seemed to be making statements more than asking questions.

"No."

"You say you looked in the cab of the truck."

"Yes."

"And that's when you found the plastic bag that's been introduced as Exhibit A?"

"Yes. It was on the floorboard."

Burnette paused and changed his line of questioning.

"Now when did you first see the defendant?"

"He was walking on the edge of the road, coming toward the truck, in the rain."

"And when he got to where you were, you questioned him?"

"Yes."

"Did he tell you where he was going?"

"No. He didn't seem to know."

Burnette flipped the page of his yellow pad and looked at Carlson over his glasses. "Now the name on the title to that truck you came upon in the ditch is Fairlee Dickson, isn't it?"

"Yes."

"You got that from the registration card?"

"Yes. It was clipped to the sun visor."

"The defendant isn't Fairlee Dickson, is he?"

"No, but he's his nephew."

"But you didn't know that at the time, did you?"

"No."

"No further questions."

What did he mean, no further questions? All Burnette had done so far was confirm everything the solicitor had already brought up to convict him. Rob sagged inside, as weary as if he'd been the interrogator.

The solicitor was on his feet again. "That's the evidence for the State, Your Honor."

"Any evidence for the defense?" the judge asked, looking glum.

"At this time the defendant would move to dismiss, Your Honor," Jason said.

I would? Rob asked himself. He pushed his shoulders back as straight as Carlson's had been, his heart pounding.

"I'll hear you," the judge said, leaning back in his chair so he almost disappeared behind the bench.

"The only evidence the State has presented in this case, Your Honor, is that someone ran a pickup truck into the ditch on Sparrow Creek Road," Burnette began, as if he were delivering a sermon. "The officer has testified that he never saw the defendant driving the truck, or even inside the truck. The State has not put the defendant behind the wheel. The only evidence the State has presented is that the defendant was walking in the rain toward the truck while the officer was at the scene. Even if the defendant had been driving the truck—not that we admit that, because there's no evidence to prove it—the State has failed to prove *when* the accident took place or that the defendant was actually under the influence of any illegal substance at the *time* of the accident.

There is simply *no* evidence to support a conviction of driving while impaired.

"As to the other charge, possession of marijuana, once again the State presents no evidence that the bag introduced as Exhibit A containing the remnants of two marijuana cigarettes belonged to the defendant. The truck belonged to someone else. Perhaps the marijuana belonged to someone else, too. At any rate, there is no evidence that this defendant was in control of the truck when it ran off the road or that the contents of the truck, namely this plastic bag, belonged to him." Burnette pressed the tips of his fingers on the tabletop and Rob watched them turn white.

"I submit therefore that there is no evidence to support a conviction on either charge, Your Honor, and we ask that both charges be dismissed."

The judge leaned forward, his arms planted on the bench. "What do you have to say, Mr. Solicitor?" he said, peering down on the courtroom.

"This is a very clear case, Your Honor," the solicitor said carefully, weighing every word. "The officer came upon the scene of an accident. He saw the defendant walking back toward his uncle's truck. He found marijuana inside the truck. There's no doubt about who was driving the pickup that night. The defendant was. The State has proven its case on both charges."

The judge leaned back again and stared at the ceiling for a moment, his hands locked on the edge of the bench. Then he pulled himself forward and looked straight at Rob as if suddenly they were the only two people in the room.

"All right, Mr. Dickson," he said, his voice cold and grim, as if he had just had a terrible thought, "stand up." He paused, waiting for Rob to force his knees to straighten, his muscles to support his weight. He clenched his fists at his sides, willing himself not to topple over.

"It is the judgment of this Court in cases numbered 1296 and 1297 that the charges be dismissed," Judge Tyson said solemnly to the room at large.

Far behind him, Rob heard Leanna gasp, then the shifting of bodies as tense limbs relaxed. He felt his hands trembling as his fingers released from the tight knots he'd held for the past hour. His face loosened, his mouth nursing a slight smile.

"Now, Mr. Dickson," the judge said sternly, ignoring the relief in the room, "although the law dictates that I dismiss the charges against you, I feel compelled to warn you that if you continue on this path of flirting with trouble, if you continue to indulge in the use of illegal substances, eventually you'll find yourself back here in this or some other courtroom, and sooner or later you'll have to pay for your actions. I sit here day after day and see young people like yourself in one kind of trouble or another, and I've found that unless they take their first brush with the law seriously, unless they decide the kind of fun and games that brought them here aren't worth the trouble, not to mention the pain they cause their families, I see them again. And I have to punish them.

"Fortunately for you, nothing that happened here today will go against your record. You have your whole life in front of you, and I urge you to use this as a lesson. I hope I never see you in my court again." He was still staring at Rob. His gaze was like a laser beam holding him fixed.

"Thank you, Your Honor," Burnette said, his hand already gripping Rob's sleeve.

"Thank you, sir," Rob repeated, mechanically.

"Let's move it," Burnette whispered in Rob's ear.

Rob was in the lobby with no memory of the steps he had taken to get there. The sun had pierced the fog, and he blinked in the bright light, holding back tears, the sniffles of relief that itched in his nose, the grin that pulled at the corners of his tightly held mouth.

"Thanks," Davis was saying, pumping Burnette's hand while he kneaded Rob's shoulder, as if to make sure his son was actually at his side.

"My pleasure," Jason said, rapping Rob lightly under the chin. "Stay out of trouble, kid," he said.

"He will," Leanna said solemnly. "I'll see to it."

Travis was grinning as he pulled Rob away from Davis to give him a big hug. "All right!" he kept saying. "All right!"

"I'm going back to the office," Burnette said. "Take care, Rob."

Davis said, "I'd better call Fairlee and Coralee. I know they're in a state by now. And your mother, Rob."

"Mama too," Leanna said, tugging on Travis. "Let's call her, Travis, before she has a conniption fit. She claims she didn't close her eyes all night long."

Ginny was standing in front of Rob, her face glowing. "Well, now things can get back to normal around here," she said. "I'm just delighted for you, Rob."

"Thanks," Rob said. Her hug felt like his mother's

would, as warm and powerful as that. Rob wiped his eyes and stood there feeling foolish. Ellery was beside him. He knew without looking.

"I didn't think you'd come," he said when the others had moved away toward the block of pay phones.

"Then you don't know me very well," Ellery said lightly. "You really don't, you know."

He could feel her sleeve against his jacket. The incredibly slight pressure sent a chill through him. He felt himself shiver with it.

"Are you all right?" Ellery asked. Her hand slipped under his, warm knuckles close under his palm. Her fingers were trembling until he closed his hand around hers.

"I'm better," he said plainly, "but I reckon I've got a ways to go, as Fairlee would say."

"I think he'd say you're doing just fine."

"And you, Ellery? What do you say?" The words were hard to come by. They challenged his old fearfulness, his familiar careless slouch.

"I was so frightened. I thought I was losing you forever," she said.

He sighed and tightened his grip on her fingers. He still hadn't really looked at her. What if her eyes told him something different from what he was hearing? What if he were dreaming?

He forced himself to look. "Oh, Ellery, I've missed you so much," he whispered, seeing her open face. No subterfuge, no punkishly madeup caricature. Just Ellery.

"I wanted to call you," she said. "I almost went to the

hospital when I heard about your grandfather, but I thought you didn't want to see me."

"I can be so stupid," he said.

"We've both made mistakes. We brought a lot of junk with us, but lately I've been getting rid of some of mine," Ellery said. "There's no going back to Charlotte."

"Dad and I haven't even talked about what I'm doing next," Rob said. "I guess we both thought there was no point in discussing it."

"And now you can do whatever you want." Ellery pulled her hand away slowly and pressed her forehead against the window. The town was sparkling. The trees on the surrounding ridges were so brilliant they hurt her eyes.

"Fairlee's doing better than anyone thought he would. He really doesn't need me anymore," Rob said. He was looking at the mountainside, too. How could it be it looked like home to him? "Grandpa's getting out of the hospital in a couple of days. I think they'll be okay."

"So you're going?" Ellery said to the glass. She could see her breath on it, the opaque circle that would disappear in a moment.

"Dad would let me stay," Rob said. He wanted to touch her, to know by the feel of her shoulders under his hands the concreteness of what was happening between them.

"Then it's up to you," she said softly, but he heard longing in it.

Davis had joined them at the window. "You ready to go, son?"

"Yep." He was looking at Ellery.

"It's a shame to miss the rest of this gorgeous day," Davis went on eagerly. "Let's go by the hospital and give Pa the good news; then we'll take Fairlee and Cora out for lunch, maybe even for a ride on the parkway."

"You wanta come?" Rob asked Ellery, who was moving away from him toward where her mother waited.

"This is a school day, remember?" Ginny put her arm around Ellery. "You two will have plenty of time."

"See you later," Ellery said as she disappeared down the stairs.

"You're a goner, kid," Davis said, grinning.

"Looks like it," Rob admitted. "Do you think I'll survive it?"

"Probably not." Davis laughed. "But I can't think of a better way to go."

Later that afternoon, while the dusk of early autumn was bringing the sky close and the trees were darkening to black hulks of shade, Rob ran the ridge. The night raced with him, catching up in the swags where thick branches blocked the purple horizon. He knew where the road would take him, remembered the course that zigzagged through the trees, then turned back on itself to bring him full circle. It was a trail Ellery had made.

Above him, perched like a nesting bird, was the Colliers'. He could see the soft spiraling light Ginny had set in the yard. Leaves lifted and turned on a slight breeze above his head, shattering the light and changing the shadows around him, but he hardly noticed.

Surefooted although the gravel tossed and rumbled beneath him, he started down, making his own path toward the hidden farmhouse below where his family waited with supper. His lungs and heart found that magic rhythm that put new spring in his legs, released his tight shoulders so his arms lifted like wings. Finally he could see the lights in brilliant, solid squares. Only he moved. There was no sound except his drumming heart and heavy breath, the dry rustle of leaf and stone beneath his feet. The world was still, waiting for him. And it seemed to him that for the first time in his life he knew where he was going.